Secretly, he was glad things hadn't worked out but he didn't tell her that. Instead, he simply listened as she told him of another friend that had just gotten engaged. Ray could hear the longing in her voice and his heart went out to her.

She deserved to be loved and he wanted that for her as badly as she did, but there was something else that bothered him and he didn't know how to handle it. Usually, he talked things over with Claudia when he couldn't figure them out on his own, but this time was different. This time it involved her and he was at a loss for what to do.

SOMEONE TO LOVE

Alicia Wiggins

Genesis Press Inc.

Indigo Love Stories

An imprint Genesis Press Publishing

Genesis Press, Inc.
315 Third Avenue North
Columbus, MS 39701

ISBN: 1-58571-098-9
Manufactured in the United States of America

First Edition

Visit us at www.genesis-press.com
or call at 1-888-Indigo-1

Big thanks to my cuz Debbie Jackson for burning the midnight oil with me and being one of the best critique partners I've ever had.

Thanks to my aunts, Mildred Washington, Jessica "Wavy" Byrd and Joan Bullock, for providing me with endless places to go to promote my books.

Daddy, Darryl, Jevey and Lena, you guys have helped me out in more ways than you will ever know and I would truly be lost without you.

Burch, thanks for all the special reasons and the usual ones, too. To my friend, Michael Jackson (the original), even though you're hundreds of miles away, you always manage to send a little sunshine my way.

Brantley, Elliot and Alexandria, I know it's not easy being my children, but you all are doing a wonderful job at it. Keep up the good work!

Shawnta Spence, sometimes I don't know what I would do without having you there for a little "girl talk". Thanks!

And finally, thanks to all of the readers and booksellers who continue to enjoy and promote my work.

CHAPTER ONE

Scented candles, Chardonnay, roses and seductive music. The mood was just right and the evening would be perfect. Ray had carefully chosen everything that would make it so. The finest wine, beautiful roses and candles whose very scent aroused the senses.

He ran his hand over his closely cut hair and surveyed the room. He was satisfied with the results. The setting was perfect and Ray knew she would be pleased. He smiled. Filling the wine glasses would be the final step to phase one and the beginning of a night filled with pleasure.

Ray heard the key in the lock and the front door opened. It was time to put phase two in effect.

He pulled her into an embrace. She felt so good in his arms. "Hey, baby. What took you so long to get home? I've been looking forward to this evening all day." He wanted to spend all evening loving her and hated to waste one minute due to traffic jams or last minute tie-ups at work.

"There's a winter storm warning in effect and I think we're in for a big snowfall this evening. It started snowing just when I left work and you know how traffic gets when that happens."

After he took her coat and hung it in the closet she closed her eyes and inhaled the wonderful aromas that drifted from the kitchen. "I would have been here sooner if I had known you were cooking dinner."

"Everything's almost ready. Here you go," he said, handing her a glass of wine. "Just a little something to help you wind down.

Let's make a toast while we wait."

"A toast to what?" she asked already knowing that she would like the answer.

Ray placed his glass on the table and replied, "To passion." He began to unbutton her sweater. "To longing." He moved his hands down to her waist and unhooked the clasp on her skirt letting it fall to her feet. "To quenching one's thirst."

She moaned when she felt his strong fingers dancing up and down her spine.

"To the sexiest, sassiest, most voluptuous woman this side of the Mississippi." Ray's voice was barely a whisper when he spoke. When he touched her lips with his, no more words were needed.

Her kisses were intoxicating and delicious and spoke clearly of the love she felt for him. He didn't need wine, as there was nothing sweeter than the kisses from the woman he loved and planned to love for the rest of his life. Just thinking about what they shared left him speechless and his heart full.

"Aren't you going to propose a toast?" she asked with a seductive smile.

"I just did."

"Have I told you lately that I love you?"

"Even if you said it a thousand times a day I would never get tired of hearing it."

"I love you," she whispered.

Ray was leading the way to their bedroom where he planned to show her love in its purest and most vulnerable form. As the clothing barrier was eliminated, he laid his woman on scented sheets that he had previously covered with hundreds of rose petals. The weight of their bodies crushed the delicate petals, releasing their subtle yet distinctive scent as the couple set about creating a scent and mood all their own.

Reaching over to the nightstand, Ray clicked off the bedside lamp and the soft glow of the candles illuminated the room.

"I like what you've done to the place."

He smiled again. He knew she would like it. "You're pleased?"

She nodded.

"Does this please you as well?" He leaned down and took a taut nipple in his mouth. He heard her moan. "And what about this?" He suckled the other nipple and felt it grow rigid in response.

Freshly manicured nails grazed the skin on his shoulders. This time it was he who moaned. Ray slowly and deliberately worked his way down the familiar path that led to treasures that were his to indulge in.

He teased her skin with rose petals and kissed the fragrant areas lovingly. He left a trail of kisses down her stomach and over her thigh, igniting a fire that burned only for him. He continued the sensual journey down one sexy leg and kissed a small scar that was right below her kneecap.

She liked it when he kissed her behind the knees. He didn't disappoint her. One long, luscious leg reached high as she offered it and he readily accepted. But as voluptuous and delicious as her legs were, he wasn't about to stop there. Her body held a roadmap of pleasures that only he knew how to travel. This would prove to be a magnificent journey.

"I need you." Her voice was soft but held an urgency that beckoned Ray.

"All in due time, my love," he promised, feeling the same urgency. Ray laid her leg gently to the side and raised himself slightly. In the soft candlelight, he could see the longing in her eyes as the love he had for her was reflected more brightly than a million candles.

He moved to join her and his lips found hers. He felt her body give in to him. He couldn't wait any longer. He needed her as much as she needed him and she couldn't be more ready to receive what he had to offer.

He heard the moan that escaped her lips when he entered her velvet walls. Slowly at first, they danced the dance that he knew only the two of them were meant to share, a coupling that stood on a rock-solid foundation. As need gave way to passion, their rhythmic dance quickened as their shared journey took them to places of magnificent ecstasy. Ray closed his eyes. He wanted to shut out the world and to be in a place where only the two of them existed. A place where dreams came true and happily ever after was the norm.

Their passion burned. Ray knew their anticipated destination was imminent. He tried to hold back, to hold in all of the exquisite feelings that seemed too incredible to be real. The force of their passion was too strong. She demanded his all and he had to give in. It was sweet surrender. There was no turning back. Their lovemaking escalated into a frenzied pairing where everything ceased except what was being shared at that exact moment.

They were as one as they reached the place where ecstasy, passion, trust and the purest form of love joined forces to seal a perfect union. And a perfect union they were.

He loved her now and always.

"I love you," Ray whispered and reached over to take her into his arms. But the place where she had been only seconds before was empty and cold. Startled, he sat up in bed and looked around the dark room.

Gone was the soft glow of candlelight and the distinct floral fragrance of the rose petals. There was no wine or music or soft words spoken in hushed whispers.

The alarm clock sounded. Ray tried to block out the intrusive and startling sound. Slowly drifting into a state of consciousness, he realized that he had been dreaming again. He fought to retain every detail. He needed to remember, although he'd had this dream before.

This time had been different from the other dreams though. Yes, as before she came to him willingly and the lovemaking was exquisite. However, this time there was no mistaking the kind of love they both shared. There was no mistaking that she was his and that they would share that bond forever.

CHAPTER TWO

The bride and groom ran from the reception hall to the waiting limousine as a light snow began to fall and well-wishers shouted their congratulations. It was five weeks before Christmas and the festive spirit of the holiday coupled with that of the wedding filled the air with gaiety, love and romance.

But Claudia wasn't feeling any of that. As the car pulled away she watched the newlyweds waving excitedly from the open window. They looked happy and deeply in love. In a matter of minutes the limousine turned the corner and was out of sight. Claudia sighed and slipped the wedding souvenirs into her purse - a tiny plastic bottle of bubbles, chocolate kisses and a miniature gold bell. She would go home and place these items with the countless other wedding souvenirs she'd accumulated over the past couple of years.

Claudia thought about her friend Lorna who that day had just married the man of her dreams. She remembered when Lorna first met Troy. According to her friend Lorna, it was love at first sight. Even though she was hesitant to admit it, that's how it appeared to Claudia as well. The same thing happened when her friend Tracy met her husband Gary.

Tracy had met Gary on a business trip. There was an instant attraction and the two of them clicked. Initially they kept in touch via email and telephone and visited each other whenever they had a free weekend. Soon the strain of maintaining a long-distance relationship became an obstacle that they needed to overcome. Gary was hopelessly in love with Tracy and she with him. They didn't want to lose each other. He eventually put in for a job transfer to Ohio and after a year and a half, the two of them were married. The last time Claudia had heard from Tracy, they were expecting a baby.

True love. Must be pretty nice if you could find it, thought Claudia. Seemed as if her pool of single friends was dwindling quickly. Pretty soon she'd be that one single friend everyone felt odd about inviting to couples' events. Even her brother Frank, the interminable bachelor, seemed to have been bitten by the love bug and had a steady girlfriend. Claudia hadn't met her, but if she liked Frank, she had to be special.

Claudia had had enough of wedding festivities for one day. She looked around for her friend Ray. The two of them had come to the wedding together. Ray was the person Claudia usually called when she needed an escort and Lorna's wedding had been one of those times. She knew she would be seeing many of her friends at the wedding and the last thing she wanted to do was to attend without a date. But now it was time to go and Ray was nowhere to be found.

Claudia sighed again. She wanted to be home, soaking in a hot bubble bath and reading a sinfully steamy romance. If she wasn't experiencing romance in real life, she might as well read about it. The last thing she wanted to do was to have to track down Ray.

Looking around the reception hall Claudia spotted Ray across the room talking with their minister. He was really engrossed in the conversation and suddenly began laughing. With his arms folded across his chest Claudia thought Ray looked particularly handsome in his navy suit and bright red tie. She was glad that he had taken her advice and wore the navy suit instead of the charcoal gray one. The cut of the jacket showed off his broad shoulders and tapered to a nice angle giving his frame a long, lean look. Even the haircut he'd gotten earlier that afternoon gave him an added touch of style – low on the sides, tapered in the back.

As Claudia approached Ray and Pastor Gray she noticed two women at a nearby table openly admiring her friend. They were a little too far away for Ray to hear them but Claudia caught bits and pieces of their conversation. "Fine" and "sexy" were two things she heard repeated a few times.

Claudia smiled to herself. She knew exactly what those women were talking about although she never acted on what she reasoned were foolish thoughts. Despite the fact that Ray was her best friend, Claudia had to admit that there were a few times that she had looked at him other than as a buddy. It was during those times she'd found herself wondering what would happen if their friendship ever took a romantic turn. But almost as quickly as she had that thought, she dismissed it. Ray was her friend and good friends were too hard to come by. Yeah, Ray was fine and sexy but there was a whole lot more to him than that. She could never jeopardize what they had for a romantic fling.

"Hello, Pastor Gray," Claudia said.

"Claudia Ryland, I have to say you get prettier each time I see you, which hasn't been very much lately." Pastor Gray winked and Claudia blushed. Since being promoted to the pricing analyst's position at the insurance company she worked for, she'd been working a lot on the weekends and especially on Sundays, when the office was quiet and she could get a lot accomplished. In the process, she'd missed quite a few church services.

Claudia smiled sheepishly and turned to Ray. "I was looking for you so that we could leave."

"You're ready to go already?" Ray asked.

"Yes, it's been a long day and I'm a little tired."

Ray and Claudia drove along in silence. He knew something was bothering her, as she was usually very talkative. He also knew she would say whatever was on her mind when she was ready, and apparently she wasn't ready. If Ray Elliott didn't know anything else, he knew his best friend Claudia.

Pulling into Claudia's driveway, Ray cut off the engine. He didn't make a move to get out of the car.

"Do you want to come inside for a minute?" she asked, hopeful that his hesitation to leave meant that he might want to hang out for a while.

Sensing that Claudia needed to talk, Ray agreed to come inside.

Claudia had only to put her key in the lock before she heard her dog Ginger on the other side barking loudly.

"It's just me, girl," she said as Ginger barked and wagged her tail excitedly at seeing Claudia and Ray, her two favorite people in the whole world.

Ray played with Ginger while Claudia went to the kitchen to put on a pot of coffee and to change out of her dress. She heard the two of them playing in the living room and hoped that Ray didn't get Ginger too excited like he usually did when they were together. Sometimes the two of them were like children and Claudia had to wonder at times if Ginger loved Ray more than she did her.

It was funny how she had acquired Ginger. She had to smile at the memory. Shortly after moving into her new house, Ray had expressed his concern for Claudia's safety living alone in a strange neighborhood. Even though the neighborhood was in one of the safer areas in the city, Ray had taken extra precautions to ensure Claudia's wellbeing by installing sturdier deadbolt locks on the front and back doors. Still not feeling one hundred percent comfortable with her safety, he soon began to suggest that she get a dog. Even though she loved animals, Claudia didn't think she would be home enough to give a dog the proper attention that it would need, nor was she sure that she wanted the added responsibility of having a pet.

Just thinking about training and housebreaking a puppy was overwhelming to her.

One afternoon Ray showed up on her doorstep wearing a mischievous grin and holding the most adorable puppy she'd ever seen. The puppy was a mixed breed with a deep golden coat that reminded Claudia of gingerbread. She was even sporting a huge gingham bow that complemented the color of her coat.

Claudia's concerns over the time and attention puppies demanded were soon forgotten when she looked into Ginger's big brown eyes. It was love at first sight and she was instantly enamored with the puppy. Ray promised to help her train Ginger, as she was instantly named, and said that if after two weeks Claudia felt that she was too much to handle, he would take her himself. That was two years ago and Claudia couldn't imagine life without her beloved Ginger.

Claudia slipped off her shoes and tucked the gold bridesmaid dress securely away in the back of the closet, putting it next to the three other bridesmaid's dresses she would never wear again. Sighing, she kicked one of the gold dyed-to-match shoes to the back of the closet and made a mental note to call Goodwill for a donation pickup.

When she joined Ray he was sitting comfortably on the couch with his jacket off and his tie loosened. Ginger rested contentedly at his feet and barely acknowledged Claudia when she entered the room.

"Now, are you going to tell me what's going on?" Ray asked. "You acted as if you were attending a funeral today instead of a celebration of marriage. You didn't even want to hang around at the reception. That's not like you at all."

Claudia picked up a magazine from the coffee table and absently flipped the pages. "What do you mean? Nothing's wrong. I'm just tired. It's been a long day."

"Claudia, you forget who you're talking to. We've been best friends since the second grade. That's twenty-five years in case you've forgotten. Don't try to give me the 'I'm tired' routine. I know when you're tired, or mad, happy, sad, irritated, bored, pissed off or giddy and right now your temperament does not lean toward any of the aforementioned items."

Claudia laughed. "You sound like you're addressing your colleagues at a planning session. And where did you come up with giddy? Have I ever been giddy?"

"As a matter of fact, yes. I've seen the giddy side of you before. Remember when you got back at Jolisa Stone for copying off of your spelling test? Mrs. Gee had become suspicious when the two of you missed exactly the same words and she accused you both of cheating."

Claudia placed the magazine on her lap, folded her arms, and nodded. "Oh, yes. I do remember that. Even after all this time I still can't believe that Mrs. Gee thought *I* was trying to get answers from Jolisa. Maybe if I'd been looking for the *wrong* answers I would have glanced over at her paper. But I did get her back, didn't I? I'll bet that little heifer will never cheat at another thing."

"Okay, let's get back to my question. What's going on with you? And I'm not just talking about today. I've noticed that pensive look a lot lately. Something or someone is bothering you."

Claudia looked at Ray and smiled, but the smile never reached her eyes. She couldn't fool him so there was no use in trying.

"Well, Ray, it's like this. I'm tired. I'm tired of seeing all of my friends fall in love, get married and live happily ever after. I'm tired of coming home every evening to an empty house with Ginger being my only companion. You know I love Ginger dearly, but it would be nice to cuddle up to something that doesn't have four paws and fur. More to the point, I'm tired of being lonely. Today, as I stood listening to Lorna and Troy promising to love, honor and cherish each other, I wondered why that couldn't be me standing at the alter pledging my love to the man of my dreams. Don't I deserve that, too? I'm a good person and I think I have a lot to offer. I'm reasonably intelligent, sane, fun-loving, faithful, a good cook, and I'm not bad looking."

Ray laughed. Claudia had had a few glasses of wine at the wedding reception and he wondered just how much of her end of the conversation was being directed by alcohol. He watched his friend's pretty face crinkle in irritation. Ray had seen that look of irritation many times, along with many other looks.

"I'm sorry. I didn't mean to laugh." But Claudia made a good point. In his book, she had it going on. A successful career, charming, well-liked by almost everyone, and armed with a fierce sense of humor, it was difficult not to be taken with Claudia. And in the looks department she wasn't bad on the eyes either. In fact, Ray had always thought she was beautiful. Clear nut-brown skin that showed no traces of the teenage acne that plagued her all through high school, chestnut hair that just touched her shoulders and pretty brown eyes that always made Ray think of the song of the same name by the group Mint Condition.

As Claudia sat across from him, Ray couldn't help but be reminded of the description offered by one of his friends when he saw Claudia for the first time: Pretty eyes, sexy thighs, and hips that gave new meaning to the warning dangerous curves.

Claudia had overheard Ray's friend and had not been amused. But Ray had to agree. The description was right on the money.

"I thought you were happy being single. You've mentioned how much you liked your independence and how empowered you feel being your own woman, living your own life, on your own terms. Nobody telling you what to do and when to do it is how you said you want to live your life."

"Don't you know a smoke screen when you see one? The truth is I do like being independent, but being in a relationship shouldn't hinder my independence. Besides, I'm not talking about changing who or what I am. The only thing I'm trying to change is this perpetual state of singleness that I seem to be cursed with."

"Claudia, you're a very beautiful, vibrant, loving woman who any man would be proud to call his woman."

"Then why hasn't it happened? The only thing the men in my life call me is friend, and frankly, I need something a little more than that."

Ray shrugged his shoulders. "Maybe the men you've been dating aren't worthy of you. Did you ever consider that possibility? The right man will come along in due time."

Claudia rolled her eyes. "You're my best friend, Ray. What just came out of your mouth was the typical friend thing to say."

"No, it was the typical truthful thing to say. Let me save you some heartache and give you some advice. You can't force love to happen. It's a process that takes time and patience. You have to know what you want in order to recognize it when it appears."

"I know all of that. Believe me, I've heard it enough from my mother and grandmother." Then Claudia's mood brightened. "But I do think we all have a certain degree of control over what goes on in our lives."

"That's true but what does that have to do with what we're talking about?"

A little smile played on Claudia's lips.

"I know that look, Claudia, and it worries me. You're up to something, aren't you?"

Claudia looked around her living room and paused for a moment while she gathered her thoughts. Maybe she could explain to Ray what she meant without him being judgmental. But before revealing her plan to Ray she wanted to unfold it a little at a time. It was something she had been thinking about a lot lately and had come to the conclusion that it was time to stop wishing and start doing. She knew she would face some opposition with what she was going to do, but she had to tell someone of her plan and who better to run it by than Ray?

"Although I agree with most of what you just said, there is one statement that I don't agree with. One can't force love to happen, but there are certainly some things that can be done to bring two people together."

"Claudia, what are you talking about? If I didn't know better, I'd say you'd mixed up a love potion. Or have you signed up with a dating service?"

"No, not a potion and definitely no dating services, at least not yet, but I do have a plan."

"I'm almost afraid to ask about the details of this plan."

"I'm serious, Ray, and I want you to listen to what I have to say. You're the only person that I've mentioned this to so I need an objective opinion."

"Okay, Claudia, let me hear what you have to say."

"First I have to get my list," she said and walked over to the far corner of the room to her computer. Ray watched as she clicked the mouse a few times and printed off a one-page document.

Ray ran his hand over his brow. Claudia's plan was beginning to worry him. What could she possible have written down that had anything to do with true love? He loved his friend dearly and didn't want to see her get hurt, so he hoped this plan of action she had was foolproof.

Claudia sat down and placed a sheet of paper on her lap. "Now, I want you to listen without being judgmental. Promise?"

Ray nodded.

"By this time next year, Ray, I plan on being in a meaningful and loving relationship. By that I mean I'll either be engaged or already married."

"And how do you propose to do this? No pun intended."

"If you could stop being corny for a minute, I'll tell you. To begin with, I've written down a course of action, if you will. I've made a list of attributes I'd like in a man. My man," she added for emphasis. "I've ranked these attributes in order of importance. That's where knowing what I want comes in to play. For instance, being gainfully employed is an absolute must. No major drama going on in their lives is another thing. No crazy ex's, no unnatural attachment to their mother, and no prison records. Good looks are a plus but won't be considered a main factor. I'm looking for a man that has something to offer and has accomplished some things in his life. In other words, he has to bring more to the table than an appetite."

"Claudia-"

"Wait, I'm not finished. I want a man who will appreciate and love me without trying to change me. He has to be a good communicator, romantic, loving, kind, considerate, hard-working, passionate, gentle and caring. And above all, I want him to love me unconditionally in spite of my flaws, as I will love him the same way."

"You actually have all of that written down on your list?"

"Yes, along with a few other things."

"What more could you possibly have on the list? Blood type and cholesterol level?"

Claudia sighed. Ray wasn't taking any of this seriously.

"No one else knows about this?"

"Not the details. But I have put out feelers to a few close friends. I wanted them to know that I'm looking but at the same time, I don't want just anybody." She didn't mention that she had posted her picture and profile on a local singles web site.

"Where did you get this idea?"

"Think about it, Ray. Why should I sit around and wait for someone to come into my life when I can take the proactive approach and go for what I want?"

"Now, forgive me for bringing this up, but I believe not too long ago you were complaining that you didn't like living in Ohio and especially Columbus because you couldn't find a good man in this town with a compass and a guidebook. So, where exactly are you going to meet these men to size them up?"

"Size them up? It's not like that. You make it sound as if this is an audition. All I'm doing is taking a somewhat unconventional approach to finding a mate. Men do the same thing and no one criticizes them for it. If I were a man looking for a woman to share my life with, you wouldn't have a problem with what I'm doing."

"Claudia, if you were a man, you wouldn't have this kind of plan or a list. Most men just let love happen. We don't go around pre-planning our romantic lives, searching for the woman of our dreams in accordance with a check list. I don't even make a list when I go to the grocery store."

"No, but you do run through a lot of inventory before you find the right product, so to speak. Look at you. You date a different woman every other month. Why? Are you sizing these women up or are you simply passing time until you're ready to settle down?"

"It's called dating, Claudia. Dinner, a play or a movie, perhaps a bit of interesting conversation, it's something fun I like to do from time to time. I'm not auditioning women to be Mrs. Raymond Elliott, if that's what you're getting at."

Claudia sniffed. "That's because you don't stay with anyone long enough for them to take the part. Besides, who would want to put up with you for more than a month anyway?"

Ray picked up a pillow and threw it at Claudia. "Seriously, Claudia, I don't want to see you get hurt. This plan of yours sounds too cold and impersonal to work. Falling in love isn't about strategically matching characteristics with a candidate. I'd hate to see you investing time, energy, and emotions into trying to snare a man that looked good on paper but in reality was far less than what you deserve. I think if you would just be patient, love will find its way into your life."

Claudia folded her list and placed it on the coffee table. "Ray, you've seen the men I've had in my life. There have been some good ones and some not so good ones. We won't even discuss the ones that fall into the 'other' category. I firmly believe that there is someone out there for me and I'm ready to meet him. If that means I have to give fate a hand, then so be it."

To Ray it sounded as if Claudia was doing more than giving fate a hand. She was about to stage an ambush. The bottom line was that she had made up her mind and there was nothing Ray could do or say to change how she felt. He knew how determined Claudia could be when she had her mind set on something. The only thing he could do was to be there for her when and if she needed him.

It was getting late and Ray was tired. This conversation was far from over but they would have to continue it another day.

Ray stood up to leave and Claudia walked him to the door. Before he left he turned to his friend and kissed her on the forehead. "Honey, you're doing a bit more than giving fate a hand. But just promise me one thing."

"Sure, Ray, anything."

"Promise me that you won't lose sight of what's really important. You're surrounded by people who love you and who want you to be happy. I'm one of them."

Claudia smiled and raised her right hand. "I promise. And one more thing?"

"What's that?"

"If you know of anyone that I'd be interested in, would you hook a sistah up?"

CHAPTER THREE

Another bad date. It was barely one week into her plan and already Claudia had been on three dates with three incompatible men. She couldn't quite put her finger on it, but there was something about her that seemed to attract the wrong type of man. Maybe it was the same type of phenomenon that enables only dogs to hear a dog whistle; only strange men were attracted to her. Just yesterday she had removed her profile and picture from the internet after being solicited on more than one occasion by men who were either looking for a fling, fantasy or something so kinky she was embarrassed just reading the suggestions.

So far her plan wasn't working very well. If she was going to find the man of her dreams, something had to change and it had to change quickly. At the rate she was going she would be old and lonely for the rest of her life.

Claudia checked her watch. It was only eight o'clock. She'd met her blind date, Marvin, downtown after work in the Arena District. The plans they'd made during a brief conversation over the phone the previous evening was to have dinner and either catch a movie or find a club where they could talk while they listened to music.

It all seemed tame enough for a first date. After all, the guy came highly recommended from an office acquaintance, and he had sounded nice over the phone. However, the date that started with a merely shaky beginning ended up a 7.0 on the Richter scale by the evening's end.

According to her friend from work, Marvin was a high school biology teacher, was tall, fairly attractive, a good conversationalist and intelligent. Claudia soon discovered that her friend had embellished some characteristics and left out a few other traits. To begin with, Marvin had the social skills of a two-year-old. At dinner he complained about everything from the restaurant's low lighting to smudges on his fork. Their poor waitress was sent back in the kitchen to change his order more times than Claudia wanted to count.

And as far as being a good conversationalist, Claudia had to wonder, *Compared to what?* She was secretly hoping that it was because he was nervous that he seemed to prattle on and on about insects, parasites and proper dissection techniques. Learning that most people unknowingly eat about thirty spiders a year didn't sit too well with her. But she was especially disgusted when Marvin attempted to demonstrate proper dissection methods using his entrée as an example.

Doing her best to salvage what seemed to be a disastrous evening, Claudia suggested that they see a movie after dinner. Since the theater was within walking distance of the restaurant, Claudia was spared having to keep up a conversation as they walked briskly in the cold evening air.

Once they arrived at the theater, they couldn't decide on what to see. Marvin only liked science fiction, which Claudia didn't mind. Since there weren't any science fiction movies showing, Marvin decided he didn't want to see anything and complained to the manager about the lack of good movies being featured at the theater. The theater incident was about the fifth time Marvin had embarrassed her that evening.

Knowing that she would probably grab him by the throat and drain the life out of his body if she was with Marvin a moment longer, Claudia decided to call it an early evening. To her surprise he seemed disappointed. She didn't quite know why. As far as she was concerned, they couldn't have been more of an odd couple. One thing was clear, Marvin Hemphill was clearly not the man of her dreams.

Ray sat in the small meeting room and waited patiently for the zoning appeals meeting to begin. He'd almost forgotten about the meeting until his partner called to remind him to bring a copy of the proposed plans for the site they were developing for their firm.

"Do you have the report from the EPA?" Ray's associate Shawn asked.

Ray's calm demeanor turned into one of near panic as he rummaged through his briefcase and prayed that he hadn't left the report on his desk. He found the survey, a copy of the proposed plans, and the letter from their law firm, but no EPA report. They needed that report. Without it their petition to be exempt from many of the zoning regulations would be denied. A lot of money was riding on this project and being unprepared at meetings was not only a waste of time, but a waste of money.

"Here it is," Ray announced with relief as he pulled the report out of the file.

Shawn patted Ray on the shoulder and advised him to relax. A small group of citizens were in attendance at the meeting and were prepared to present their list of questions to the developers. Ray and Shawn both knew that some of the people present were going to oppose their company's development of a ten-acre strip of land that abutted a small group of houses. Not only were they going to have to present the positives of developing the land to the board and the homeowners, they were also going to have to convince the zoning board to grant them exemptions on several items listed in the code.

Throughout the meeting Ray and Shawn fielded questions about the land development project, explained details of the EPA findings and continuously reassured the board and homeowners of the integrity of their firm and of their intentions on developing a site that would provide jobs to an area that lacked a solid economic base.

"You seemed pretty distracted tonight," Shawn commented after ordering a couple of beers.

Ray stretched his neck from one side to the other. He was tired. He hadn't slept well the night before and had gone to the gym for a few hours after work, before the meeting. The intended benefit of working out was lost, as Ray had overdone it a bit.

"I just have a lot on my plate right now. That's all. It's nothing I can't handle."

Shawn wasn't convinced that it was just work that was the cause of Ray's distraction and he put his theory to the test. "Does this current distraction have a name?"

Ray shook his head and smiled sheepishly. "No, it's nothing like that. I told you, I'm involved in quite a few projects and I've been burning the candle at both ends. At least after tonight there appears to be an end in sight. I'm putting the finishing touches on the South Linden project early next week and Pryor and I just signed off on the Southland extension this afternoon."

Shawn nodded. "So I've heard. Who ever thought that working for a land development firm would be so fulfilling? Building cities and neighborhoods with Legos was never this fun. By the way, the buzz around the office is that the top folks are pleased with the way you handled the Southland project. You even managed to come in slightly under budget. I drove through the area last week and was impressed by the way you incorporated the new structures with the old. I'm glad to see that you didn't have to tear down the old post office. A few more successes like that one and you'll be a partner before long."

Ray shrugged his shoulders. Making partner in the firm had been something he'd thought about a lot when he first came to Braxton-Smith, Ltd., but lately it wasn't his job or making partner that occupied his thoughts.

He had been thinking about Claudia's plan to get married. She'd called him earlier that day to tell him about her date with Marvin. He had to laugh although he knew she was disappointed.

Secretly, he was glad things hadn't worked out but he didn't tell her that. Instead, he simply listened as she told him of another friend that had just gotten engaged. Ray could hear the longing in her voice and his heart went out to her.

She deserved to be loved and he wanted that for her as badly as she did, but there was something else that bothered him and he didn't know how to handle it. Usually, he talked things over with Claudia when he couldn't figure them out on his own, but this time was different. This time it involved her and he was at a loss for what to do.

CHAPTER FOUR

Claudia stood in front of the mirror in the restroom at work. She had fifteen minutes to get ready and she needed to freshen up her makeup and run a comb through her hair before meeting Ray and his friends.

Ray had called earlier that afternoon and invited Claudia to join him and a few of his friends for dinner after work. At first Claudia had declined the invitation. Her sister Karen had arranged for her to attend a Christmas ball that weekend with a friend of their pastor's and she still needed to find a dress. But when Ray mentioned that he had someone for her to meet she changed her mind. Any friend of Ray's would certainly be worth meeting. She prayed that he wasn't another Marvin.

When Claudia arrived at the restaurant she was a few minutes late. There had been an accident and traffic had been re-routed causing an unavoidable delay. She asked the hostess if Ray had arrived and was immediately led to their table in the far corner of the restaurant.

Ray saw her approaching and stood to greet her. He gave her a peck on the cheek and whispered, "You're late."

"Traffic," she whispered back.

She took a quick scan of the people that were sitting around the table. She recognized one of Ray's associates Shawn BeVier and his wife Leslie and an attorney friend of his that she knew was happily married and expecting a baby any day now.

Taking her seat, she looked at Ray questioningly. Who was she supposed to be meeting?

Ray simply smiled, clearly pleased with himself and began chatting about downtown traffic and how much snow they'd been getting lately.

After everyone ordered drinks, Claudia asked if they were expecting anyone else to join them. Before Ray had a chance to answer she heard a deep voice behind her greeting Ray.

"Damien, glad you could join us." Ray stood and greeted his friend. After the two men shook hands, Ray took a chair from another table and placed it between Claudia and himself. Ray winked at Claudia when he did so.

"Where are my manners?" Ray exclaimed. "Damien, I believe you know Rob, Shawn and Leslie, but I don't believe you've met Claudia Ryland."

Damien turned in his seat to face Claudia and smiled brightly.

He was a cutie, thought Claudia and he smelled good, too. She found herself staring a little longer than was necessary and thinking that she had never seen a man with such beautiful skin and clear eyes. He also had the most perfect white teeth Claudia had ever seen. It was obvious that the man took good care of himself. Judging by the way he filled out his suit jacket, she could tell that he took *very* good care of himself.

"Nice to meet you," Claudia said when Damien extended his hand.

"Likewise," replied Damien as he gave her a quick once over.

Claudia thought she saw him raise his eyebrows slightly, almost as if he approved of what he saw. She wasn't sure if she should feel offended or flattered.

"Claudia," Ray began, "Damien just moved here from Pittsburgh and was saying what a hard time he was having finding a house. Aren't there several houses in your neighborhood that are for sale?"

Taking her cue, she jumped in. "Uh, yes, what exactly are you looking for?" she asked Damien, who was looking over the menu with a slight frown on his face.

"Well, I need a lot of square footage and large open spaces. You see, I entertain a great deal and need someplace that will be conducive to that. I'm also looking for a place with plenty of closet space. A finished basement would be nice and a workout room, too. Oh yes, a large yard is a must. I have two Dobermans that need room to run."

The waiter came to take their orders and when Claudia ordered the fried chicken salad with cheese and extra ranch dressing, Damien turned to her with a look of concern.

"Do you always eat like that?" he asked, clearly concerned.

A bit surprised by the question, Claudia replied, "Not always. I had to skip lunch today because of a meeting and now I'm pretty hungry."

"Do you know what all that bacon, cheese and ranch dressing will do to your arteries?"

"No, but at the moment it will satisfy my appetite," she responded, trying to keep an edge of annoyance out of her voice. *Who died and put you in charge of my diet?*

Damien began to give his take on why Americans ate the way they did. He cited several reasons for obesity in adults and especially children. Television was the number one culprit, in his opinion. To him television was a waste of time and so was reading, unless the reading material was about fitness. Why sit when you could be pumping iron, running marathons or swimming laps? All during his speech he made certain to mention several times that he worked out religiously and would never put anything into his body that would sabotage all of his hard work. He even took off his jacket and had Claudia feel one of his biceps. She had pretended to be impressed while at the same time trying to keep from rolling her eyes.

Throughout the evening the conversation touched on several different topics but Damien always seemed to manage to interject some tidbit about himself. He rather enjoyed talking about himself and clearly expected his audience to be just as interested with the topic as well.

It didn't take Claudia much time to realize that Damien was not for her. He was already in a committed relationship - with himself.

After coffee and dessert - water and fruit for Damien - everyone decided to call it a night. Damien needed his rest and Shawn and Leslie had to get home to relieve the babysitter. Their other guest had left right after dinner. Only Claudia and Ray remained.

"Was that your idea of the type of man that I would be interested in?" she asked Ray who had been strangely quiet all through dinner. "Or, was Damien your idea of a joke?"

Ray felt like a heel. He knew Damien wasn't Claudia's type, but he was trying to show her that auditioning men to be her husband was a bad idea anyway. But the whole point had missed its mark.

Damien had been more arrogant and self-centered than Ray ever imagined. Now Claudia was upset with him for trying to hook her up with an egomaniac. "I had no idea he was like that, I promise," Ray offered in his defense. "I've worked with him a few times in the past when his company completed site preparation projects for us but I've never hung out with him socially. The only reason I invited him to join us this evening was because I knew he was new in town and was probably a little lonely." He wasn't quite telling the truth but hopefully Claudia would buy it.

"Lonely? Damien? I'm sure he would have had no trouble keeping himself company without us."

"Well, don't say I didn't try. Besides, you've got to admit, most women like muscles and Damien is packing."

"You think I want to marry and spend the rest of my life with muscles? Ray, give me a little more credit than that please. Besides looks, there was nothing even remotely interesting about Damien. He was a prime example of don't judge a book by its cover, because Lord knows, the pages inside that book were absolutely blank."

CHAPTER FIVE

"Do you have any idea who you set me up with tonight?"

Claudia stormed into her sister Karen's house still wearing the black beaded gown she'd purchased for the evening's event.

"Yes," Karen replied indignantly. "Judge Gideon Thorne is a well-respected domestic relations judge, a humanitarian and a personal friend of Pastor Gray's. The man is prime marriage material. Please don't tell me that you didn't have a good time, Claudia, or worse, that you did something to send Judge Thorne away."

"Do I look like I'm wearing my man repellent gear?" Claudia turned around to give her sister the full view of the beaded gown, matching shoes and tasteful, yet elegant, accessories.

Karen gave a nod of approval.

Claudia sighed and said, "It's not as if I didn't want to have fun tonight, Karen. I spent all afternoon getting ready. I even had my nails and hair done so that I would look my best. You make it sound as if I sabotaged the date."

"Well, did you?"

"The date was sabotaged, but it wasn't my doing. Did someone forget to mention that Gideon had just gone through a messy divorce?"

"Uh, maybe I did. I didn't know it was messy but I did read somewhere that he was divorced."

"No need to mention it now. Judge Thorne filled me in on all the sordid details throughout the evening."

"So, you didn't have a good time at the Red and White Ball

with Gideon because he's divorced?"

"A good time? Are you kidding? Dating someone who is divorced is one thing. Providing therapy is another. I think I was Gideon's first date since his divorce was final six months ago. The man could talk of nothing else but that. All through dinner I had to hear about the former Mrs. Gideon Thorne. Even while we were dancing he had to mention how his wife had signed them up for dance classes at the Y eight years ago and she never thought to consider that he wasn't interested in learning ballroom dancing." Claudia sat down at the table and kicked off her shoes. She fingered the edge of the laminated place mat her nephew had made at school and sank down in her chair. It felt good to relax. She had wanted to make a good impression on her date and had been nervous all day. Now all she wanted to do was to forget about another miserable date.

"What kinds of things was he saying about her?" Karen asked as she poured them a cup of coffee. "This might be interesting."

"Trust me, it wasn't. Can you believe the man is still upset that his ex-wife never did much cooking but had the nerve to ask for the gourmet cooking set they'd purchased on a trip to Europe and half of the other appliances, cookbooks and various other cooking utensils they accumulated over the years?"

"I guess people can get kind of petty when going through a divorce. I'm sorry things didn't work out, Claudia. The man had such potential. I see him being interviewed on the news all the time and he seems so calm and collected."

"Probably lost that in the divorce, too."

"What's strange is that when Pastor Gray mentioned that he had a friend who was re-entering the dating scene and wanted to know if I knew of someone his friend might be interested in, I thought about you."

"Did you ever think to ask why his friend had been away from the dating scene?"

"No, and he never mentioned anything about his friend's divorce."

"He knew better," Claudia remarked sarcastically.

"I guess the whole divorce thing gets pretty ugly sometimes and all the pettiness surfaces and adds fuel to the fire. Do Gideon and his ex-wife have children together?"

Claudia rolled her eyes. "No, but there are two dogs that got caught in the crossfire. Pride and Joy. Guess who has custody of the little darlings."

"The former Mrs. Gideon Thorne."

"He even showed me pictures of the dogs. Can you believe that? The man carries pictures of his dogs in his wallet. He gets to see them on weekends."

Karen was trying not to laugh but she was having an extremely hard time keeping a straight face. She could just imagine her sister's face sitting across from the very handsome and suave Judge Gideon Thorne while he poured his heart out to her about cookware and dogs.

"I know this didn't turn out the way you wanted, but at least you'll be able to laugh about all of this one day," Karen offered.

"It won't be today, that's for sure."

"Is it safe to assume that there won't be a second date?"

Claudia cut her sister a quick glance. "Oh, that's a very safe assumption. Make no mistake about it, this date has been declared a mistrial."

CHAPTER SIX

Christmas was Claudia's favorite time of the year. The general hustle and bustle never seemed to bother her the way it did other people. In fact, she actually enjoyed it.

Since Christmas was a little more than two weeks away Claudia had decided to take off a half day from work to hit the malls. She was also going to meet her brother afterward for dinner.

Thankfully she only had three people left on her list to buy presents for: her sister Karen, her father and Ray. Selecting Karen's gifts would be easy. Any type of jewelry would be a big hit with her. Claudia's father would be even easier, as he was a great collector of tools and was quite the handyman. According to her mother, he'd been eyeing a new socket set at the hardware store for a few weeks now.

Ray wouldn't be as easy as the others so she had decided to leave him for last. She always took special care with his gifts, especially his Christmas and birthday gifts. She had learned early on that Ray's parents weren't much on celebrating the holidays, at least not in the traditional sense. Around the holidays, and especially on Christmas Day, his parents generally got drunk early on and would spend the remainder of the day working to stay that way or badly hung over. Before that, when Ray was even younger, he was usually pawned off by his parents onto a distant aunt. She passed away when Ray was nine and so ended any decent Christmas celebration.

When they were twelve years old and Claudia found out that Ray was planning to spend Christmas day in his room reading or listening to the radio, she decided then and there that he would never spend another holiday alone. Arriving at his house early that Christmas Eve morning Claudia found Mrs. Elliott sitting at the kitchen table with a glass of what looked like watery orange juice, with her head in her hands and smoking a cigarette. Nothing was cooking, there were no decorations or presents and everything looked dirty and gray. Nothing in that house indicated that anybody cared about anything or anyone.

Not wasting a minute and not wanting to spend any more time in the house than she had to, Claudia explained to Mrs. Elliott that she and Ray had a project to work on for school. She went on to further explain that part of the project was that they had to observe various ways of celebrating the holiday. For good measure she added that her brother also wanted to know if it was all right for Ray to spend the night at their house. In actuality, Frank didn't know about Claudia's plan, but if he did she knew he would probably go along with it. Claudia didn't dare mention the annual Christmas Eve party her parents always hosted for fear that Mrs. Elliott would invite herself. That might prove to be disastrous and embarrassing for Ray. Those two things Claudia wanted to avoid at all costs.

Ray's mother didn't seem to have a problem with him being gone for Christmas and almost seemed relieved that he would be away from the house. Claudia wondered if she even knew what day it was or if she cared.

Ray had been surprised and a little embarrassed when he answered the timid knock on his bedroom door and saw Claudia standing on the other side. She rarely came to his house and he preferred it that way.

Once Claudia told Ray that his mother said it was all right for him to spend Christmas with them the two friends set off on what would become the first of many memorable holiday seasons for them.

Claudia's shopping was almost done. After buying Karen a gold bracelet with matching earrings and her father the socket set he wanted and a pair of slippers and new robe, she checked her watch and noticed that it was almost time to meet her brother. If traffic wasn't heavy and she went a little over the speed limit, she wouldn't be late. Frank was the most punctual person Claudia knew and she wanted to be spared a lecture from her big brother on valuing other people's time if she could help it.

It had started to sleet and the parking lot of the restaurant was crowded. Claudia had to park far away from the entrance and her feet were cold and wet by the time she reached the restaurant's front door. She hoped Frank had already gotten a table for them.

Weaving through the small crowd of people at the entrance, she looked around for Frank, who at six feet five inches tall was hard to miss, even sitting down. She spotted him waving to her from a booth about halfway into the dining room.

Making her way to the table, Claudia passed a group of women who seemed to be rating some of the restaurant's male patrons. Apparently they'd already taken full advantage of the half-price happy hour drinks. One of the women made a comment about the tall, serious brother sitting all alone at a nearby booth. Claudia had to giggle when she realized it was her brother they were talking about. She wanted to stop at the table and tell the women not to waste their time trying to get Frank's attention. Unless they lived in a petrie dish or beaker, Frank wouldn't notice them.

"What were you doing that you couldn't be here on time?" Frank asked his baby sister as she plucked his ear and sat down across from him.

"Relax, Frank, I was busy. Besides, I'm only a few minutes late." Claudia leaned in and whispered, "Don't look now, but I think you have a fan club over there at that table."

Frank looked over his sister's shoulder and inadvertently caught the eye of one of the anxious young women. He returned her smile but nothing else.

"Too young, too eager and too-"

"Good for the likes of you," Claudia finished. "I wish you would stop being so boring and get out and enjoy life a little. You're the only man I know that would prefer to sit and watch mold grow instead of cuddling up in front of a warm fire with someone special. I don't know how Sharon can stand dating you."

Frank snapped open his menu and frowned.

Instantly Claudia was sorry she had teased her brother. She sensed something was wrong.

"Sharon and I broke up," Frank announced matter of factly.

"What happened? You two seemed to really be hitting it off."

Frank closed his menu and shrugged his shoulders. "Yeah, I thought the same thing, but I guess I read that one wrong. Let's order," he said motioning for the waitress and putting an end to the conversation about his failed relationship with Sharon.

All through dinner Claudia did her best to cheer Frank up, who was doing his best to pretend his break up with Sharon wasn't affecting him.

"I saw Ray at the gym the other day. He asked about you," Frank said, trying to change the subject.

"Really?"

"Yes, and I thought that was pretty strange."

"What's so strange about that? Lots of people go to the gym, Frank. We don't all get our kicks from experimenting on lab rats."

Frank didn't think his sister was funny. "I thought you two were joined at the hip. He said he hadn't seen you in a while. What's up with that? Are you growing tired of Ray after all these years?"

Claudia thought about what Frank said. She really hadn't seen

Ray in a while. They'd had dinner together the night she met Damien but that had been the last time she saw Ray. She'd meant to call him after she cancelled their standing Wednesday lunch date, but had gotten so busy doing other things that she'd ultimately neglected to do so. He probably thought she was still upset with him about Damien.

"I guess I've gotten so busy with work and volunteering at the church that I haven't spent very much time with Ray." Claudia didn't mention to Frank that the real reason she'd been busy was because she'd been on several dates. She also didn't mention how bad some of her dates had turned out. She was beginning to wonder where all the good men were hiding. It had to be somewhere on another planet.

"Good friends are hard to come by, Claudia. Don't be so careless with the ones you have."

It always annoyed her when Frank acted and sounded like their father. This time was no different even if he was right.

"Spare me the lecture, Frank. I'll make it up to Ray."

When the waitress placed the check on the table, Claudia snatched it up before Frank had a chance to grab it. "My treat," she announced. "It's the least I can do to cheer up my big brother."

Frank smiled at the effort his sister was making to bring him out of the dumps. He loved both of his sisters very much, but it was his youngest sister Claudia that no matter what could always make him smile.

"That's good for starters, baby sister. But don't forget that generous attitude when you're picking out my Christmas gift," he joked on their way out of the restaurant.

CHAPTER SEVEN

Ray's meeting had ended early. He was glad since he had been unable to give his full attention to what was being discussed. He hoped that his partner had taken good notes and would be able to address any issues pertaining to the meeting if questions arose.

Ray was distracted and unable to concentrate. Maybe it was the holiday season or the fact that the general work atmosphere was more relaxed with everyone concentrating on taking time off as opposed to getting any real work done. Maybe it was because it was Friday and the weekend was too close to think seriously about work. Whatever it was, for some odd reason he found himself doing a great deal of reflecting and way more daydreaming than he should have been doing.

Whenever he felt like this it always helped him to talk to Claudia. He had hoped talking to her would help this time and he had been trying to call her for the past two days. He'd left messages for her at work and at home. She hadn't returned any of his calls and he had begun to get worried. When she finally did call him back, it was to cancel another Wednesday lunch date. Their conversation had been brief but she did manage to tell him that she was having lunch with a man she'd met at a business seminar. He was only going to be in town for a few days, and the only day they could have lunch together was on Wednesday.

Their Wednesday, thought Ray glumly.

He knew this plan of Claudia's was going to mean trouble. She rarely cancelled their lunch dates and for the strangest reason, this time it seemed to really bother him.

He'd tried to get information from Claudia on her latest prospect but she had declined to give him too many details while promising to fill him in later. The only thing he managed to get out of her was that this guy lived in Indianapolis and was the vice president of marketing for a mid-sized insurance company. She also made a reference to him not being anything like Damien.

Ray was used to Claudia dating and he never really had any problems with the men she dated, although he thought some of them had been a complete waste of her time. But he and Claudia had made a pact a long time ago not to interfere in each other's love lives. At times this had proven to be a bit difficult, especially on Claudia's part, as she tended to be a little more vocal about Ray's choice in women. But he knew she meant well and she never actually interfered, she just let her opinions be known.

Ray sat at his desk and tried once again to concentrate on the notes his partner had given him for an upcoming project but he still couldn't seem to focus. He was restless and he didn't know why. His mind wandered back to Claudia. He wondered about the latest prospect from Indy. Would this guy be worthy of her? Would he treat her the way she deserved to be treated? Would he laugh at her jokes, know her favorite song, enjoy her cooking or know how to cheer her up when she was down? Would he appreciate all the wonderful, crazy and unique things about her that made her special? How could he?

"Enough already," he said aloud. This was ridiculous. He couldn't sit there all day thinking about Claudia and whom she was dating. This had never been an issue before and he wasn't about to let it be one now.

Ray shut down his computer and grabbed his coat and briefcase. He was going to take the rest of the day off and his first stop would be the gym. Working out always cleared his head and that was exactly what he needed today.

Claudia woke up Friday morning feeling as if she had been hit by a truck. Her throat was sore and scratchy, every muscle in her body ached, and she was nauseous. She stuck her head out from under the covers and looked at the clock. It was almost eight-thirty. Just thinking about getting up to look through her medicine cabinet exhausted her. There was no way in the world she was going in to work today.

After she called to tell her manager that she was not coming in, Claudia sat on the side of her bed. Her head was spinning and she was hit by a wave a nausea.

She needed some aspirin and ginger ale. Neither of which she could recall having in the house. She picked up the phone to call her mother but remembered that she and her father had gone to Cleveland for the day. Karen was working and her brother was teaching a class all week and would be difficult to reach.

"Where's everybody when you need them?" Claudia asked Ginger who stared at her with a puzzled look.

Ray. Maybe he wouldn't be too busy at work and could make a drug store run for her on his lunch break. She called him at work but he wasn't at his desk. Claudia left a brief voice mail message and crawled back into bed. Her head pounded relentlessly and she was freezing and just couldn't seem to get warm.

Around noon Claudia woke up and wondered why it was so warm in her room. It felt as if someone had cranked up the heat. Throwing off the covers she dragged herself down the hall and into the kitchen to get something to drink. She felt no better than she had earlier that morning except that the nausea had subsided a bit and her pounding headache had downgraded to a mere dull ache. Not being very hungry she knew the important thing to do was to stay hydrated. She had phoned her doctor earlier who advised that it sounded as if she had the flu and to call him if the symptoms worsened.

Claudia sniffed. She didn't feel like getting dressed and going into his office but at least he could have pretended that she was serious enough to need to be checked out. As far as she was concerned he might as well have said, "Take two aspirin and call me in the morning."

She was thirsty and her throat was still sore and dry. Scanning the shelves of her refrigerator she found very little that would be of benefit to her in her present state. A quart of milk that may or may not be spoiled, cranberry juice, eggnog and a bottle of wine. Claudia poured herself a glass of juice. It tasted awful. Apparently her taste buds had been affected by her illness. She decided to go back to bed and later, if she felt better, she'd go to the store for provisions.

Just as Claudia headed down the hall to her bedroom, the doorbell rang. Ginger ran to the front door and barked once.

"Hush, Ginger. We don't want to scare away whoever is on the other side of the door, especially if they would be willing to make a run to the pharmacy."

Knowing she probably looked a mess and not really caring, she opened the door and found Ray on the other side. Carrying two large grocery bags, he took one look at Claudia and realized she was indeed sick.

"You have no idea how glad I am to see you," she said.

Ray stepped inside and took the packages to the kitchen with Ginger leading the way. "I was in a meeting when you called. Luckily I checked my messages before going to lunch. Don't take this the wrong way, but you look and sound awful."

Claudia sneezed and adjusted her robe. "If that had come from anyone else I would have been offended. But come to think of it, the way I feel right now, being offended is the last thing on my mind."

Ray dug to the bottom of one of the grocery bags and produced a bottle of aspirin. "Here, take this with some juice and go back to bed."

Claudia gladly did as she was told and remembered to thank Ray for coming to her rescue.

"Have you called the doctor?" he asked before she left the kitchen.

Claudia sneezed again and nodded her head. "He gave me a phone diagnosis of the flu and told me to drink plenty of liquids, take a pain reliever and to call if my symptoms worsen." Claudia turned to leave and told Ray that he could leave everything on the counter and that she would put it up later. She thanked him again and headed back down the hallway to her bedroom.

Once inside her bedroom Claudia laid her robe at the foot of the bed and climbed under the cool comfort of the sheets. She heard Ray puttering around in the kitchen even though she told him that she would put everything away later. She was too tired to fuss and drifted off to sleep instead.

The clock read eleven forty-five P.M. when Claudia got up to turn up the heat. Still feeling tired and achy she knew she should try to eat something but didn't have enough energy to make the effort of foraging through her cabinets for food.

Before she reached the end of the hallway she saw the flickering lights from the television coming from the living room. Ray must have left it on when he was watching TV earlier, she thought.

Claudia stopped just inside the entranceway of the living room when she not only saw that the television was still on but that Ray was fast asleep in the recliner. Ginger had been sleeping under the Christmas tree and looked up when she heard Claudia.

Had Ray been there since earlier that afternoon? Claudia picked up the remote from the coffee table and turned off the television.

Sitting up in the chair, Ray mumbled groggily, "Hey, I was watching that."

"No, I think the TV was watching you, Ray."

He checked his watch. "What are you doing up? Don't you feel any better?"

"Not really. I just got up to get something to drink and to turn up the heat." Claudia pulled her robe tightly around her frame and rubbed her arms. "It's freezing in here. You're not cold?"

"No, and I'm not sick either. Seems as if your internal thermostat is going haywire."

Ray took Claudia by the shoulders, turned her around and headed back down the hallway to her bedroom.

"Here," he said, pulling the covers back, "you need to be in bed." He went to the cedar chest at the foot of the bed and retrieved a blanket. "Sit tight for a few minutes. I'll get you something to drink. Don't let her leave this room," Ray instructed Ginger who had followed them into the bedroom and seemed to be standing guard at Claudia's bedside.

Claudia pulled the blanket up to her chin and snuggled deep under the covers in an attempt to fend off the chills.

"Do you feel like eating anything?"

Claudia shook her head no.

After fifteen minutes had passed Ray returned with a tray. "I want you to drink this," he said handing her a cup of steaming liquid.

Claudia stuck her head out from under the covers and eyed the steaming cup of yellow liquid suspiciously. "What in the world is that?"

"The pharmacist said it's hot flu therapy. She said a steaming cup of this will help with body aches, fever and most of the other symptoms that you have. Plus it will help you sleep."

"It looks nasty and I'm sure if my sense of smell were working, I'd be repulsed."

"Repulsed or not, you need this. Besides, it's not bad. I tasted some. It's lemon flavored."

Claudia wrinkled her nose and took a sip. "Tastes like hot water and medicine."

"That's because your taste buds aren't working. Just finish it. And eat this, too."

Ray had scrambled some eggs and made toast. Claudia really didn't want to eat but was touched that Ray was making such an effort to help her feel better.

She finished the medicine and ate her eggs and toast without a fuss. Ray was satisfied.

"Have you been here all afternoon?"

Ray nodded. "I knew you were probably feeling pretty awful and I wanted to hang around in case you needed something. I'm going to put this stuff back in the kitchen and I'll be back to tuck you in."

Claudia was still cold and snuggled as far under the covers as she could. She knew Ray had turned up the heat because she heard the furnace kick on, but she still couldn't shake her chills. When Ray returned from the kitchen he found Claudia shivering slightly.

"I was supposed to have a date tonight," she said in a muffled voice. "What a time to be sick."

"Date or no date, there's no good time to be sick. The best thing for you to do is to get some rest."

"Are you getting ready to go home?"

"I don't have to. Do you need something?"

"Yes, a little heat."

Ray resisted the temptation to lay next to her and wrap his arms around her. "You'll be warm soon. Just relax and try to get some sleep."

"Would you mind doing me one more favor?"

"Sure. Anything."

"Could you sit with me until I fall asleep?"

"Of course I will," Ray said as he moved some clothes off of the chair across from Claudia's bed.

"You know what this reminds me of?" Claudia asked as she tried to stifle a yawn.

"What?"

"The time you had your tonsils out."

"And you sneaked into the hospital to sit with me so that I wouldn't have to be alone." He didn't mention how infrequent his parents' visits had been, but they both remembered that, too.

"It never occurred to me that you'd have a roommate and that the nurses would be in your room every fifteen minutes."

"Or that I'd have all that ice cream, popsicles and Jell-O."

"Or that my parents would have a fit when they found out that I'd taken two buses to get across town and had sworn Karen to secrecy about my whereabouts."

"If my memory serves me correctly, you didn't swear Karen to anything. You threatened to tell your mother that she had a boyfriend if she didn't keep quiet about your journey across town."

"Hey, I was only ten years old. I had to use whatever tactics I could in order to ensure your safety and welfare."

Ray laughed. "Was it my safety and welfare you were concerned about or the fact that I could have all the popsicles and ice cream I wanted?"

Claudia yawned again. "I don't know why you keep mentioning that. Mere treats had nothing to do with my concern for you."

"Yeah, right."

"Okay, since you're forcing me to fess up, I guess I'm a big enough person now to admit that I was just a tad bit jealous of all the attention you were getting. But let's not forget the most important thing that keeps getting overshadowed; I really was concerned about you."

"I know," Ray said. "And I was touched, even when you tried to hide in my room so the nurse wouldn't see you when it was after visiting hours."

"Yeah, and you know I became scarred for life because of you."

"How was I supposed to predict you'd hit your knee on the side of the bed and end up having to get stitches?"

"My parents were furious. How long was I confined to my room after that whole ordeal?"

Ray crossed his arms and thought. "Till high school graduation?"

"Seemed that long. Until today, you still owed me big time. However, I think now we're even."

"That makes me feel a whole lot better."

"Even though I'm still scarred for life." Claudia yawned. "Ray," she continued in a sleepy voice, "thanks for taking care of me today. I don't know what I would have done if you hadn't come over. I clearly don't deserve you."

"No problem," he replied. The combination of the flu medication and Claudia's fatigue caused her to quickly become drowsy. When she was sleepy, she tended to ramble.

"One day someone will realize what a wonderful catch you are and snatch you right up from under my nose. Next thing I know you're going to be married, have a house full of kids, a minivan and a dog, and you'll forget all about little old me."

"Never."

"Hmm, that's what you say now. A wife and kids and no time for Claudia. I can see it as clear as day. I'll be an old spinster and I'll have no one to look after me, not even Ginger. I think if given the choice, she would leave me in a heartbeat and move in with you. Maybe I should get a couple of cats. They're supposed to be good companions. I'll become the crazy old lady with a house full of cats to keep me company."

"Go to sleep, Claudia," Ray said leaning forward and kissing her on the forehead.

"Is Spike a good name for a cat?"

After a few moments Claudia became quiet and her breathing was deep and steady. She had finally drifted into a peaceful sleep. Ray leaned forward and moved an errant strand of hair from her forehead. His fingers brushed against her skin slightly but she was not disturbed. However, Ray was.

He studied the face of the one woman who knew everything about him except for what was in his heart.

CHAPTER EIGHT

Jewel hung up the telephone and sat down at the table with a cup of coffee.

Looking up from his newspaper and munching on the donuts he'd brought over on his visit, Frank noticed a puzzled look on his mother's face.

"Is something wrong with Ray?" he asked.

"No."

"Weren't you just talking to him on the phone?"

"Yes, but I called Claudia's house and he answered the phone."

"What's wrong with that?"

"He said Claudia was in bed with the flu and it sounded as if I'd roused him out of his sleep."

"Mom, Ray has stayed at Claudia's before. I don't know what you're getting at."

"He answered the phone on the first ring."

Frank looked at his mother and wondered when she was going to get to the point.

"There's no phone in the guest room," she replied. "Which makes me wonder where Ray slept last night."

Ray had gone home Saturday afternoon and returned later that evening to check on Claudia. Her illness proved to be short-lived and by Sunday she was feeling much better although she still had the sniffles and was a little tired.

Sunday evening Ray showed up at Claudia's front door with dinner and some videos.

"What's all this?" she asked, helping him unload the bags of food.

"I thought you might not feel up to cooking and I didn't feel like eating alone tonight. So this seemed like the perfect solution." Suddenly realizing that Claudia may have had plans, he asked, "You don't mind, do you?"

"Of course not. I was just about to order something to eat."

Ray spread all of the Chinese food containers on the counter. "I didn't know what you would feel like eating, or could tolerate, so I brought a little bit of everything."

He wasn't kidding. It really did look as if he'd gotten a little bit of everything. There was egg drop soup, sweet and sour chicken, shrimp fried rice, egg rolls, pot stickers, barbecued spareribs, and almond cookies.

Claudia wasn't quite sure herself what she could tolerate so she just had a little of the soup and an egg roll. Ray, on the other hand, ate heartily and didn't miss at least tasting some of everything.

After they ate Claudia helped Ray put the leftovers away.

"This was nice, Ray. I can't remember the last time we spent this much time together. I'd forgotten what a fun date you can be," Claudia joked.

"And I'd forgotten how sappy you get when you're sick."

"Sappy? What do you mean?"

"Just something you said when you were under the influence of flu medication."

Claudia tried to remember what she'd said. She remembered they were talking about the time he had his tonsils out and that she still blamed him for the scar on her knee, but other than that, she couldn't think of what else they'd talked about.

"I just want you to know that I'm not that kind of guy," Ray said with a serious expression on his face.

Worried about what she may have said, Claudia asked, "What kind of guy? Did-did I do something?"

Ray looked at Claudia with a straight face and then burst out laughing. "I'm just teasing. You'd didn't do anything, except snore like a bear."

Claudia wadded up a napkin and threw it at Ray. "If you hadn't bought over such a nice selection of goodies, I'd put you back out in the cold."

Ray was still laughing.

"You're terrible. And I don't snore."

Ray and Claudia sat on opposite ends of the couch with Claudia resting her feet on his lap. There was a comfortable silence between them.

"You're right," Ray said. "Despite the fact that what led up to this evening was your being sick, this was fun. We haven't hung out together in a long time."

"Yeah, this was nice."

Ray had missed being with Claudia. Their schedules hadn't allowed them to just spend time doing the simple things they loved doing together, especially with Claudia concentrating so hard on finding a husband.

They were quiet for a while as they watched the movie. Then Ray picked up the remote and turned down the sound.

"I need to talk to you about something, Claudia."

"What is it?" she asked, slowly turning her attention away from the movie.

"It's something I've wanted to talk to you about for a long time but I never really knew how to say it, or even if I should say it."

Picking up on the serious tone in his voice, Claudia took the remote from him and switched off the TV. "Is something wrong?"

"Depends on how you look at it."

"Well, first tell me what it is and how you're looking at it."

Ray looked down at his hands and then at Claudia. Sitting on the couch in a sweatshirt and sweat pants with her hair in a ponytail, she looked as beautiful as ever. Claudia had absolutely no clue as to how she made him feel. There was nothing in the world that he wouldn't do for her. Taking care of her when she was sick had been his pleasure and he would gladly do it again.

Ray's expression was serious and he seemed nervous as he began, "I guess I should start out by saying-." The doorbell rang before he could finish his sentence.

"Hold that thought," Claudia said as she got up to answer the door.

"Hi, sweetie," Jewel greeted her daughter. "A little bird told me you weren't feeling well and I stopped by to see if you needed anything."

"No, Mom. I'm fine now. On Friday I was really out of it, but Ray came over with some food and a bunch of other stuff that I needed. He's actually been taking very good care of me since then."

"I see."

Ray came out to greet Jewel when he heard her voice.

"Hello, Ray. How's our patient?"

"Almost as good as new," he reported. "One more day of rest and she should be absolutely perfect."

Jewel looked at the expression on Ray's face and wondered if she had interrupted something important. Ray looked uncomfortable and Jewel thought she saw a trace of perspiration on his brow. Sensing an odd tension in the room, she decided it would be best to leave.

"Here," she said holding up a bag. "I brought you some fruit.

I've got to get going. I need to pick something up for your father on the way home. Take care and call me if you need anything."

Claudia thought her mother's behavior was a little odd but decided not to pursue it. Besides, she wanted to get back to her conversation with Ray. He was just about to confide in her about something and she wanted to know what it was. Probably met someone he was interested in and wanted her opinion, she mused.

After Jewel left, Ray, too, decided it was time for him to leave. He wanted to talk to Claudia about what was on his mind but maybe it was too soon.

"I thought you wanted to talk to me about something," Claudia said concerned.

"It can wait," he said standing in the doorway and zipping up his coat as the chilly wind encircled them. Before he turned to leave Ray reached out and touched Claudia's shoulder and pulled her into an embrace. He held her tightly and was amazed at how wonderful she felt in his arms. Just as if she belonged there. "You'd better get back inside before you catch a chill," he said abruptly and left.

Claudia watched Ray's car pull out of the driveway and wondered what had just happened. Why had Ray hugged her that way? It was different from the way he normally hugged her, although, she had to admit, it felt nice. Shrugging her shoulders she went back inside and turned on the TV. Despite being puzzled by his behavior at times, she thought again how fortunate she was to have Ray in her life. She hoped that when she found the man of her dreams, he would be as good to her as Ray had always been.

Ray pulled into his garage and cut off the car's engine. *What's wrong with me?* He had just let the perfect opportunity slip by. He needed to tell Claudia how he felt about her and tonight would have been the perfect time, but he'd convinced himself that it was too soon. When would he have that opportunity again? Claudia was actively dating and looking for a man to fall in love with. And here he was right here! Why hadn't she considered him to be the man of her dreams? And why didn't Claudia recognize the love he had for her?

Looking back it had taken everything Ray had to keep quiet when Claudia had initially revealed her plan to him. He'd wanted to tell her right then how he felt about her, but the time wasn't right. Besides Ray didn't know if Claudia felt the same way about him that he felt about her.

He loved her. For him their friendship had turned into a love deeper than he could ever have imagined. For a long time he tried to deny his attraction to Claudia and at one point even speculated that his feelings for her stemmed from a past rejection. But deep down once he stopped trying to analyze what he felt for Claudia, he was able to accept it for what it was. True love.

She was everything that he had ever wanted, even when there was a time in his life that he wasn't sure what he wanted. Claudia was someone he trusted implicitly and knew would never let him down, and that meant a great deal to him.

On top of everything else he had to admit that she knew him better than anyone else and he could always be himself around her, especially if that meant showing his vulnerable side which she never took advantage of.

When Ray was a teenager he witnessed first-hand how destructive his parents were to each other all the while confessing their love. Their relationship was plagued by manipulative, deceitful and at times, downright violent behavior. Seeing that he was afraid that he would never be able to be close to anyone for fear that he would one day end up like them. Luckily he had other examples of what love was supposed to be and knew that his parents had no idea of the true meaning of the sentiment. Claudia didn't know it and neither did he early on, but there were many times she showed Ray that love meant respect, adoration and commitment, all of which she gave without hesitation.

Of all the women he had dated over the years, none could compare to Claudia. It was never actually his intention to compare anyone to her but it always boiled down to that. Maybe it was because he knew she cared enough to want to know all the little things about him. Most people knew that his favorite color was blue. It was Claudia who knew it was *royal* blue. She knew that he loved warm chocolate chip cookies and action movies. She also knew that a relaxing evening to him was listening to jazz as the sound of rain fell gently against the window. She even knew how embarrassed he was the time his parents showed up at one of their school functions so drunk that the principal had to escort them out of the building.

Even at that young age, Claudia had known what to say to make Ray feel better. However, now the one thing Ray wished with all his heart that Claudia knew she was completely unaware of. She didn't know how much he loved her.

He needed to find out what Claudia's feelings for him were. But how? He couldn't just come right out and ask her, could he? What if she still only thought of him as a friend and he confessed his love for her? Not only would he look like a fool but the results could be disastrous and no matter what, he didn't want to lose the one thing he was sure of – Claudia's friendship.

CHAPTER NINE

It was Christmas Eve and the usual downtown hustle and bustle were replaced by a quiet calm that seemed to have blanketed the city in a matter of a few hours. Most of the downtown offices had closed earlier that afternoon and the retail stores had long since rung up their final sales. Several inches of snow had fallen earlier in the day guaranteeing a much-coveted white Christmas.

Claudia stood in front of her bedroom mirror admiring the way her new outfit looked. From the elegant gold hoop earrings to the blue knit dress down to matching blue boots, she was a sight to behold. She rarely wore blue but had found the outfit at a sale when she was shopping for Ray's gift and couldn't pass up such a great bargain. It was the perfect outfit to wear to the Christmas Eve service at church. Afterwards she was going to her parents' for their traditional Christmas Eve party.

Claudia ran her fingers through her hair and wondered if she should bump it a little or leave it straight. Deciding that she liked how it looked straight, she gathered her purse and coat and headed for the door leading to the garage. But before she could turn the door handle, the phone rang.

"Hello?"

"Hey, Claudia," Ray said through the static of his cell phone. "I'm on my way to the Christmas Eve service. Do you want me to swing by and give you a ride?"

"No thanks. I'm on my way out right now. My mother called earlier to find out if you were coming to the party. I told her that as far as I knew you'd be there. She complained that she hadn't seen much of you lately and then went on to chastise me for not bringing you around. Like it is my fault that my parents haven't seen you."

"Tell your parents that I'll be at the party, but I really called for another reason."

Claudia shifted her purse and a tray of deviled eggs she'd made to take to the party. "What's the other reason? Is it something that can wait until I see you at church?"

"Viveca is in town."

"Viveca Roberts?" *What rock did she crawl out from under and why had she headed in their direction*? Claudia thought as she tried to keep a stream of hatred from coursing through her consciousness.

"Her mother is ill and she came back to help take care of her."

"Knowing Viveca she's probably waiting for her mother to die so that she can collect on the insurance."

Ray knew he had opened a can of worms when he mentioned his ex-fiancé Viveca Roberts, but he didn't want Claudia to run into her and be caught off guard. Theirs was truly a case of no love lost and he didn't want to think about what would happen if they accidentally ran into each other.

"Come on, Claudia, don't allow yourself to get upset about Viveca. For all we know she could be a changed person. There's nothing to worry about if you're worrying about me. Besides, I'm a big boy. I can handle whatever comes my way from the cunning Ms. Roberts. I just wanted to give you a heads up in case she attends church this evening. Look, I've got to get some gas before I run out and I need to find a grocery store that's still open. I'll see you at church."

Claudia sat the tray of deviled eggs on the counter and sighed. Viveca Roberts. That woman was bad news and Claudia didn't think for a minute that anything short of a lobotomy would change her.

She hoped that her visit would be short. But more importantly, she prayed Ray would be careful.

The Christmas Eve service was packed. By arriving a little before the service started, Claudia was able to get a seat in the main sanctuary with her parents and sister. Ray, she later learned, had to watch the service on closed circuit television in the overflow room with the other late arrivals.

Claudia ran into people that she hadn't seen since last Christmas Eve's service. Even though she didn't attend church as regularly as she should, she still managed to attend more than the Christmas, Easter and Thanksgiving services.

Several people mentioned to her that Viveca Roberts was back in town. *Had her arrival made the evening news?* Claudia wondered wryly. She was surprised that Viveca hadn't made an appearance at church. Missing an opportunity to be seen wasn't like her at all.

When Claudia turned down the street that led to her parents' house, she was surprised by the number of people that were already there. She ended up having to park halfway down the block and instantly wished she had worn more sensible boots to walk through the freshly fallen snow. She prayed she wouldn't slip and fall, scattering deviled eggs all over the sidewalk, not to mention the embarrassment she'd feel if someone actually saw her fall.

Christmas music, the delectable aromas of many of Claudia's favorite foods, and familiar faces greeted her when she stepped inside her parents' home. Bright lights flickered on the enormous Christmas tree standing in the far corner of the living room, mistletoe hung over the entranceway of the kitchen, and everywhere she looked Claudia was reminded of how wonderful it was to be surrounded by family and friends, especially this time of year.

"Hey, baby girl, go in the kitchen and see what's taking your mother so long bringing out more ice," instructed Lawrence Ryland of his daughter before going over to the stereo and putting on an Etta James CD.

Claudia went into the kitchen with the tray of deviled eggs that she was thankful hadn't ended up decorating the sidewalk. She found her mother standing in front of the open oven basting chicken wings and humming along to Etta.

"Honey, put those eggs in the dining room on the long table. And take this bag of ice and fill the ice buckets before your father has a heart attack," Jewel Ryland said to her daughter.

Claudia did as her mother asked and then came back into the kitchen to offer her help.

"I think that's all I need right now," Jewel said, looking around the kitchen. "As soon as the wings are ready to come out of the oven, I'm going to join the party."

"Where are Karen and Frank?" Claudia asked, munching on a piece of celery.

"Frank called right before you got here. He said he had to finish up something at work before coming to the party."

"On Christmas Eve? He's a research scientist, for goodness sake. Were there mold cultures that had to be analyzed tonight? Somebody needs to get that boy a life."

Ignoring her daughter, Jewel continued, "Karen had to run back home and change Candace's clothes. I don't know why your sister doesn't just carry a change of clothes for that child at all times. She's five years old. How does she expect her to stay clean for any length of time? The standard rule is if you have a child under ten, always be prepared for accidents. Keep extra clothes and moist towelettes handy." Jewel paused and took a breath. "With that said, I'm sure Karen will be back as soon as she can."

Jewel wiped her hands on a dishtowel and turned to Claudia. "Where's Raymond? I didn't see him at church tonight."

"You would have seen him if you had been in the overflow room. He arrived late and had to watch the service from there. I'm sure he'll be here soon."

"Where has he been hiding lately? I haven't heard from him except for that one day he called here looking for you."

Claudia shrugged her shoulders. "I have no idea what Ray's been up to. I'm not married to the man."

"No, Miss Smarty, but he is your closest friend and I would think you would treat him as such. Didn't you have lunch with him Wednesday?"

"No, I had to cancel. I had another, uh, engagement."

"Engagement? By that do you really mean a date?"

Claudia looked at her mother suspiciously. "Depends on what you've heard."

Jewel pretended to look sternly at her daughter. "Don't play with me, girl. I asked you a question."

Claudia folded her arms and was about to roll her eyes but thought better of it. "Yes, Mom, what I really meant to say was that I had a date."

Unmoved by her daughter's theatrics, Jewel asked, "And is this someone from work?"

Claudia took another piece of celery and dipped it lightly in a container of ranch dressing. Her mother was waiting for an answer and she wondered just how much she should reveal to her. She really didn't want to get into a long, drawn out discussion about her social life but she guessed it wouldn't hurt to tell her a little bit about the man she was seeing. "No, I don't work with him but he is someone I met through work. He's from Indianapolis and so far seems really nice. Good job, nice manners and quite attractive."

"Don't talk with food in your mouth. So, does he have all of the attributes you're looking for in a husband?"

Claudia stopped chewing and looked at her mother. "What do you mean by that?"

Jewel filled a bowl with ranch dressing and didn't even bother to look up when she answered, "Your sister told me about your plan."

This time Claudia did roll her eyes. "I asked Karen not to say anything. That's why I never tell her what's going on in my life. She has no idea what it means to keep something in confidence."

Jewel stopped what she was doing and walked over to her daughter. "Sweetheart, don't be upset with Karen. She's just concerned about you, that's all. We all love you and are concerned about you."

"Concerned about what? I don't see what the big deal is. I'm thirty-two years old, not twelve. I don't see anything wrong with what I'm doing." Claudia's voice softened when she said, "Mom, I know what you're going to say about my plan, that it's a hair-brained scheme. But look at things from my point of view for a minute. Every time I turn around one of my friends has announced their engagement, celebrated an anniversary or announced the arrival of a new baby. It's not that I'm jealous or anything, but I have to admit, I want those same joys in my life. Being single was fine before. Now I need more. It gets a little lonely going home night after night with no one to spend time with besides Ginger. I don't think I'm asking for a lot. All I want is what you and Daddy have together, what Karen has with David. I want a husband and family to come home to in the evenings. I want someone to care whether or not I had a bad day at work or who wants to snuggle with me on cold winter evenings. I want to have Christmas Eve celebrations with my husband and children and a house full of people laughing, loving and enjoying life. The bottom line is that I want someone to love who loves me back."

Jewel's heart went out to her youngest daughter. "Honey, there's nothing wrong with wanting those things. You deserve that and a lot more, and it's out there for you. However, you're looking at this strategically and that may not be the best approach."

"Then what is? 'Cause I can't seem to find that magic formula for finding someone that I want to spend the rest of my life with and Lord knows I've looked."

Jewel walked back to the counter and placed the bowl of dip in the center of the vegetable tray. When she walked by her daughter she leaned over, kissed her on the cheek and said, "There's no magic formula or pills or potions. The best advice I have for you is to simply open your eyes. Sometimes what you're looking for is right under your nose."

"Ahem."

Claudia and Jewel looked up simultaneously. Ray stood in the kitchen doorway with a devilishly handsome grin on his face.

"Raymond Elliott, come over here and give me a hug."

Ray gave Jewel a hug and kiss on the cheek after she sat the tray down.

Jewel stood back and looked at Ray. "Don't you like us anymore?" she asked. "We hardly ever see you and we miss you terribly."

Ray laughed. "Of course I like you, Miss Jewel. You're the best family a person could have. And I've missed you all, too."

"Then what's the problem?"

Ray looked over at Claudia and shrugged his shoulders. "I've been a little busy. That's all."

"Well, you'd better not get too busy for family."

"Claudia, seems like your father has pulled out his solid gold blues collection," Ray remarked, glancing over his shoulder.

Claudia rolled her eyes as she listened to a gravelly voiced singer talking about big legs and mini skirts. "I know. I wish he'd let someone else choose the music. Everyone is going to leave if we don't get some better music in this joint. Mom, can you do something about that?"

Ray snapped his fingers and bumped Jewel with his hip. "What's wrong with you, girl? Don't you know good music when you hear it? Feel like going out there and getting' your groove on, Claudia?"

"To that?" Claudia asked, nodding in the direction of the living room.

"Ah, go ahead," Jewel said. "Here, take this vegetable tray out to the dining room and tell you father that I need help here in the kitchen. And as soon as he turns his back, change the music."

Ray and Claudia did as they were told but Lawrence was a little reluctant to leave his duties as DJ. After he was safely in his wife's care, Ray traded Koko Taylor for more fitting dance music and danced with Claudia until she was forced to kick off her boots.

"You look nice tonight," Ray said admiringly.

"I'm sorry. What did you say?" Claudia had been watching her niece and nephew trying to dance like their grandparents.

"I said, you look nice tonight. That shade of blue is certainly your color."

"Thanks. You don't look too shabby yourself."

Claudia did look nice. In fact, she looked absolutely beautiful, Ray thought. He watched as she left him and joined her nephew on the makeshift dance floor in her stocking feet. As she swayed to the music her knit dress clung seductively to all her luscious curves. Ray wiped a few beads of perspiration from his forehead.

Everyone was laughing and having a good time, including Ray. There was nothing like Christmas Eve at the Ryland house.

Ever since Ray had walked into the house that evening he could feel the love and warmth that dwelled there. It had always been that way and he knew he could count on it remaining so. When he and Claudia were kids they would hang out at her house most of the time after school since both of his parents spent the majority of their time making each other as miserable as possible. Ray loved his parents but he'd learned at an early age that they simply were not cut out to be parents, or husband and wife. Jewel was more of a mother to Ray than his real mother ever was. Jewel would fuss over him, always making sure his homework was complete, attended most of his basketball games and track meets, and when both of his parents were killed in a car accident right before his high school graduation, it was Jewel who encouraged him to attend college and pursue a career in architecture. Ray truly loved Jewel and Lawrence Ryland and they loved him the same.

When someone put on a slow song, Ray took the opportunity to cut in on Claudia and her nephew.

"Hey, little man," Ray said tapping the six year old on the shoulder, "may I?"

Little Eric looked confused and asked, "May you what, Uncle Ray?"

Ray knelt down and spoke to Eric and nodded his head in Claudia's direction. "May I have a turn dancing with the pretty lady?"

"You mean Aunt Claudia?"

Ray nodded and Eric wrinkled his face, shrugged his shoulders and ran off to find his sister.

"This is fun," Ray said. He held Claudia close as they danced to "This Christmas" by Donny Hathaway. Even though he'd never mentioned it, he always enjoyed dancing with her. There was just something about the way they fit and moved together perfectly. It just seemed so right.

Ray laughed.

Claudia leaned back and looked at him quizzically. "What's so funny?"

"I was thinking about our prom and how long it took for you to teach me how to slow dance."

Remembering the lessons, Claudia joined in the laughter. "I still can't figure out how you could be so graceful on the basketball court but have two left feet when it came to dancing." She leaned her head back down against Ray's shoulder. He smelled nice, very nice.

He shook his head and sighed. "And to think, after all those lessons, my date came down with chicken pox two days before the prom."

Claudia chuckled. She remembered frantically trying to find a prom date for Ray after his date became ill but eventually convinced him to go stag. It was a good thing too because Claudia's date abandoned her shortly after they arrived at the dance.

"Thinking about Buck Evans?"

Claudia nodded. Buck Evans. The prom date from hell. Once Claudia realized Buck had abandoned her to hook up with his ex-girlfriend for the remainder of the prom, she did her best to act as if it didn't bother her. She had laughed and pretended to have a good time but deep down inside she was hurt. Ray had contributed to the performance and pretended to be Claudia's intended date. In fact, they'd put on such a convincing production that the following Monday everyone wanted to know if Claudia and Ray were dating, but she had refused to answer. After his girlfriend had dumped him again Buck even had the nerve to ask her if she was dating Ray.

High school hadn't been the only time people thought Claudia and Ray were dating. Their relationship somehow affected every relationship Claudia had been involved in. Most men didn't understand her friendship with Ray. Some saw him as competition and others simply felt uncomfortable with the whole situation. They all assumed that at some point they'd been lovers or eventually would be.

Being friends with Ray wasn't easy to explain even though they had been friends for ages. Over the years he had filled many voids in Claudia's life. He was her confidant, best friend, sounding board and in-a-pinch date. But never her lover.

She couldn't imagine their relationship taking that particular turn. Although, there was a time or two that she'd let her mind wander in that direction, but nothing ever went further than her imagination. The main thing she wanted to avoid was losing what she had with Ray. The thought of risking everything on becoming his lover only to have things end badly was something she simply did not want to chance.

It wasn't that Ray wasn't good boyfriend or husband material. In fact, he possessed many of the qualities Claudia was currently looking for in a husband. He worked for a successful land development firm, was active in the community, and her parents adored him. He was also educated, moral and passionate about causes that were near and dear to him. For the past five years Ray had volunteered as the boys' football coach at their church. Claudia had seen him work with some of the neighborhood boys that had been labeled incorrigible by the authorities and their schools. But Ray had refused to believe that these were bad kids. He felt that they simply needed an outlet for their energies and frustrations. But more than anything they needed to know that someone cared about them. Ray provided that care and a lot more.

He pushed his kids hard and he expected a lot from them, on the field and off, especially in the classroom. It wasn't out of the ordinary for him to show up unannounced at school and sit in the back of one of his players' classrooms. A parent or teacher simply had to call him if one of the kids was acting up in school or at home and he would deal with it. Education and respect were serious business with Ray and the kids knew he would not tolerate poor grades, apathy, drug or alcohol use, fighting or skipping school. He let his players know from day one that it would be a good education, hard work and perseverance that would take them places beyond their wildest dreams, and that cutting corners or looking for the easy way out was not the way to go. There was never a question that Ray's players admired and respected him.

For the right woman Ray was certainly a complete package. At first glance most women saw a tall, mocha-hued brother who could dress to kill, walk with confidence and had a style that was all his own. But for those who had the opportunity to look a little deeper, it was evident that Ray had a lot more going for him than just good looks. Even though Claudia would never admit it to him, she sort of liked the envious glances she received when they were out together.

Yes, Ray would be a good candidate if they weren't such good friends. But why risk messing up what they already had?

"Are you still reminiscing about the prom?" Ray asked as the song ended.

Claudia started toward the kitchen and stopped in the doorway. "No, I just thought of something else."

"Care to share?"

"I was just thinking, if it weren't for the fact that you've elevated the state of bachelorhood to an art form, don't have a romantic bone in your body, hate cleaning up after yourself and wouldn't know a good woman if she fell directly in your path, you'd be decent marriage material."

Ray looked at the smile on Claudia's face as she counted off the list of his unfavorable, but untrue, characteristics on her fingers.

He was a bit surprised by her statements but he wouldn't let her know that, at least not yet. She thought she had everything, and especially him, all figured out. Well, Claudia may be smart, but when it came to matters of the heart, he was more than qualified to teach her a thing or two.

"So, what you're saying is that I don't fit the criteria on your list? I don't quite measure up."

Claudia continued to smile and tilted her head to the side as if she were posing a challenge. "Afraid not," she said teasingly.

It was time to give Miss Claudia a little insight. Ray leaned in closer so that only she could hear what he was about to say. "First of all, being a bachelor is not something I absolutely love, but it's my current situation, not my permanent one. Secondly, if I make a mess, I clean it up. Third, but most important, I look at being romantic as more than just giving your woman flowers and candy. It's treating her like a precious flower and letting her know that she's sweeter than the finest chocolate. It's knowing that after she's had a rough day at work, when she gets home, and more precisely, once she walks into your arms, that rough day is nothing than a passing memory. Being romantic is lying in bed at night with the lights off and being turned on by simple conversation about absolutely nothing but it means something because someone who loves you is there to listen. It's also knowing how and where your woman likes to be kissed and caressed and never disappointing her. And when it's time to show her how much she's desired, stopping at nothing short of total, mind-blowing satisfaction."

Claudia's smile faded as she stood before Ray stunned. Under normal circumstances she would have snappy comeback, but she couldn't think of one intelligent thing to say. Ray had never spoken to her that way before. All she could do was to stare at him and wonder where he learned all those things he just mentioned, and if he really did them.

Ray looked at Claudia with her wide eyes and before she came to her senses, he closed the small space between them and said, "Speechless? Good." He then leaned down and captured Claudia's slightly parted lips with his own. His tongue danced the width of her delicious mouth, taking what he wanted and teasing and caressing and beckoning her to also give in to her need. He wanted to brand her taste into his memory and never forget its lush sweetness, and he wanted her to know, without uttering the words, that the kiss they shared was a small sample of what he had to offer if she would open her heart and let him enter.

Claudia felt her arms fall to her sides as Ray's strong hands held her shoulders, pulling her as close to him as was humanly possible. She wanted to make her arms move to embrace Ray but they hung at her sides like lifeless appendages. Heat rushed through her body and threatened to engulf her as the passionate kiss continued.

What was wrong with her? This was Ray she was kissing. Her buddy, her pal, her best friend. And she was liking every bit of it!

Almost as quickly as it had happened, Ray released her and ended the kiss. Standing under the mistletoe Claudia looked dazed, delighted and downright confused.

Ray opened the closet door next to the kitchen and took out his coat. Before leaving, he turned to Claudia and said, "Put *that* on your list."

CHAPTER TEN

Jewel Ryland looked out of her front room window and checked once more for her daughter. "Where is your sister?" she asked her oldest daughter, Karen.

"I have no idea. You know how Claudia is. Have you ever known her to rush to get anywhere? I suppose we should have gone by her place to pick her up," Karen said, clearly unconcerned about her sister's lateness. "We'll give her a few more minutes. Maybe she got caught in traffic or something."

Just then the two women looked up when they heard a car pulling into the driveway.

"Finally," Jewel said looking out the front room window.

"Hi." Claudia rushed into the living room and immediately noticed the displeased look on her mother's face. "Sorry, I'm late. A friend of mine called and I got carried away with a bit of gossip. Karen, you will never believe who's getting married."

Jewel frowned. She hated gossip no matter how harmless and she gave Claudia a displeased look.

"This isn't really gossip, Mom, it's just news," Claudia said in her defense, but Jewel maintained her frown. Karen and Claudia exchanged looks which meant Claudia would give her the news later.

"Good thing you came when you did," Karen said, changing the subject back to her sister's tardiness. "Mom was about to send out a search party."

Jewel crossed her arms and sighed. "You girls don't appreciate a New Year's day sale like I do. I just wanted to get to the stores before all of the good stuff is gone. By now we've missed most of the door buster bargains."

Karen grabbed her purse and started toward the door. "Don't worry, Mom. I'm sure there will be plenty of good stuff left when we get to the mall. I seriously doubt all of those people who arrived at the mall when it opened this morning at seven A.M. managed to buy everything."

After growing tired of looking through racks and racks of clothes and finding nothing of interest, Claudia and Karen finally left their mother to shop on her own while they went to the food court to get ice cream. Jewel promised to meet them there after she'd finished trying on the cache of dresses she'd been carrying around for the past twenty minutes.

"So, who's getting married?" Karen asked with anticipation.

"I'll give you a hint. Think Valentine's Day, dimples and base-ball."

Karen wrinkled her nose and repeated, "Valentine's Day, dimples, baseball. Valentines, dimp - oh my goodness. Reggie Fisher."

Reggie was the boy practically every girl in high school was in love with, especially Karen and Claudia. Tall, athletic and smart, he was the stuff adolescent dreams were made of, and to top it all off, his birthday was February 14th.

Even though he was the object of desire for most of the high school's female population, Reggie never noticed any of the girls and had only one thing on his mind - baseball. For a while after graduating from college he played for the Columbus Clippers, the farm team for the New York Yankees. Karen and Claudia had attended more of those games than they would ever dare mention to anyone. But no dates and barely even a glance ever materialized from it. Reggie was eventually moved up to the majors and far away from Columbus.

"Who told you about Reggie, and is he marrying someone we know?"

"Frank heard it from somebody at work. He didn't mention who Reggie was marrying."

"Frank? I didn't think he and his colleagues talked about anything except dead lab rats."

The two sisters laughed. They knew their brother was a well-respected research scientist but they liked to joke about his job and lack of sense of humor.

"So how's your friend from Indianapolis?" Karen asked, swirling her strawberries and whipped cream together in her sundae.

"Fine."

"Just *fine*? Didn't the two of you go out again after Christmas?"

"Yes, and I'm glad we did. It was an eye-opening experience."

A frown creased Karen's forehead. "I'm confused. You don't sound happy about going out with him. Did something happen?"

"You could say that." Claudia moved the cherry around in her sundae with her spoon and tried not to remember how disappointed she was with the way things had turned out between her prospective Mr. Right and herself. "Let's just say, he's been disqualified as a candidate."

"That doesn't sound good. What happened?"

"Well, Mr. Wonderful told me he was separated, but he forgot to tell me he still lives under the same roof as Mrs. Wonderful."

"Oh, I see," Karen said. "So, is there another candidate?"

"Well, sort of. Kelly Lyle, the call center manager from my job, has a cousin who just moved here from North Carolina. She arranged a little dinner party at her house next weekend for the two of us to meet."

"Sounds good."

"We'll see. The way my luck has been going, I'm a little afraid to get my hopes up."

"Hey, you've got to keep hope alive."

"Hope is beginning to need CPR. What's strange is that I've been meeting a lot of men, and while some of them look good on paper, in reality, they are so far removed from what I'm looking for."

"Maybe you should stop looking on paper and start looking with your heart."

"Don't start with that, Karen. I get enough of that from Mom and Ray. I know what I'm doing. My plan may not be the most conventional method of finding true love but I think it will serve me well. Eventually."

"If you say so. I'm surprised Ray hasn't voiced his opposition to this plan a little more loudly. The poor man cringes at the thought of blind dates or even matchmaking."

"Oh, he's voiced his opinion all right. He recently made the suggestion that I come up with a written questionnaire for future candidates to fill out on the first date. If they answer all the questions to my liking then they would proceed to the next level."

"That sounds so-"

"Cold and calculating," Claudia finished for her sister. "Ray was being sarcastic and trying to make a point."

"Which was?"

"That my plan is a waste of time."

Karen ate a spoonful of ice cream to keep from offering an opinion that she knew her sister didn't want to hear. "Speaking of Ray, what happened at the Christmas Eve party between you two?"

"What do you mean?" Claudia asked a little too quickly. Had Karen seen what happened in the kitchen? No, she couldn't have. Maybe someone else did and told her.

"I went upstairs to get something and when I came back Ray was gone. He usually closes down the party. Mom said he had a strange look on his face when he left." Karen left out what else her mother had said about Claudia.

Claudia pretended to look in her purse for something.

"Well?"

"Well what?" Claudia asked.

"What happened? Were the two of you arguing or something?"

There was something all right. Claudia wasn't ready to talk to Karen about the kiss she'd shared with Ray, or her reaction to it. She still hadn't gotten a handle on the whole thing herself.

No one had ever kissed her with such longing and passion before. Why did that first someone have to be Ray? And why did she like it so much? She couldn't help but wonder if Ray had really been trying to prove a point, or did the passionate kiss he gave her mirror his true feelings?

She'd spoken to Ray on Christmas day when he called to wish her a merry Christmas, but neither of them mentioned the kiss and she hadn't spoken to him since. There was too little information to form any type of intelligent conclusion, Claudia later decided after much thought. She was going to have to sit down with Ray and find out what was going on. She had to admit one thing to herself, that had been one hell of a kiss. She couldn't seem to get it out of her mind or the other things he'd said to her. *Where did he learn to kiss like that?* she wondered again.

The kiss Claudia and Ray shared on Christmas Eve hadn't been their first. Once when they were both on break from college, they'd gone out to the movies. Afterward when they sat in Ray's car and talked about all the things going on in their lives, out of the blue, Ray had leaned over and kissed her. That kiss had been sweet, not filled with fiery passion like the most recent one. Claudia was surprised then, too. Ray later explained that he'd kissed her because he'd been so homesick and he had really missed her. This time there was no explanation and Claudia had concluded that it was best to let sleeping dogs lie, for now.

"Earth to Claudia."

"Huh?"

"Are you ignoring me or do you just not want to talk about Christmas Eve?"

"Both," Claudia said half joking.

"Well, since you obviously want to change the subject, guess who I ran into at the grocery store the other night," Karen inquired when she realized her sister was not going to tell her what was going on.

Claudia shrugged her shoulders.

"Joe Caldwell."

"So."

"So, he asked about you. He wanted to know if you were you were still single or in a relationship, and if you had children. You know, the typical is-there-a-chance-for-me questions."

"Did you tell him I was married with five kids and three more on the way?"

Karen put down her spoon and stared at her sister. "What is your problem? You used to be crazy about Joe. Now you're acting as if you could care less about the man."

"For starters, I was never crazy about Joe. I had a crush on him in the ninth grade. That's all. Besides, Karen, the man has been married three times and has six children."

"Well, excuse me for trying to hook you up."

"Oh, that would be a hook-up all right. Thanks, but no thanks."

"Claudia Ryland."

Karen and Claudia looked up in unison toward the sound of the voice.

Viveca Roberts.

Viveca turned to Karen and smiled. "Hello, Karen, long time no see."

Not long enough, Claudia thought.

"How are you, Viveca? I didn't know you were in town," Karen said, glancing sideways at her sister.

"I'm only here for a short time. My mother has been ill and I came back to take care of her until she's better."

"Well, you're looking good. I guess the beautiful weather in California agrees with you."

Claudia still hadn't spoken and Karen was doing her best to keep the conversation pleasant and brief.

"Thank you. I couldn't be better," Viveca offered, looking at Claudia. "I was just out running a few errands. Ray is taking me out to dinner tonight and I needed to pick up a few things before our date. You know how important it is to look your best when on the arm of a handsome man."

Claudia's smile was as tight as it was phony. Her hands were clinched in her lap as she tried like crazy to squelch thoughts of grabbing Viveca's slim throat and draining the life out of her. Just remembering the way she'd left Ray when the two of them had broken up made Claudia's blood boil.

"Well, ladies, I've got to run. Ray is coming by around five and you know how he hates to wait. See you around," she said and sailed off in the direction of the west exit.

Claudia had been smiling and clenching her teeth so hard her head was beginning to hurt. Once Viveca left she was able to relax.

"That's why you've been so crabby," Karen exclaimed. "Why didn't you tell me Viveca was back in town?"

"Because I didn't want to waste my breath mentioning her name."

"She said she's having dinner with Ray tonight. Did you know about that?"

"No, I don't monitor Ray's social calendar. Can we please change the subject, Karen?"

"All right, but one more thing."

"What?"

"Don't get in Ray's way if he still wants to have a relationship with Viveca."

"If he wants to have a relationship with Viveca?" Claudia repeated incredulously. "You have got to be kidding. After the way she treated Ray and then left him, I'm surprised he can even stand to be in the same city with her. And for the life of me, I don't know what would possess him to have dinner with her. I hope somebody hides the sharp utensils."

"Claudia, there's nothing you can do about Ray's feelings for Viveca. I know he is your friend and you care about him, but you can't control who he chooses to have a relationship with, especially since you're busy pursuing your own romantic interests."

Unfortunately, Karen had a point. "I know that," Claudia said, trying to keep the edge out of her voice. "But what happens when Viveca gets tired of playing with him and dumps him like she did before?"

"Then you'll still be there to be his friend. Unless-"

"Unless what?"

"Unless you're jealous of his relationship with Viveca."

Claudia's head shot up and she glared at her sister. "That is the dumbest thing I have ever heard come out of your mouth. And it couldn't be more untrue."

Unaffected and sure she'd hit on something, Karen continued, "Is it? I know you don't like Viveca-"

"No. I don't like peas or shoes that are too tight. I loathe

Viveca," Claudia interrupted.

"I know you *loathe* Viveca, but you're trying to protect Ray as if he didn't have sense enough to steer clear of a bad situation."

"Where Viveca Roberts is concerned, I have to wonder."

Karen's voice softened and she looked closely at her sister to gauge her reaction. "Are you afraid Viveca is going to take Ray away from you?"

Claudia was angry. "What are you trying to say, Karen? I'm not afraid of anything. What I don't want to see happen is for Ray to get hurt. That's all. Four years ago Viveca lied, cheated and manipulated her way into Ray's life. And for what? To see how much she could get out of him before she moved on to the next victim? And poor Ray was crushed. In the whole time I've known him, I've never seen Ray more devastated. He loved that woman and she used his feelings for her to her benefit. She's a user and I don't want to see Ray get used again."

Karen was taken aback. She knew her sister and Ray were best friends but for the first time she wondered if there was something more to Claudia's feelings for Ray. Claudia was angry and Karen decided not to press the issue. At least for now.

Claudia sighed and leaned back in her chair. "I'm sorry, Karen. I didn't mean to blow up at you. There's just something about Viveca that brings out the worst in me. Come on, let's find Mom before she buys out the entire mall."

And before I hit upon the real truth, Karen thought as she glanced at her sister.

CHAPTER ELEVEN

Ray pulled his car into a parking space at the Halifax Hotel and turned off the engine. He wondered again if he was making the right decision getting involved with Viveca. Did they share too much emotional baggage to have a relationship now? During the time they were together he had given her everything: His undying devotion, unconditional love, and foolishly, his heart. But over time he'd forgiven her and moved on with his life, to a point.

Ray had once thought that Viveca had hurt him so deeply that he would never be able to feel about another woman the way he'd felt about her. At least he'd thought that until now. In the three years since Viveca had ended their relationship, Ray had not been seriously involved with anyone. That was by his choice. Claudia often accused him of running away from love. She brought it up every time it seemed as if he were getting too close to someone, only to quickly end the relationship soon after. But she couldn't have been further from the truth. Ray wasn't running away from love. He'd made a big mistake in the past giving his love to someone who did not love him. The next time he made such a move he wanted to be sure before he put his heart on the line.

After lightly knocking on the door to her suite, Ray heard Viveca unlock the door. She looked excited to see him when she opened the door and planted a kiss on his cheek.

As he stepped inside, Ray noticed that very little had changed about the woman he had once been head over heels in love with. She still wore the same perfume, still kept him waiting and still looked beautiful, even in the silk bathrobe that wrapped around her slim figure like a hug.

It wasn't hard to see why men enjoyed looking at Viveca. She was a complete package; honey-kissed skin that was fragrant and soft to the touch, thick chestnut hair that hung down her back, and the kind of figure that most women would die for. But there was something Viveca lacked that made Ray wonder if it had always been missing or if he had been too blind to notice before - warmth and compassion.

"As punctual as always," Ray commented, taking a seat on the arm of the sofa.

"Now, Ray, you know you can't rush perfection. I'll be ready before you know it," Viveca said and hurried off to the bedroom, leaving a trail of perfume behind her.

Ray picked up a magazine and absently flipped through the pages while he waited for Viveca. Tossing the magazine on the coffee table, he looked around the hotel suite. Posh was the best word to describe the décor.

Viveca was staying at the Halifax until her mother was released from the hospital. She had told him that she didn't like staying in her mother's empty house all alone and opted for the comfort of a hotel for the time being.

Ray wondered which one of Viveca's admirers was footing the bill for her elaborate digs.

"Do you know who I ran into today at the mall?" Viveca asked from her bedroom.

"Who?"

"Your buddy, Claudia Ryland and her sister."

Ray held his breath and waited for the details of the meeting with Claudia and Viveca. She offered none.

"Did you and Claudia speak?" he asked, knowing that Claudia would have been polite but brief.

"Not exactly," Viveca answered coming out of the bedroom completely dressed except for her shoes, which she carried in her hand. "Would you zip me up please?"

She turned around for Ray to zip up her dress when he noticed she wasn't wearing any undergarments. With somewhat unsteady hands he managed to zip up the dress without making a complete fool of himself.

"Were the two of you at least civil to each other?" Ray asked in a voice which was much stronger than he felt.

"I suppose. Mostly she just glared at me and pretended that she didn't want to pull my hair out at the roots."

Ray helped Viveca on with her coat. "You're exaggerating, Viveca."

"Maybe I am just a little but you have to admit, there's no love lost between the two of us."

Being the wise man that he was, Ray decided to leave well enough alone.

Over dinner Viveca talked about her job in California, her divorce and her mother. She mentioned to Ray that she had taken an extended leave of absence from her job as a buyer for a small chain of department stores. Ray couldn't imagine that a buyer's salary would work with her expensive tastes. However, knowing Viveca she had a supplement to her income.

When discussing her divorce, Ray was surprised to learn that Viveca's husband had been the one to file the action. He'd been under the impression that she was the one who had wanted out of their marriage.

"So, tell me, Ray, whose heart do you have wrapped around your little finger these days?"

Ray smiled and poured a dollop of cream into his coffee. "What makes you think I'm seeing someone?" he asked innocently.

"Because, you've got the look," she answered smiling.

"What's *the look*?"

"Dreamy eyes, distracted, and in the last five minutes you've looked at your watch at least four times."

He laughed, completely unaware that he'd checked his watch that many times. "I think you're letting your vivid imagination get the best of you."

"Oh, am I? I'd like to think I was the one that put those stars in your eyes, but I have a feeling that that's not the case."

"Honestly, I'm not seeing anyone in particular," Ray said, taking a sip of his coffee.

"What about Claudia?"

Surprised, Ray looked up from his coffee. "What about her?"

"The two of you have been buddies for so long that I kind of figured one day you'd just end up being lovers."

Ray leaned forward in his chair and tilted his head to the side. "Oh, really? Is that why you broke my heart and ran off to California to pursue other interests?"

Caught off guard by his words, Viveca gently sat her cup down on the saucer and lowered her head. "I guess I deserved that one."

Ray shook his head. "I'm sorry. That was uncalled for."

"No, no, I deserved that and a whole lot more. I was the bad guy, Ray, and I did some things that I'm not very proud of. I know this is long overdue, but I'm sorry for the way I treated you. I hope you can see it in your heart to forgive me."

"I already have, Viveca."

Viveca narrowed her eyes and looked at Ray. "Have you? Really?"

"Yes, I have. Really."

"Good, because I need someone like you in my life right now. As a friend," she added cautiously. "With my divorce and my mother's illness, it has been a huge emotional drain."

"I'm here for you as a friend if you need me, Viveca." Ray was careful to make his intentions clear to her. He didn't want there to be any misunderstanding about his commitment to her.

"Despite everything, you've never let me down. And I knew this time would be no different."

After Ray dropped Viveca off at her hotel he drove by Claudia's to see if she was home. All through dinner she'd been on his mind. He needed to check on her, probably more for his sake than hers.

Her lights were on and he could see the faint flickering light from her television through the window when he pulled into her driveway.

He rang the doorbell and soon after heard Ginger barking loudly on the other side of the door.

"Who is it?" Claudia called and at the same time attempted to quiet Ginger.

"It's me," Ray answered.

She opened the door and held Ginger by the collar with the other hand. "What's up, stranger?"

"I just thought I'd drop by on my way home," he answered, ignoring Claudia's sarcastic tone and walked into the living room and took a seat on the loveseat. At least Ginger was happy to see him.

"You look nice," she said already knowing the reason he was dressed up.

"Thanks. What's on?" he asked nodding toward the television.

Claudia picked up the remote control and turned the television off. "Nothing of any importance," she said. "What's on with you?"

"I just dropped Viveca off at her hotel," he began.

"And?"

"And nothing. We had a nice dinner. She talked about her life in California, friends, ex-husband, her mother. I told her about some of our mutual friends and what was going on here."

"Did she mention anything else?"

"Like what? Why she threw my marriage proposal in my face and ran off to California?"

Claudia was instantly sorry that she had pushed Ray to discuss what went on between him and Viveca. She knew she'd hit a sore spot.

Ray leaned back on the loveseat and looked up at the ceiling. "She apologized."

"She did what?"

"You heard me. She said she was sorry for the way she treated me and asked if we could be friends."

"What did you say?"

"I told her yes."

Claudia sniffed. "Be careful, Ray. You know how Viveca operates. She's a user and schemer and she is not to be trusted."

"I know all of that, Claudia. Believe me, I know that better than anyone. But it's like I said before. I'm a big boy. I can take care of myself."

Claudia decided not to comment.

"So, how's the man hunt going?"

Claudia tried to keep the irritation out of her voice when she answered, "Fine. Thanks for asking."

"I ran into Karen when I stopped to buy gas and she told me the contender from Indy is out of the picture."

Claudia sighed and said, "Karen seems to be doing a lot of talking lately about things that don't concern her."

"Any new prospects?"

Ray was being flippant and Claudia refused to show him that it irritated her.

"Now that you mention it, I do have a dinner party that I'll be attending next weekend. A friend of mine has a cousin that just moved here from North Carolina. He sounds really nice and from the physical description she gave of him, he sounds delicious." Claudia stood. "I'm going to fix myself something to drink. Do you want anything?" *Let him stew over that comment*, she thought.

Ray shifted uncomfortably in his seat. *Delicious?* What did she mean by that? "No thanks," he answered mumbling.

"Oh yeah," Claudia called from the kitchen, "my friend says her cousin worked in construction when he lived in North Carolina." She rejoined Ray and sat down with her glass of soda. "If he's looking for the same kind of work here, maybe you could put him in touch with some of the people you know in the business."

"Yeah, maybe."

"You know, I'm excited about this dinner party. From the other things my friend told me about her cousin, he seems to have it going on." Claudia took a sip from her glass and looked up at the ceiling. "Good looking, hard working, southern charm, sounds like a good prospect to me. And you know what they say about southern men; they treat their women very well. I wonder if he's a good kisser."

"Look, I've got to go," Ray said abruptly. "I'm pretty tired. It's been a long day."

Claudia placed her glass down and reached for a book on the side table. Without looking up, she said, "All right, Ray, I'll catch up with you later. Have a good evening. Would you mind locking the door on your way out?"

Before he walked out of the room, Ray turned to look at Claudia who seemed to be completely engrossed in her book. She seemed not to notice, or care, that he was leaving. Or that a wave a jealously had just washed over him with such force, that it took him by surprise.

CHAPTER TWELVE

It was Karen and David's wedding anniversary and Claudia had agreed to babysit so they could enjoy an evening on the town without the children. Candace and Eric were five years old and six and a half years old, respectively. With their parents gone and their Aunt Claudia in charge it seemed to Claudia that her niece and nephew were on a mission to get her to let them do all of the things their parents never allowed them to do.

Claudia had ordered pizza for them and later, made root beer floats. Candace insisted that they were allowed to eat in the family room but Claudia knew her sister had just put new furniture in that room and barely allowed them to sit on it, let alone eat on it. The last thing she wanted to have to explain was why she'd let a five year old spill ice cream and pop on the new couch.

After the kids had settled down after their snacks and had their baths, Eric asked Claudia if she would read them a story. When she said yes she then had to referee an argument as to which book she was going to read.

Candace pulled out a book that looked as if it had seen better days. The back cover was missing and the pages were bent.

"No, Candy, Aunt Claudia is not going to read that story. Dad reads that to you every night and I don't want to listen to a baby story anyway."

"It's my favorite story and it is not a baby story."

"Well, she doesn't want to read it," Eric protested. "Read this one, Aunt Claudia."

Claudia took the book from Eric and quickly skimmed through the pages. The story was about a little boy who was afraid of the dark. Seemed tame enough, she thought, but Candace wasn't having it.

"That story is dumb. You only want her to read it because you're scared to sleep in the dark. I'm not going to listen to that one."

"I am not scared to sleep in the dark. You are."

"Okay, you two, either you compromise and come up with one or two stories that you'd like for me to read, or you can go to bed without a story."

The argument stopped and Candace and Eric looked at each other defiantly.

"Why don't you make up a story," Eric suggested after he realized that his aunt's threat was real. "Sometimes Mom does that when Candy is acting like a baby and won't pick out something we both like."

"Okay, I guess I could do that."

Claudia thought for a minute and then began to tell the story of a boy and girl who just happened to be around the same age as Candace and Eric, except the girl was the older of the two. Throughout the story Claudia interjected little lessons about being good and kind and not talking to strangers and any other childhood lesson she could think of. When she was wrapping up the story she added a special part for Candace's benefit. The little girl was really a princess and didn't know it. At the end of the story when she found out that she was a princess she learned that she had to be good and kind to all of her subjects and got to live in a magical castle happily ever after.

Sitting wide-eyed and excited Candace said, "That was good, Aunt Claudia. I liked it a lot especially the part about the princess. Can you make up another story?"

Claudia checked her watch and recognized Candace's stalling techniques for what they were. It was thirty minutes past their bedtimes and they were beginning to wind down.

"I'll tell you what, after you get your teeth brushed I'll tuck you into bed. Deal?"

Eric and Candace groaned in unison. They were sleepy but would never have admitted it in a hundred years.

"Can't we stay up a little longer?" Eric asked hopeful that Claudia was a softer touch than his mother when it came to staying up late.

"Nope, I promised your mom and dad that I would have you guys in bed at a certain time and we're already past that time. I'd hate for them to walk in the door and find the two of you still awake."

"We could run and jump in bed when we hear the garage door open," Candace offered.

"Or, you could just be in bed when they get here," Claudia said and laughed at the disappointed looks on her niece and nephew's faces.

After taking what seemed like an excessive amount of time to brush their teeth, Claudia was finally able to get the kids in bed and settled. First she went in to Eric's room to tuck him in. He had just finished saying his prayers when he told Claudia that he had liked her story even though some parts of it were girly.

Claudia smiled and kissed her nephew on the cheek. Now it was time for Candace. She wouldn't be as easy to tuck in as her brother had been. Twice already she'd been up to get water.

"All right, missy, time to stop stalling and get to sleep," Claudia announced from Candace's doorway.

"Aunt Claudia, I had fun. You make the best root beer floats. Mommy doesn't stir the ice cream up and it gets stuck in the straw."

"Well, I'm glad you liked it. Now, it's time to go to sleep."

"Okay," Candace said with a sigh. "But can I ask you something?"

"Sure, honey, what would you like to know?" Claudia came into the room and took a seat on the edge of Candace's bed. Knowing her niece, this was probably going to take a minute.

"Why don't you have any kids?"

"Well," Claudia began, searching for the right words. "I'm not married for one thing."

Candace raised herself up on one elbow. "My friend Kyle's mommy isn't married. He said his daddy lives really far away and he only gets to see him sometimes. I feel kind of sorry for him because he doesn't get to do all of the things with his daddy that I get to do with mine."

Claudia didn't really want to get into a deep discussion with a five-year-old as to why she wasn't married and especially about why some kids didn't live with both of their parents.

"Sometimes kids only have a mommy or daddy because-" she didn't really know how to explain it. "What I mean is that everybody has a mommy and daddy it's just that sometimes the mommies or daddies don't live with them."

"Oh," Candace said with the clarity that only a child can achieve from the simplest of explanations.

Claudia stood to leave but Candace stopped her. "Can I ask you one more thing?" she said.

"This is the last thing, Candace, then it's lights out, okay?"

Candace nodded. "Are you going to marry Uncle Ray?"

Surprised by her niece's question, she asked, "Why do you ask that?"

Candace smiled and looked around the room to make sure that Eric hadn't sneaked into her room to hear the secret. Her voice was a whisper when she said, "I saw you and Uncle Ray kissing. Does that mean you're going to get married?"

Claudia flushed. Someone had seen Ray kissing her and it was Candace. She wondered if the child had mentioned it to her mother. Surely Karen would have said something by now, wouldn't she?

"Um, honey, Uncle Ray and I are just friends."

"I know," Candace said, sounding exasperated. "You can't marry a stranger, it has to be somebody that you know. I know that. But does that mean that you can't marry somebody that is your friend?"

"Um, no. That's not what I meant."

"I think Uncle Ray likes you," Candace said as if sharing a secret. "I bet he would like it if you married him. Then you could have a baby and the baby would have a mommy and daddy that lived in the same place."

This was getting to be too much for Claudia. It was time to end this conversation before she ended up having to explain to Candace where babies came from.

"Okay, Candace, enough girl talk. It's time for you to go to bed."

Satisfied that she had given her aunt something to think about, Candace conceded and laid her head down on her pillow. Claudia kissed her niece good night.

"Did you say your prayers?" Claudia asked hopeful that the child was too tired to ask any more questions.

"Yes," Candace replied after a big yawn. "Do you want to know what I said in my prayers?"

"That's okay, you don't have to tell me."

Candace went on anyway. "I prayed for all the mommies and daddies that were too far away to be with their kids."

"That's good, sweetie, now good night." Claudia was inching out of the room.

"Aunt Claudia?"

"Candace-"

"This is the last thing, I promise. I asked God to make you married. So get ready, okay?"

Claudia smiled and turned off the bedroom light. As she tiptoed down the stairs she thought with amazement how cute and perceptive her niece could be at times.

Claudia laughed softly when she thought of Candace's prayer. She'd asked God to make her married. Although Candace didn't know it, Aunt Claudia had prayed that exact same prayer.

CHAPTER THIRTEEN

Nearly a week had gone by and Claudia hadn't seen or heard from Ray. He was annoyed with her, but she was not going to let that ruin her evening. Besides, she should be the one who was annoyed with him. She couldn't understand Ray. After everything he'd been through with Viveca, he let her waltz right back into his life as if nothing ever happened. What could he possibly be thinking? Would he expect her to be there for him to help pick up the pieces after Viveca broke his heart again? Probably.

Claudia checked her makeup in the rear view mirror. She had on her favorite perfume, a new shade of lipstick and a sexy, yet tasteful knit ensemble that clung to her curves in all the right places. The deep, rich cranberry color of the outfit brought out the warm tones in her skin.

As she walked up the driveway to Kelly's house, Claudia willed herself to put thoughts of Ray and Viveca out of her mind. She took a deep breath, held it and then let it out slowly before she rang the doorbell. Time to meet the man Kelly couldn't stop talking about.

"Don't you look absolutely divine," Kelly commented when she took Claudia's coat. "Girlfriend, that outfit puts the X in sexy. My cousin is already here and has been anxiously awaiting your arrival. Boy, is he going to be pleased."

Kelly went to hang up Claudia's coat. While she waited for her to return Claudia walked into the living room and covertly scanned the small group of people trying to figure out which one was Kelly's cousin. She had spent the better part of the afternoon mentally preparing for this meeting. Kelly had been hyping her cousin all week and Claudia was beginning to wonder if the man could actually walk on water. But, she had decided, good, bad or indifferent, she was going to have a good time tonight.

"Mark is in the kitchen. Just follow me," Kelly instructed.

Claudia followed Kelly into the brightly-lit kitchen where two men leaned over the counter with their backs to the doorway. One of the men Claudia recognized as Kelly's husband, Craig. The other had to be Mark and if his front looked half as good as the back view, she was going to be in deep trouble.

Wide linebacker shoulders, a tapered waist, and tailored dress pants that couldn't quite conceal a tight rear end that connected to long legs.

Kelly cleared her throat and both men turned around. "The lady of the hour is here. Mark, I'd like you to meet Claudia Ryland."

Mark walked toward Claudia and extended his hand. "Well, my cousin has told me a lot about you but she failed to mention how beautiful you were."

Not only did the brother possess a magnificent combination of good looks and a slamming body, he was also a charmer with a hint of a southern accent. That was an extremely appealing combination, one in which Claudia liked a great deal.

Standing in front of Claudia she noted that Mark was tall but not towering. She guessed the he was about six-two, give or take an inch. He had cinnamon brown skin that had been bronzed by the sun, dark eyes framed by long, curly eyelashes and a neatly trimmed moustache. She liked that, too.

Mark's cashmere sweater seemed to have been made to fit his exact measurements. Kelly said that Mark had worked in construction in North Carolina. Perhaps that was where he had developed his nice physique.

"It's nice to finally meet you," Claudia said politely as she let her hand slide out of his strong grasp. She could tell his hands were strong and used to doing hard work, but he was gentle when he took her hand in his own.

"Craig, I need you to help me in the dining room." Kelly turned to Claudia and said, "I didn't invite you to my dinner party to put you to work, but would you mind helping Mark in here for a few minutes? I'd really appreciate it."

Claudia almost laughed out loud. Kelly's attempt to leave her alone with Mark was blatantly obvious. But she would be a good sport and play along. "No, I don't mind helping out."

After Kelly and Craig left, Mark turned to Claudia and smiled. "Please let me apologize for my cousin. She takes her job of matchmaking very seriously."

Mark had a nice smile. And she liked how his moustache framed his upper lip. She bet the moustache would tickle her when they kissed.

"No apologies necessary. I think it's kind of cute. So, what am I supposed to be helping you with?"

"Hmmm." Mark looked around and asked, "Would you look in the drawer by the stove and get out the pastry brush? When I take the rolls out of the oven you can brush butter over the tops."

Surprised, Claudia looked over at Mark and asked, "You know what a pastry brush is used for?"

"I certainly do. And when you taste my rolls you'll know that I know a thing or two about making bread."

"Oh, I'm impressed."

"You haven't even tasted the rolls yet."

"I don't need to. The fact that you know cooking utensils is enough for me."

༄

Kelly had invited a total of ten people to her dinner party. Beside Kelly and Craig Claudia only knew one of the other couples.

At the dinner table Kelly seated Claudia and Mark next to each other. Throughout dinner the conversation flowed easily between the two of them. Claudia was a little surprised to find out that Mark had never been married. Who wouldn't want to marry a man that looked this delectable and knew his way around the kitchen? She also found out from Kelly that Mark had not only made the rolls, which were absolutely divine, but he had also prepared the dessert. Claudia had never had tiramasu but after one bite it had instantly become one of her favorite desserts.

As everyone enjoyed their dessert and coffee in the living room, Mark and Claudia sat next to each other on the couch and continued their earlier conversation from dinner.

"Where did you learn to make rolls that light and fluffy?"

Mark was pleased that Claudia had enjoyed his cooking and was secretly hoping to impress her with some of his other talents. "My grandmother taught me. She lived with us when I was little. I used to love to sit in the kitchen and watch her mix the dough for rolls and lay it out on our kitchen table. She would have her flour spread out as she kneaded the dough and got it just right. It amazed me how she would use up every bit of flour as she kneaded that dough. Sometimes she would let me help. Of course, I'd have flour everywhere and have dough stuck to my hands and clothes, but eventually I became less messy and picked up a technique or two from my grandmother."

"Well, it sounds like you were a very attentive student."

Mark shrugged his broad shoulders and smiled. "When it's something I'm interested in, I tend to pay close attention to details."

Claudia wondered if they were still talking about cooking.

"So, tell me why someone as beautiful and charming as you is available. I can only imagine that the cold Ohio weather has affected the judgement and eyesight of the men who live here."

Claudia laughed. "I could ask you the same question. Why are you still single? I'd marry you just to have homemade rolls every day."

Mark laughed.

Claudia liked his laugh. It was deep and rumbling and not the least bit phony. She quickly learned that Mark had an easygoing way about him. He was easy to talk to and not the least bit pretentious or strange. *Damien and Marvin should be here to take notes,* she thought.

"There's more to me than being a decent cook. To be honest with you, this is the first time I've baked anything in over a year." Mark took Claudia's empty dessert plate and placed it on the coffee table on top of his.

"I'm still curious as to why you're not happily attached to some lucky woman."

"I guess to answer your question I'm still single because I haven't found anyone that I really want to share my life with. But I'm hoping that will change soon."

Kelly's dinner party had been a success in more ways than one. Mark was everything Kelly had said and then some. Claudia had enjoyed herself more than she thought she would.

As it neared midnight, Claudia reluctantly decided it was time to go home. Being the gentleman that he was, Mark walked Claudia to her car.

"I can't believe how cold it gets here," Mark commented as

Claudia started her car.

"It's not so bad. After a while you get used to it."

"That's hard to imagine. It's going to take me a while to get used to the cold and I'm not sure if I'll ever get used to all this snow."

"Well, you'll either love it or hate it. Most people think I'm crazy, but winter and fall are my favorite times of the year. For me the snow is a bonus. When I was a kid my brother and I couldn't wait until the first heavy snowfall. We'd spend what seemed like hours outside building snowmen, making angels and having snow-ball fights. We had so much fun. I'm going to have to show you how to enjoy the winter weather, Ohio style."

"How, by driving as far away from it as possible?"

Good sense of humor, Claudia thought as she mentally scanned her list.

"I'll tell you what. The next time we have a big snowfall, I'll take you to Big Run Park and we can go sledding."

"How much snow will we need for that?"

Claudia looked through the windshield at the light dusting of snow on the ground. "Well, most of what we had earlier has melted but we will need a little more than this," she said. "Two to three inches at least."

Mark secretly made a wish for a heavy snowfall. Even though he wasn't particularly fond of snow and cold weather, he kind of liked the idea of falling into a snowdrift with this pretty lady.

"Sounds like a date. But, in the meantime, just in case we don't get snow tonight, what are you doing tomorrow?"

"I need to go into work for a couple of hours, but I should be free around noon. What did you have in mind?"

"Work? On Sunday? What kind of boss do you have that makes you come in on a Sunday?"

Claudia suddenly felt guilty about working on Sunday. But she had some work to finish before Tuesday and she didn't want to stay late finishing it on Monday.

"Nobody makes me, I just find it easier to get some things done when no one else is around."

"Well, once you get finished with your work, would you like to see a movie and maybe have dinner afterwards?"

Claudia couldn't think of any reason not to and in fact, she found that she really wanted to see Mark again. "I'd like that," she said sincerely. She took a business card out of her purse and wrote her home number on the back.

"Then it's a date." Mark took the card and flipped it over. Reading the front he said, "Tomorrow you can tell me exactly what a product analyst of an insurance company does."

"I will. Now, you'd better go back inside before you freeze to death."

Mark was cold but he didn't want Claudia to leave. But it was late and they had made a date for tomorrow. He would be counting the minutes until then.

Claudia was just about to raise her window when Mark stopped her. "Before I go in, I want to tell you how much I enjoyed this evening."

"So did I," Claudia said.

"I'm looking forward to tomorrow. Have a good evening."

With a smile on his face Mark watched Claudia drive off. Once her car's taillights faded out of sight he went back into his cousin's house.

Kelly was placing dishes in the dishwasher when she heard her cousin come in. "Was she everything I said and more?" she asked, clearly proud of herself.

Mark folded his arms and nodded his head. "You've outdone

yourself, Kel."

Craig had just walked in from the dining room and remarked, "Don't hurt your arm patting yourself on the back, sweetie."

Kelly waved her husband away. "Any plans to see each other again?"

"Funny you should ask; we're going to the movies tomorrow." Mark tried to hide his smile, but for some reason when he thought about Claudia he couldn't help but smile.

Kelly practically beamed. "I've got good vibes about this," she remarked.

"So do I, cousin. And I hope it isn't just wishful thinking on my part," Mark added cautiously.

CHAPTER FOURTEEN

Viveca sat next to her mother on the couch. They had been watching a movie together, but from her mother's rhythmic breathing Viveca knew she had fallen asleep. Gently placing an afghan over her legs, she was careful not to wake her.

The room grew quiet once Viveca turned off the television. Even outside on the streets it was quiet. More snow had fallen earlier that morning and most folks probably thought it a good idea to stay home. The snowfall hadn't been heavy, just messy.

Viveca was bored. She missed her life in California and it hadn't taken her long after her arrival back in Ohio to realize one of the reasons she'd left Columbus in the first place. She hated cold weather and she especially hated snow.

After restlessly flipping through the pages of a magazine, she thought about calling Ray and inviting him over but decided against it. It was Sunday morning. He was probably at church.

Ray Elliott. He hadn't changed much over the years. Three years can bring about great changes in a person's life, but Ray only seemed to get better. Since she hadn't seen him since the breakup, Viveca was initially a little unsure of his feelings for her. She expected that he might hate her for the way she'd treated him. But she couldn't have been more wrong. Ray still cared for her. That was clear. She just wasn't sure how much he cared, but she knew his feelings for her ran deep. You never forget your first love, she thought, and she was pretty sure that she had been Ray's first real love.

There weren't many things that Viveca felt that she'd done right in her life. Ray had been the one thing that had seemed right. But she had blown it by taking his love for granted and running away from him when he offered all of the things she should have wanted but didn't–marriage and stability. She was the type of person who always looked for that greener grass on the other side and the excitement that went along with it, never satisfied with what she had. That's what her mother had often accused her of and she was right.

Viveca wanted to be satisfied. She wanted stability, at least financial stability. She wanted someone who cared about her and what made her happy, but with no strings attached. And she didn't necessarily want to be tied down to that person. Freedom was important. Freedom to see whomever she wanted or do whatever she felt like was how she liked to live. Most men couldn't get with that.

Searching for freedom had led her to Clayton. Thinking about her ex-husband, she wondered how or why the two of them ever thought they could form a stable relationship. Viveca had left Ray for Clayton and she had regretted it not long after.

At first things were fine. Viveca had met Clayton one weekend when Ray was out of town. She was bored and had decided to put on her party clothes and frequent one of her favorite bars. From the moment she entered the bar Clayton hadn't taken his eyes off of her. He sent a drink over and from there the two of them struck up a conversation.

Clay, she learned, was from California and ran an import business. He was generous and charming and not the least bit arrogant. Everything about him reflected a certain confidence and style that Viveca was drawn to. His tailored suit, manicured nails and even the way he spoke indicated to Viveca that he was someone she wanted to get to know.

Throughout the evening Clayton dropped subtle hints about how well he lived in California. He made it clear that he wasn't rich but that he was quite comfortable. Following that evening the two of them continued to see each other, unbeknownst to Ray. Once Clayton returned to California Viveca could not stop thinking about him and they continued to keep in touch by phone.

Clayton knew all the right things to say and Viveca heard exactly what she wanted to hear. It was just a matter of time before he began to promise her the good life and all the things she craved. What she didn't know at the time was the high price she would pay to accept his offer.

She had mistakenly thought that with Clayton's busy work schedule and his financial standing she could have the best of both worlds – freedom and money. But what she realized after arriving in California should have been enough to immediately send her back home. Clayton was a hustler. Everything he had and probably everything he would ever have was obtained by the latest game he was running. She also realized that he was as restless and selfish as she was, maybe even more so. He wanted the good life but at someone else's expense and he wanted to involve Viveca in his games. He had expected a lot from her, more than she was willing or able to give.

After hearing for nearly two years how grateful she should be to have someone as wonderful as him, she'd had enough. Viveca laughed softly. Clayton had known Viveca was ready to leave, so in an attempt to save face he was the one to file for divorce. He claimed that no woman had ever left him and it certainly wouldn't be a hick from Ohio that claimed that accomplishment. Viveca didn't care one way or another who filed. She didn't even bother to contest the divorce. She just wanted out and as far away from Clayton as possible.

The last thing she heard, Clayton had found himself a meal ticket who didn't mind his mean spiritedness, wandering eye or expensive tastes. Viveca hoped his new woman would come to her senses before being stripped of her money, self-respect and dignity. She almost hadn't.

Viveca's thoughts went back to Ray. He was nothing like Clayton and was morally incapable of being that way. But Ray puzzled her. When they were last together he seemed distracted. He kept checking his watch and she found herself having to work at keeping the conversation going. She'd like to think she was the cause of his distraction but, unfortunately, she knew she wasn't. The question was, who was occupying Ray's thoughts?

Claudia stared at the spreadsheet on her computer screen and wondered why she had decided to come in to work on a Sunday. She really should have emailed the spreadsheet to herself at home and prepared the basics of her presentation from there, but somehow coming into the office seemed liked the thing to do. It was peaceful and quiet and all of the resources she needed were at her fingertips. Even with that in mind, she now wished that she was at home sitting in her favorite chair, wrapped in a fluffy robe, drinking a cup of coffee and reading the Sunday newspaper.

Claudia yawned. It was past time for a cup of coffee. She needed a caffeine fix and she needed it soon but she cringed at the thought of getting a cup from the downstairs vending machine. But at this point vending machine coffee would have to do.

Claudia yawned again on the way to the break room. She had gone home after Kelly's dinner party and had been unable to sleep. Thoughts of Mark kept her awake most of the night. She wondered why such a great guy was still single. Maybe he'd been thinking the same thing about her, assuming he thought she was great. She hoped he did.

Claudia fished some change out of her pocket and pushed all the right buttons on the vending machine. While she waited for the cup to fill with coffee she wondered what Ray would think about Mark. Would he accept her relationship with Mark? Would Mark accept Ray? There really was no reason why the two men shouldn't get along. At this point Claudia didn't know a great deal about Mark, but the little she did know indicated that he was easygoing, a pretty good conversationalist and pleasant. He was also fine, but Ray wouldn't care anything about that, she mused.

Claudia carefully removed the cup of coffee from the metal grips that held it upright inside the vending machine. Peering into the cup she had to wonder how anyone could call the murky brown liquid coffee. It vaguely resembled something she and Karen had mixed up in their backyard after a heavy rain, she thought as she walked back to her desk.

Since she wasn't getting much accomplished, Claudia tossed the cup of coffee into the trash bin and decided it was time to go home. It looked as if she was going to have to come in early Monday morning in order to finish her work. She was tired anyway and wanted to take a nap. She also wanted to talk to Ray. They had to clear the air.

Ray awoke with a smile on his lips even though he had over-slept. It was almost eleven o'clock and too late to go to church. But it wasn't church that was on his mind. Ray snuggled under the covers as a passionate feeling from only moments before still wrapped him its comforting cocoon.

He'd had that dream again. Candles, wine, and this time a hot, steamy bubble bath. The lovemaking had been as exquisite as ever and more intense than before. And just as before, he couldn't shake the feeling that segments of his dream appeared to be so real.

Sitting up in bed Ray looked around the room half-expecting to see Claudia. Maybe she'd be walking into the bedroom carrying a breakfast tray and wearing a sexy number from her favorite lingerie boutique, Debbie's Gems. Maybe she would just be coming out of the shower wrapped in a towel with her skin damp and fragrant.

Ray groaned inwardly and closed his eyes. He could only imagine what it would be like to make love to Claudia on a lazy Sunday morning like this.

He laced his fingers behind his head and rested back against his pillow allowing himself to get caught up in the fantasy. If he and Claudia were together on a morning like this he'd probably be the first one to awaken because Claudia was a sound sleeper who also liked to sleep in whenever possible. He'd try to arouse her by first nibbling on her neck. Then shoulders. If that didn't garner the results he hoped for, he would then pull the covers back to reveal her sexy body and be taunted by the outline of her breasts through her thin nightgown. Knowing Claudia she would probably complain about the sudden loss of heat, but he would take care of that. Running his fingertips over each nipple until they peaked with interest, she would soon forget about being chilly as Ray warmed her with his body. She wouldn't be able to deny her need. Her body would reveal the secret desires that were his to discover and it would be his pleasure fulfilling every single one of those needs.

As the sun would begin to rise, so would Ray and the fervor of their passion would consume their thoughts and bodies as they joined together, mind, body and soul. He would love to see how passion shown on her face. Lips slightly parted. Skin warm and glistening and pretty brown eyes reflecting love. There was nothing like early morning lovin'.

"Why am I torturing myself like this?" Ray said aloud. He was driving himself crazy with thoughts of Claudia. She was everywhere, on his mind at work, in his thoughts while he was driving, and constantly in his dreams. It was there, in his dreams, that she came to him without reservation and with unmistakable love in her heart, the kind of love that lifelong unions are built on.

Ray pulled back the covers and swung his long legs over the side of his bed. He could almost smell Claudia's perfume as he tried to recall details of the dream that was quickly fading from his memory. Although, without having to think too hard, he could vividly remember the taste of Claudia's lips and feel her soft skin. His skin still tingled from her touches that only came to him in his dreams. She had gentle hands that knew his body like her own and wasn't afraid to use them.

Ray let out a long, slow breath. He wanted more than anything for his dreams of Claudia to become their reality.

Sitting on the side of his bed, he reached over and picked up the phone. He dialed Claudia's home number.

There was no answer. He punched in the number for her cell phone.

Claudia wasn't home and she wasn't answering her cell phone. *Just how well did last night's dinner party go?* he wondered as jealously reared its ugly head.

What's wrong with me? Jealousy wasn't a part of his make up but on more than one occasion it had made an unexpected and unwelcome visit. He knew he would have to get a handle on that.

Ray thought back to Christmas Eve when he'd kissed Claudia under the mistletoe. He'd only meant to show her that what she was looking for was standing right in front of her if she'd only open her eyes, but somehow the point behind the lesson had been lost once his lips had touched hers. Those soft lips. He was the one who ended up being schooled that night.

He knew Claudia had felt something from the kiss. He certainly had, more than he would have imagined. That evening it had taken a long drive, an hour on the treadmill and a cold shower to squelch the desire that had touched him down to his very soul. And that night he'd had a passionate dream about loving Claudia and pleasing her in a way that he knew would be fulfilling for them both. That hadn't been the first such dream, but it had certainly been remarkable.

Ray sighed and rubbed his hand over the back of his neck. *Why were the simple things in his life becoming complicated while the complicated things were becoming simple?*

His friendship with Claudia had always been simple. It was something he could depend on no matter what and there were some pretty clear boundaries. They were buddies. Pals. Comrades. They'd played kickball together, rode bikes in the park, shared secrets, developed career plans and confided in each other whenever needed. Now he could see all of that was changing and he didn't know exactly how to handle it.

He wanted Claudia. Plain and simple. It wasn't just about sex or fulfilling a fantasy. What he felt for her was reality at its best.

Then there was Viveca. There was no doubt in his mind or his heart that he'd gotten over her, but he wasn't so sure of her intentions. He knew that she needed emotional support while her mother was ill. He also sensed that there were other personal demons that she didn't seem to want to share with him at the moment, but Ray was a little unsure of what else Viveca wanted from him.

Their dinner and subsequent conversations had been light and friendly, although there was an underlying sadness in Viveca that Ray didn't know how to handle. Part of him wanted to reach out to her and be her friend, but another part knew that Viveca was a survivor and would land on her feet no matter what. And in Viveca's book, if landing on her feet meant that she had to step on someone else, then so be it. Ray had been that someone else before and would not play that role again.

Ray couldn't afford to get emotionally tangled up with Viveca right now or ever. More to the point, he didn't want to.

The phone rang, jarring Ray from his thoughts.

"Good morning, sleepy head."

Ray's heartbeat quickened when he heard Claudia's voice.

"I wasn't asleep but if I was could you blame a brother for sleeping in? This is the perfect kind of morning for lounging around." *Or making love.* "Where have you been? I've been trying to reach you."

"I went in to work for a little while but couldn't seem to concentrate. I was on my way to Karen's to see if she would be nice enough to make her favorite sister some breakfast."

"I've got a better idea. Why don't you meet me at Spivey's in about forty-five minutes for brunch."

Claudia put her hand on her stomach as it grumbled. "Forty-five minutes? I'm hungry now. I don't know if I can keep up my strength for that long."

"Stop being a baby. You can wait that long. Besides, if you're just coming from work, you're on the other side of town. By the time you get through the detour on I-71 it'll take you at least twenty minutes to get to Spivey's. If you get there before I do, get us a table by the window."

Claudia looked out the restaurant window to see if she could catch a glimpse of Ray's car. She was on her second cup of coffee and was about to start eating without him. The waitress had placed a basket of hot biscuits on the table along with butter and strawberry jam. She'd eaten one biscuit and was drawing on every ounce of reserve she had not eat another one. To add to her misery, she was sitting within ten feet of the buffet table and it was killing her. Despite his claim that he would meet her in forty-five minutes she knew Ray wouldn't be on time, and she was starving. The buffet attendant had just put out a bowl of mixed fruit. Fresh strawberries, cantaloupe, grapes, and kiwi were beckoning her.

Finally hearing Ray's familiar baritone as he greeted the wait-ress, Claudia looked up from her coffee and frowned.

Ray lifted his hand to stop her from saying anything. "I know I'm a few minutes late. I had to run an errand." He didn't dare men-tion that Viveca had called him after he hung up from talking to Claudia. She had invited him to lunch, but he'd declined by telling her that he was meeting a friend for brunch. He wasn't quite sure why he didn't just tell Viveca that he was meeting Claudia, but he felt it was better to keep that bit of information to himself.

After satisfying her hunger with made to order waffles, bacon and scrambled eggs, all was forgiven. Claudia was in a much better state of mind than she had been earlier and now she could sit back and enjoy coffee and conversation.

As usual, Ray was still eating and he ate heartily. Pancakes, sausage, eggs, grits hash browns and coffee. Claudia was used to Ray packing away a lot of food at one time. She had stopped won-dering long ago where it all went.

Ever since she'd known him, Ray had been a big eater. But long gone was the lanky boy who had been all arms and legs and who never seemed to gain an ounce. Luckily, routine visits to the gym and keeping active with his football team kept him in top shape.

Claudia sipped her coffee and watched Ray under the veil of thick eyelashes. No, Ray was not a boy anymore and hadn't been for a long time. He'd matured in more ways than one.

"What? Do I have syrup running down my chin?" Ray asked jokingly when he caught Claudia staring at him. *Had he just seen longing in her eyes?* he wondered.

Uneasily, she looked way.

"So, how was the dinner party?" he asked, feeling a need to change the subject.

"It was nice," she answered nonchalantly.

Ray pushed his empty plate aside and sat back in his seat. "And your friend's cousin?"

This time Claudia smiled. "Also very nice."

Ray's jaw tightened slightly. "Care to elaborate?"

"What would you like to know?"

"For starters, is he a known felon?"

Claudia tilted her head and frowned.

"It was just a joke. Don't get upset. Okay, what about a name?"

"His name is Mark Bishop and he just moved here from North Carolina, but I told you that part already."

That's right, a southern brother, Ray thought wryly. Women liked southern men. He tried to smile. "Sounds nice."

"What sounds nice? His name or where he's from?"

"Both," Ray replied wearing a fake smile. "Will you and Mr. North Carolina be seeing each other again?"

Claudia checked her watch. "As a matter of fact, yes. We're supposed to be going to the movies and out to dinner this evening."

"I see."

Claudia sat down her coffee cup and looked squarely at Ray. "What do you see, Ray?"

"I see that you're moving ahead with this plan of yours," Ray answered, sounding a little more serious than he had intended.

"And why did you think otherwise? Correct me if I'm wrong, but I believe we've gone through this before and I told you that if you have a problem with it, then-"

"Then what?"

Claudia thanked the waitress for refilling her coffee cup and turned to Ray. "Then I guess you're going to have to either get with it or deal with it. You make the call."

Ray leaned in closer to the table. "This just seems so strange, Claudia."

"About as strange as that kiss you placed on me Christmas Eve?"

Ray sighed and rubbed his hand across the back of his neck. Up till now, neither of them had mentioned the kiss. Maybe it was time to bring it out in the open.

"I've been meaning to apologize for that."

"Forget the apology, I would just settle for an explanation."

"The explanation happens to be pretty simple. I was just trying to make a point."

"Which was what? That you know how to kiss a woman?"

No, that I know how to kiss my *woman.*

"Look, Claudia, I just got carried away with the whole holiday, food, fun and family thing that night."

Claudia narrowed her gaze and thought before continuing. "That's your explanation? Ray, you kissed me like we have a thing going on and all you can say is that you got carried away with the festivities that night."

"Look, Claudia, I-" Ray stopped. There was so much he wanted to say, but this wasn't the right time or place. He needed to get his thoughts and emotions in check before he revealed to Claudia what he felt about her. She wasn't ready to hear what he had to say and he wasn't ready for a possible rejection. Time to flip the script.

"This whole dating thing is just strange. That's all."

"Why are you getting so serious? There is nothing strange

about me going out on dates. Grown folks, heck, teenagers, do it all the time. If my memory serves me correctly, I believe you and Viveca shared such an occasion recently."

"That was not a date."

"Call it what you like," Claudia said flippantly. "I always heard that if it quacks like a duck and walks like a duck, folks tend to call it a duck. And don't ducks fly to warmer climates in the winter?"

"Claudia, you have got to get over this thing you have with Viveca."

"Just for the record, Viveca and I don't have a *thing*. And unless the two of you are getting married I don't see any reason why she and I have to be friends."

Ray didn't want to argue about Viveca, or anything else for that matter.

"Are the two of you getting married?" she asked half-jokingly.

"You know that part of our relationship is over. And how did we get on the subject of Viveca? I thought we were talking about us?"

Surprised, Claudia asked, "Us? Now I'm confused."

Ray caught himself. "What I meant to say is that I just want you to be careful. That's all. You mean the world to me, Claudia, and I don't want to see you get hurt, that's the bottom line."

"Ray, you keep saying that. I'm just dating. I'm not going to get hurt."

Ray reached over and covered Claudia's hand with his own. "You're right, Claudia. Forgive a brotha for trying to look out for his friend."

She knew that Ray meant well and she really couldn't be upset with him for caring. "I guess all's forgiven," she said. "Just remember, Ray, I'll never let anyone come between us. You're my best friend and I'll always love you."

Ray looked across the table at his friend and wished that she could see into his heart. He wished that he had the courage to tell her that she meant more to him than she would ever know. But her vision didn't allow for that type of insight. The words would have to remain buried for now, deep in his heart where they would stay safe until it was the right time.

"And I'll always love you," he said. *With all my heart and soul.*

CHAPTER FIFTEEN

Viveca looked around the hospital room at the various pieces of equipment that were designed to monitor blood pressure, oxygen saturation and heart rate. Some machines displayed numbers and emitted beeps at different intervals, while printing out wavy lines on strips of paper that only trained eyes could decipher. Others pumped a steady flow of essential fluids into her mother's weakened body.

Viveca hated hospitals. She hated the sound of the machines that hummed and buzzed and beeped with precision, knowing that at any given time a patient's very life depended on its functionality.

Joyce Roberts had suffered a mild heart attack and a stroke. So far there was no paralysis but the doctor wanted to run a few more tests to assess any possible damage.

Earlier that afternoon Joyce had been resting comfortably. When she got up from her nap she complained of a headache, dizziness and chest pains. Fearing the worst, Viveca called the paramedics to rush her mother to the hospital. Thankfully, the emergency room doctors acted quickly.

Perfect way to spend a Sunday afternoon. If things had gone as planned and Ray hadn't been busy, she'd have had lunch with him and they could have enjoyed each other's company for the rest of the afternoon. Maybe even getting in a little adult fun while they had the chance.

Despite everything she had gone through with her mother that afternoon, the thought of spending time with Ray brought a smile to Viveca's beautiful face. Ray had always been a good lover. Eager to please, willing to learn and monogamous. Three important factors that made up part of Viveca's pleasure principle. And since Ray was a successful member of his development firm, the ever-important monetary factor was present as well.

She could have a lot of fun with Ray if he weren't so old-fashioned. But lately Viveca noticed that a lot more men were exhibiting some of the same old-fashioned values that Ray had. It surprised and irritated her at the number of men who wanted to settle down and have families. Maybe it had something to do with age. Whatever it was, she wasn't affected. Viveca simply wanted to have fun. She wasn't really in the market for a good man, just a man to be good to her followed by a good time.

Was that asking too much? She didn't think so. The last thing in the world she wanted right now was to be tied down to a husband and a bunch of children that would place constant demands on her time, attention and energy. Being a soccer mom, wiping runny noses and singing lullabies was not on her agenda. However, living the good life and having fun along the way were two things that she wanted most, at least for now. Maybe that would change as she became older, but she didn't foresee it happening any time soon.

Her mother had chastised her over and over again for her lifestyle, yet Viveca wouldn't back down. What did hard work and love get you? If she had to use her mother as an example, she'd say hard work and love were nothing more than the vehicle that led to heartache, old age and misery.

Viveca could never remember one time when her father was living that they had ever gone on vacation or spent money on anything other than necessities. There weren't pleasant dinner conversations, only a few kind words here and there and very little affection.

Her parents seemed to work so hard and were so unconcerned about anything that didn't involve their jobs or bills that at first that was the way Viveca thought everyone lived. Growing up she didn't have a lot of the trendy or fashionable clothes her friends had or the money for movies, parties and other outings. Her parents provided the necessities and very little else.

After her father died and as soon as she was old enough to work, she did. And every bit of money she made, she gave to her mother to help with the bills. Viveca learned to hate hard work, especially if she couldn't reap the benefits from it. In high school she wanted more than anything to have extra money for makeup, clothes and going out with her friends. Unfortunately, extra money was almost non-existent in the Roberts' household. Determined not to live a life filled with the kind of hard work that yielded little, if any benefits, Viveca sought a way out. At the time she thought it would be a good education that would provide her with a better life. That was when she met Clarence. He was the first man that ever really paid attention to Viveca.

Clarence bought her trinkets, took her to nice restaurants and gave her money to spend on herself. Those were things Viveca had never experienced before and quickly grew to love.

It didn't take long for Viveca to outgrow Clarence and to eventually move on to bigger and better providers. Discovering that her good looks and charm could get her almost anything she desired she used both to her full advantage. It took no time at all to find another man who was willing to provide even more for her than Clarence ever had.

Exotic trips, designer clothes and jewelry were just some of the perks Viveca scored by being charming, seductive and making sure she never fell in love. After dropping out of college, she returned home to Columbus while deciding what she wanted to do with her life. Working for a time as a marketing rep, she soon grew tired of the daily grind of a nine-to-five job. While she was working full-time she missed the exotic trips and other luxuries she had enjoyed when she was away at college.

Then she met Ray. He was well on the path to a promising career and was the kind of man all of her girlfriends were looking for. Ray was nice and all, but Viveca was looking for bigger and better fish.

Using Ray to pass the time until she found someone more willing and able to provide the lifestyle that she had become accustomed to, Viveca was unaware that Ray was falling in love with her. By the time she realized how deep his feelings were becoming, it was too late. He was hooked.

Ray wanted to get married, buy a house and live happily ever after. Viveca tried to explain to him that those things did not hold the same value for her as they did for him.

Sensing that he might lose her, Ray set out to win her heart in whatever manner he could. He bought her beautiful and expensive clothes, took her on romantic getaways and spent more on her than his salary could comfortably accommodate. The more he did to win Viveca's heart, the more trapped she felt. Seeing no other way out, she did the only thing she thought she could do. She left town and left Ray brokenhearted.

Despite everything, Viveca felt like dirt for hurting Ray. Yet she knew marrying him wasn't the right thing to do.

The nurse came in and smiled in Viveca's direction. She was young, probably fresh out of college, and seemed very excited about caring for her patients. Viveca could never remember being that cheerful or pleasant, unless she absolutely had to be.

"I'm going to be taking a break in about fifteen minutes," the young nurse said. "If you or Mrs. Roberts need anything, just hit the call button and one of the other nurses will be in to assist you."

The nurse left the room and Viveca heard her and another nurse in the hallway discussing a patient that had just been brought on the floor. It was a young woman who had been beaten up by her boyfriend. Apparently the injured woman had suffered broken ribs, a fractured wrist and a few other ailments that Viveca couldn't decipher from the conversation.

Viveca cringed inwardly. At this point in her life she could not imagine taking abuse from a man or anyone for that matter, especially physical abuse. It had been enough that her ex-husband thought it acceptable to belittle her when things were going wrong in his life. She knew he suffered from low self-esteem and greed, a dangerous combination, yet she had refused to be the means by which he used to boost his ego and his bank account.

Viveca was tired of sitting in the room listening to the monitors and machines. She needed some fresh air and a cup of coffee. Making sure her mother was sound asleep, she slipped quietly from the room.

As she walked down the hallway to the cafeteria, Viveca kept her eyes focused straight ahead. She didn't want to accidentally look into a room and see something that would depress her for the rest of the evening.

Then, something caught her attention. It sounded like crying. Instinctively, she turned toward the sound.

Viveca found herself staring into the open room of a patient. A young woman lay in the bed closest to the entranceway and the privacy curtain was partially open. Viveca could see the woman's face was bruised and swollen and her arm was in a sling.

It had to be the woman the nurses were talking about. Viveca turned to walk away and bumped a cart with her purse. The woman turned toward the sound. As their eyes met momentarily a sadness that Viveca had never seen reflected in such young eyes shone painfully through. Viveca's breath caught and she tried to turn away. For a split second her ugly past had resurfaced.

At one time she had been that woman lying bruised and battered.

Before she met Ray, Viveca had been involved with a man that she learned too late was extremely controlling and violently jealous. When they first met, he was exactly what Viveca thought she was looking for. Good-looking, suave and very generous, she had used every bit of charm that she could muster to get him to notice her. And notice her he did. In the beginning Viveca was so taken with this man that she didn't see the warning signs of danger. The two of them became involved quickly and before long Viveca began seeing signs of jealously mixed in with his generosity. At the time she had convinced herself that dealing with jealous feelings was a small price to pay for the lavish lifestyle she was leading.

But things became progressively worse. Once the jealousy turned into false accusations which then exploded into heated arguments, she knew she had made a mistake getting involved. Each argument and accusation became more frightening and no matter how expensive the gifts were that followed, Viveca knew it was time to get out.

The night she decided to leave, they'd had another heated argument. This time it turned violent and left Viveca with a broken wrist and a black eye. After pressing charges and putting her offender behind bars, Viveca vowed never again to be a victim. She learned that she had to be more selective in the men she chose. The first sign that something wasn't right, she was gone.

Viveca found herself standing inside the doorway of the young woman's room. She couldn't have been more than twenty-two or twenty-three years old, she thought as she walked cautiously over to her bed.

Her lips were trembling and tears ran down her bruised cheek. Taking a tissue from the box on the nightstand, Viveca offered it to her.

"You don't have to be a victim," she said quietly to the woman. "The choice is yours."

Viveca stood staring out the window on the sixth floor of the hospital and wondered how she had managed to turn her life into such a mess. A failed marriage, no friends and a strained relationship with her mother rounded out the list of elements that summed up her sad life. Seeing the battered young woman earlier reminded her that she hadn't come much further than that. Although she bore no physical scars, emotionally she was numb.

Viveca found an area of the hospital where she could use her cell phone, but after scrolling through a list of numbers she couldn't think of one person to call.

She sighed. Viveca couldn't ever remember feeling so alone and so unloved. And the saddest part of all, she had no one to blame but herself.

"Claudia, I asked if you wanted more cream in your coffee?"

Claudia looked up from her coffee cup and stared blankly at Mark.

"Is something wrong? You seem a bit distracted."

"No," Claudia replied. "It's just a little noisy in here and I didn't hear you."

Ever since he'd picked her up from her house, Mark had noticed that Claudia wasn't the same chatty and cheerful person he'd met the night before. Maybe she was tired, he reasoned. After all, she'd stayed up late the night before and had gone to work earlier that morning.

"Did you like the movie?"

Concentrate on one man at a time.

"Yes, I did. I'm glad you chose that one. Lately many of the action movies I've seen have been all action and no plot, but I have to admit, this one kept me on the edge of my seat and the story was pretty interesting." Claudia hoped Mark didn't ask her about any of the movie's particulars as she had spent the majority of time in the theater thinking about her earlier conversation with Ray.

"Claudia?"

Claudia looked up into Mark's questioning eyes and realized he had asked her another question. "I'm sorry, Mark, what did you say?"

"I asked if you wanted dessert."

Claudia pushed her coffee cup away and folded her hands. *Snap out of it,* she chastised herself. "Mark, you must think I'm Dr. Jekyl and Mrs. Hyde."

"No, I think you're either bored to death by me, hate how I look in broad daylight or you're mentally making out your grocery list."

Claudia shook her head and smiled. "No, it isn't any of those things. I guess I'm just a little tired. That's all. I should never have gone into work this morning after staying up so late last night."

"Would you like for me to take you home so that you can get some rest?"

Claudia checked her watch. It was still early and despite the lack of attention she was paying toward their date, she really did enjoy Mark's company. "No," she replied smiling, "I've got a better idea. How are your video game skills?"

Mark smiled and cocked his head to the side. "Well, I'm a little rusty, but I guess my skill level depends on what you have in mind."

Claudia intertwined her fingers and extended her palms outward, cracking her knuckles. "Let's see just how skilled you are when you're up against the Mole Patrol."

Mark chuckled. He had no idea what Claudia had in mind, but he was willing to go along with it, as long as it afforded him the opportunity to spend a little more time with her.

Ray scanned the sports pages of the newspaper as he sat at the bar of the restaurant waiting for his carryout order to come up. He'd decided to stop by on his way home to grab a hamburger and fries after spending the better part of the afternoon hanging out at the gym with his buddies.

The restaurant was noisy. It seemed as if someone was having a birthday party in the back of the restaurant in the game room. Usually noise didn't bother him but today everything seemed to aggravate him. He was hungry, tired and in a lousy mood. The only thing he wanted to do was to go home with his food, sit down in front of the TV and hopefully fall into a deep, dreamless sleep.

Ray checked his watch. He wondered if Claudia was still out with her new prospect. He could just see her right now, being charmed out of her socks. At least that was all he hoped she was charmed out of.

Ray saw the waitress approaching with his order and he pulled a few bills out of his wallet. As the waitress counted back his change and attempted to flirt with him, he turned when he heard a familiar voice.

It was Claudia. And she wasn't alone.

The man Claudia was with had to be the man she'd met at the dinner party the night before. Mark. The two of them were laughing and seemed to be having a terrific time. They didn't even seem to notice Ray.

A wave of jealousy washed over Ray so suddenly that it caught him by surprise. He immediately noticed the way Mark looked at Claudia. He seemed to be hanging on to her every word. It wasn't hard to see that Mark was taken with her and that bothered Ray immensely.

Fully turning from the bar, Ray approached Mark and Claudia.

Caught by surprise, Claudia asked, "Hey, Ray, what are you doing here?"

"Picking up something to eat on my way home," he replied, never taking his eyes off Mark.

Claudia noticed the strange expression on Ray's face. She gave him a questioning look but he continued looking at Mark.

"Uh, Mark, I'd like you to meet Ray Elliott."

The two men shook hands, with Ray's grip being a little more firm than necessary. Undaunted, Mark matched the firmness of Ray's grip without wavering.

The two men stood face-to-face shaking hands until finally Mark said, "It's nice to meet you."

"Yeah, likewise," Ray mumbled.

The three of them stood in awkward silence until again Mark spoke up. "Well, Ray, Claudia and I don't want to keep you. Besides, I'd hate for your dinner to get cold."

Forgetting about the bag of food he was holding, Ray simply nodded and bid his friend and Mark good night.

After successfully beating Mark in five out of six games of Mole Patrol and having been beaten by him in a game of pool, they decided to have dessert before calling it a night.

"So tell me, pretty lady, what do you do when you're not raising the blood pressure of the male population here in Ohio?"

Claudia laughed. "I don't have it going on like that."

"You're being modest. I'm a very good judge of people and from what I can tell, you are truly a woman that has a lot going for her. You're fun to talk to, when you're paying attention."

Claudia blushed.

"You're also pleasant to be around and have a wonderful sense of humor. And my cousin thinks the world of you," he continued. "You're intelligent and, if you don't mind my saying so, absolutely gorgeous."

Fanning with her paper napkin, Claudia replied, "And you're the biggest flatterer that I've ever come across."

"It's not flattery that's given lightly either."

Claudia leaned her elbow on the table and rested her chin in the palm of her hand. "I'm curious. What makes you think I'm intelligent?"

"Kelly told me what you do for a living. Crunching numbers all day long, dealing with complicated insurance terms. Heck, I'm doing good to figure out when my payments are due and what's covered under my policy and what isn't. Thank goodness I have an agent that I can trust."

"It's really not that complicated. Most people think what I do is boring and to be honest with you, sometimes it gets to be a little mundane. But, I like what I do. When I started with my company I knew numbers and how to analyze them. And in the beginning I was just like you. I didn't know anything about insurance. But I studied and learned everything I could about the industry. I worked closely with different departments and learned what functions they provided so all of the reports and analysis that I generated made a little more sense to me."

"What made you decide to take your skills into the insurance field?"

"One summer after my freshman year I interned as an underwriter assistant. But I didn't like it very much."

"Why not?" asked Mark, taking a sip of coffee.

"For one thing, there was a great deal of phone work and a ton of paperwork. Mostly I had to deal with agents looking for an exception to write a risk that they knew really wasn't eligible for our company or explaining why their client's premium had gone up. I learned a lot but the work wasn't very challenging. Another reason I didn't really like working in underwriting was because there were times I had to be the bearer of bad news and cancel someone's policy."

"Yeah, I can see that part of the job being tough. No one likes to be the one that has to give out the bad news."

"So, what about you? I've pretty much monopolized the entire conversation. Tell me about yourself and what brought you here from North Carolina."

"Well, my two brothers own a construction business in Charlotte and I've worked with them for the past eight years. But for about a year now I've wanted to do something different."

"I remember you telling me that last night. Did you get tired of construction work?"

"Well, it's not so much that I'm tired of the work, I just want to do something different. A buddy of mine from back home moved up here a few years ago and we've kept in touch. When I told him that I was looking into a career move he suggested that I move up here and that the two of us go into business together."

"Oh, really? Construction?"

"No," Mark said sheepishly. "We're thinking about going into the restaurant business."

"Really? I guess I shouldn't say I'm surprised. As long as you have your homemade rolls on the menu, the restaurant should be a huge success."

"Now who's the flatterer?"

"It's not flattery that's given lightly," Claudia repeated with a smile.

When Mark returned Claudia to her house he told her that he would be going out of town for a few days and promised that when he got back to Columbus he would prepare some of the dishes for Claudia that the restaurant planned to feature. He wanted to get her opinion.

"Thanks for tonight," Mark said as he and Claudia stood on her front porch.

"No, thank you. I promise that the next time we go out I will be better company."

"On the contrary, I enjoyed your company very much."

Claudia wasn't sure if he was just being nice or if he really meant it. Hopefully he was sincere because she really did want to see him again.

Before he left that evening Mark leaned down and gave Claudia a brief kiss good night. But thoughts of his moustache tickling her lip were lost when images of the kiss she shared with Ray under the mistletoe sprang forward. Disturbed by the memory and even more so by the timing of its appearance, Claudia quickly bid Mark good night and retreated inside her house.

CHAPTER SIXTEEN

It was cold, rainy and downright miserable outside. The weather matched Claudia's mood to a T. She couldn't wait to slip out of her clothes and drop into bed. Her day had begun with one meeting and then another followed by a deadline that she had made just under the wire. She didn't even bother about dinner. She wasn't hungry anyway. It had been a long day at work and food had taken a backseat to her need for some serious downtime.

As she peeled off her clothes along with the day's stress, she decided to check her voice mail for messages before getting too comfortable. There were two. One message was from Mark giving her a number where he could be reached in North Carolina and letting her know that he was thinking about her. The other was from Jewel, inviting her to a luncheon. Not feeling up to talking to anyone she decided she would call Mark and her mother later.

Slipping under the warmth and security of her down comforter and wearing her favorite flannel pajamas, Claudia lit a few candles, turned off the lamp beside her bed and tuned into her favorite blues station. Ginger settled in at the foot of the bed and for the first time that day, Claudia felt herself relax.

A song by B.B. King floated over the airwaves. Claudia let the rhythm of the guitar relax her as she listened to the lyrics of a love gone bad. It was the perfect music to end a not so perfect day.

Claudia had inherited her love of the blues from her father and grandfather. Karen and Frank called it old folks' music and used to tease her for listening to Bobby "Blue" Bland, Etta James and

Denise LaSalle, but Claudia didn't care what her brother and sister thought. She liked what she liked. Sometimes her mood called for hip hop, sometimes jazz and other times the blues.

Some of Claudia's fondest childhood memories included sitting with her father on Saturday evenings while he listened to some of the greatest blues artists of that time. He always told her that amongst all music the blues gave one a fitting perspective on life. Listening to a blues artist describe the love of a good man or woman in song was better than reading the advice columns. One could learn what to do when being cheated on, mistreated or lonely.

Blues songs were also good at lauding the benefits of being in love. Real love. The kind of love that has the power to make you forget all of life's hang-ups and bad times, but at the same time giving you hope and strength to carry on one more day just because you have someone to love.

Claudia smiled and snuggled deeper under the covers. If only life were really that simple.

She wondered what kind of song lyrics could be penned from her life. Right now the words would reflect loneliness, longing and confusion. All of that seemed like fitting material for a blues song. But she hoped to change all of that very soon.

She liked Mark and she could tell that he liked her, too, although it seemed as if Ray was trying to throw a kink into her plans. For what reason she had no idea. Didn't he want her to be happy? He said he did, but his words and actions proved otherwise.

For a while now she had been receiving signals from Ray that she didn't know how to decipher and these signals had started before the kiss under the mistletoe. Ray had always been concerned about what went on in her life, but now he'd kicked that concern up a notch. He was even getting a little nosey, wanting to know who she was seeing, where she was going on her date, and other things that only her mother and father had a right to ask.

Men. Who could figure them out?

Claudia listened to the rain beat against her windowpane. The wind had picked up a little and made a low howling sound as shadows from the tree branches outside her window were thrown across the bedroom walls casting shadows of various shapes and sizes.

This would be the perfect night to cuddle, she thought. She found herself wondering if Mark liked to cuddle and what type of music he enjoyed. Ray liked listening to jazz, especially when he needed to relax and unwind. She didn't have to wonder if he also enjoyed cuddling. From a previous conversation, she knew that he did.

She could only imagine what it would be like to be wrapped up in big, strong, loving arms. It had to be a wonderful feeling to be held in the protective and loving embrace of someone who you knew loved you with all their heart and soul. But when she pictured that scene in her mind, it wasn't Mark that she imagined cuddling with. It was Ray. And in her imagination, he was very good at it.

Although Ray tried to play the part of the quintessential male around most people, she knew the man behind the mask very well. Around the people he cared about Ray never hesitated to show his sweet, kind and gentle side. Unlike Claudia, Ray rarely forgot a birthday, anniversary or other special dates. He was also the type of man who paid attention to details. He would notice whether or not Claudia's toenails were painted, if she was wearing a new outfit or even a new shade of lipstick. He cared if she'd had a good day or not and seemed to always pay special attention to what made her happy or sad. There were many times when Ray sought Claudia's advice about important issues in his life and she knew that he truly valued her opinion. Some of her female friends didn't have that type of connection with their husbands.

If she ever allowed herself to seriously think of Ray as something other than a friend, she would have to admit he would probably be a good catch and decent husband material, not to mention a good lover.

"Stop it," she said aloud. The last thing in the world she wanted to do was to fantasize about Ray - again. She had a mission to accomplish and getting sidetracked by inappropriate thoughts of Ray would not help her reach her much-desired goal.

CHAPTER SEVENTEEN

Rolanda Beckham had been an outstanding college student. Excelling academically while actively participating in service organizations, sorority life and various other campus activities. She held many fond memories of her life at college. Most of her fondest memories included her college roommate, Claudia Ryland. The two women had formed a bond during their freshman year and after graduation continued to keep in touch by phone, email, cards and letters.

Rolanda was in town for a business seminar and had contacted Claudia to arrange a get together for later that evening. The two of them hadn't seen each other in over a year and had a great deal of catching up to do. The last email message Claudia had received from Rolanda had informed her of a job promotion, the finalization of a long, drawn out divorce and a new lease on life.

When Claudia arrived at the hotel to pick up Rolanda, she found her friend flirting with a bellhop and looking better than she had looked in years.

After exchanging hugs Rolanda stepped back to get a good look at Claudia.

"Girl, you look fabulous," Rolanda exclaimed. "If I were two sizes smaller that outfit would be mine!"

"You're looking pretty fine yourself."

Rolanda stood at least three inches taller than Claudia and was slimmer through the hips, but with a more ample bust line. Honey colored skin with a spattering of freckles across her nose, she no longer wore glasses and had apparently switched to contact lenses. *A good move,* Claudia thought to herself. She always loved Rolanda's dark, mysterious eyes but they always seemed to be hidden behind a pair of thick, unflattering, glasses.

Since the last time they saw each other Claudia noticed a few other things that had changed about her friend's appearance. Sporting short dreadlocks and looking at least twenty pounds slimmer, Claudia thought that Rolanda looked even better than she had when they were younger. She definitely was more confident and poised.

The plan for the evening was dinner at Claudia's with hours of girl talk to follow. Claudia and Rolanda unpacked bags of groceries from Claudia's car and chatted incessantly about boyfriends, past and present, the weather and current events.

"I see Ginger's still watching over you," Rolanda commented as they maneuvered the sacks of groceries around the over-excited dog. She had been barking from the time the garage door opened until they entered the kitchen.

"What can I say? Besides you, Ginger's my girl. She sticks closer to me than cellulite."

Rolanda folded her arms and looked at Claudia mockingly. "That would be funny if you actually had a speck of cellulite on you."

Claudia and Rolanda donned aprons, rolled up their sleeves and started preparing the meal. It was going to be simple but filling-grilled chicken, baked potatoes and salad. Rolanda didn't know it but Claudia had picked up a cheesecake for dessert. Rolanda's favorite.

Claudia handed her friend a glass of wine and went over to put the potatoes in the oven. "I can't get over you, Ro. You really look good. Your skin is glowing, your eyes are sparkling and there's a certain little something in your step, like you're walking around with a million dollars in your pocket."

Rolanda took a sip of wine and laughed. "A million dollars, huh? Well, life is good, but it's not quite that good."

Claudia walked back to the table to join Rolanda. "Before we get caught up in girl talk, I want to tell you how excited and proud I was when I heard about your promotion." Claudia held up her glass and said, "Congratulations."

Rolanda touched her glass with Claudia's.

"Chief Financial Officer. Kind of has a nice ring to it, doesn't it? Whoever thought all of those boring accounting and business math classes would lead to this?" Claudia said jokingly.

Rolanda placed her glass on the table and looked at her friend. "I can't tell you how happy I am with this new position. Lord knows I worked like a slave to get it. This is going to sound like something a high school guidance counselor would say, but hard work and perseverance are finally paying off. On top of everything else, this has been a rocky year but this promotion has been the big, fat cherry on top of the sundae I know was made especially for me, and I am enjoying every bit of it."

"If anyone deserves this, you do. So enjoy."

The salad was tossed, the dressing made and the chicken was cooking on Claudia's indoor grill. Claudia put out some fruit, crackers and cheese to snack on until dinner was ready.

"I know I've said this before, Claudia, over the phone and in writing, but now I want to thank you in person. I don't know how I would have made it through this past year without having you to talk to when things were going crazy and seemingly falling apart. I know I joked before about losing two hundred and seventy-five unsightly pounds when I divorced Greg, but let me tell you, divorce is no joke and it's something I don't ever want to go through again."

"It was my pleasure to be there for you, Ro. Besides, I knew you would make it through that whole ordeal and would emerge stronger and better than before. And I was right."

Rolanda smiled. "Maybe I have it together right now, but there was a time or two that I did not know what I was going to do."

Claudia nodded her understanding. After Rolanda's husband had walked out on her she'd had to face one of the toughest times in her life. With raw emotions and feeling more vulnerable than she had ever felt before, there had been many nights that she'd called Claudia looking for encouragement, a laugh, or even to hear her friend say that everything was going to be all right. Claudia had been there for her every step of the way.

"I find that the strangest thing about the breakup of my marriage was how lost and alone I felt without Greg. When we were dating, that man did everything within his power to get me to marry him and then after everything we put into the marriage he decided he wanted out."

"Ro, it's not every day that the man you're in love with and plan to spend the rest of your life with comes home and tells you that he's not in love with you anymore. It takes a lot to handle that kind of news."

"Trust me, I know and it was a lesson punctuated with an exclamation point. Let me tell you, that was some serious heartache and more than one of those in a lifetime can take a person out."

"Well, that's all behind you now. You've come through this like the beautiful, independent, take-no-mess sistah that I always knew you were."

"And what about you, Miss Claudia? Looks as if life has been treating you well, too. You're going to have to tell me who put the sparkle in your eyes. Not to mention who you're dressing all cute for. 'Cause, girl, you're wearing that suit. I always said you knew how to work a knit skirt with those hips."

Claudia laughed. Rolanda was still one of her best girlfriends and just as crazy as she'd always been. It felt good having Rolanda here and seeing that everything was working out for her.

Throughout dinner the two friends continued discussing their jobs, mutual friends and anything else they could think of. Claudia told Rolanda about Mark. And although it was too early to designate him as the man she wanted to spend the rest of her life with, she did mentioned that she had been seriously thinking about the whole marriage and family thing. However, no mention of her plan was made. She wasn't sure what Rolanda's reaction would be and she decided that she really didn't want to find out. She had enough feedback from plenty of people already.

"So, how's your gorgeous friend?"

Claudia knew Rolanda was referring to Ray. Ever since he had shown up unexpectedly for her birthday during their freshman year Rolanda had wisely advised Claudia to hold on to him as a friend.

"He's the same wonderful person now that he has always been, give or take a few annoying habits."

"Still keeping him at arm's length?"

Surprised by the question, Claudia stopped eating and looked at her friend questioningly. "What is that supposed to mean?"

Rolanda shrugged her shoulders. "It means that you've always treated Ray as a buddy and there's clearly a lot more there than you're willing to admit."

"What makes you say that?"

"Because I have two perfectly good eyes and ears. They allow me to see through people and hear more than what is being said."

"I don't know what you're imagining but I think you might want to seek help from a professional."

"You can joke if you want to, but during the course of our conversation this evening, you've mentioned your new friend Mark once, two times at the most. Yes, there was a small glimmer in your eyes and a certain fondness when you spoke of him, but when I brought up Ray, I saw something more. What I saw tells me that there's more between you two than just friendship. Something has developed over the years, Claudia, hasn't it?"

"No. You're seeing things that aren't there, Ro. Maybe I should have served iced tea instead of wine. There is nothing between us other than friendship." Claudia rested her chin on her hand and sighed. "Why do I sound like a broken record when I say that?"

"Maybe it's because you're busy trying to convince yourself."

Claudia dropped Rolanda off at her hotel around two A.M. She had tried to convince her friend to spend the night but Rolanda had declined. She had to facilitate an early morning session and needed to catch her flight back to Chicago shortly afterward.

The two friends parted and promised that they would try to get together again soon. Rolanda had also made Claudia promise something else, to stop looking at Ray as a buddy and start looking at him as a man.

CHAPTER EIGHTEEN

Joyce Roberts sat up in her hospital bed staring out the window. When she heard someone coming into her room she turned to see her daughter entering and holding a vase with a small floral bouquet.

Viveca looked into her mother's tired eyes and again promised herself to never let life beat her down the way it had her mother.

"I hear they're springing you today," Viveca said, trying to force a cheerful tone in her voice.

Joyce sighed and folded her hands in her lap. "And not a moment too soon either. I'm more than ready to go home. I haven't been able to get any rest in this place. Every time I manage to drift off to sleep, someone comes in here to check something or other. I think that's the hospital's way of keeping you sick, by not letting you get any rest."

"Well, you won't have to wait much longer to leave. The nurse said your doctor should be in here in a few minutes with some final instructions and your prescriptions."

Viveca helped her mother get dressed and gather the few personal belongings she had in the hospital room. She had suffered very little damage from her stroke and was able to move around quite easily but still needed just a little help from her daughter.

"Hello, Mrs. Roberts."

Both Viveca and her mother turned toward the male voice coming from the doorway.

"Dr. Hammond," exclaimed Joyce, "I thought Dr. Gibson was the one sending me off today."

"He was called away on an emergency," Dr. Hammond said, continuing the banter with Joyce as he glanced over at Viveca as she packed her mother's bag.

Viveca had been quietly observing the good doctor as he and her mother chatted. Over the years she had become quite skilled at assessing a potential suitor and Dr. Hammond certainly had potential. No wedding ring. Manicured nails. Expensive Italian leather shoes. Well-spoken. He wasn't as attractive as she would have preferred but she was sure his financial assets would make up for any shortcomings in the looks department.

Yes, the good doctor certainly had potential.

"Where are my manners?" Joyce exclaimed when she noticed the doctor looking at her daughter. "Dr. Hammond, I'd like you to meet my daughter, Viveca Roberts. She came all the way here from California to look after me."

Viveca may have been mistaken, but she thought she detected a note of pride in her mother's voice. She stood and extended her hand to the doctor.

"It's a pleasure to meet you, Dr. Hammond," she said in her most charming voice. "Please let Dr. Gibson and the rest of the staff know how much I appreciate the wonderful care my mother has received."

Viveca was practically oozing sexuality and Dr. Hammond was no match for her charms.

He smiled broadly and said, "Well, thank you. I'll be sure and pass the message on."

Viveca smiled seductively.

Dr. Hammond cleared his throat and remembered what it was that he should be doing. After scribbling down a few notes on the chart he handed Viveca two prescriptions along with a copy of the discharge papers. "Just in case of an emergency or if you have any questions, here is my pager number. I can also be reached through my service," he added, catching Viveca's gaze. "Please, don't hesitate to contact me if you need me."

"I'll do just that," she practically cooed.

Viveca and Joyce rode along in silence until they reached the drug store.

"I'm going to get these prescriptions filled and pick up a few other things. Would you like me to get you anything while I'm in the store?" she asked her mother.

Joyce stared out the passenger side window and shook her head.

Viveca had left the car's motor running so that her mother wouldn't get cold. When she returned to the car she found her still peering out the window.

After a few seconds Joyce turned to her daughter. "Why aren't we leaving? Did you forget something?"

"No, I didn't forget anything. I'm just waiting."

"For what?"

"For you to tell me why you're upset."

"What makes you think I'm upset?"

"Because I know you and I know that when you're giving me the silent treatment that all hell is about to break loose. Now, would you please just say whatever it is that's on your mind so we can get this argument over with."

Joyce pursed her lips. "I'm not going to argue with you, Viveca. But I do want you to know that I thought it was shameless the way you flirted with Dr. Hammond."

Viveca threw her hands up in exasperation. "What's wrong with a little harmless flirting? It's not as if I threw the man on the ground and ripped his clothes off."

"There is nothing wrong with flirting, except that with you it

137

won't be harmless."

"What do you mean by that?" Viveca asked angrily.

"You know perfectly well what I mean. Don't think I didn't see how you were sizing that poor man up. I'm sure you've already calculated in your head how much he paid for his pants, watch and sweater, and whether or not his shoes were Italian leather."

Viveca tightened her jaw.

"Don't sit there like you're innocent. Viveca, I know how you use men."

"Oh, you do? What is wrong with getting what I want out of life the best way I can?"

"Nothing, as long as you're not using someone else to get it."

"That's a matter of opinion."

"No, sweetheart, that's a statement of fact. Just remember, what goes around comes around. The person you misuse today might return the favor to you someday."

"When you were younger, I watched how you used the men in your life to get the kind of material things you thought were a symbol of happiness. But you weren't happy then and you're not happy now. Then you were simply greedy and I don't believe that has changed at all."

Viveca sat and listened to her mother as she became angrier with each stinging accusation.

Joyce continued without regard for her daughter's feelings. Viveca needed to hear what she had to say and it was long overdue.

"I should have spoken up a long time ago, especially after the way you treated Ray Elliott. You made me ashamed. That man loved you dearly and all you did was use him. And to add insult to injury, you ran off to marry that good-for-nothing gigolo, Clayton."

"Don't hold your tongue now, Mom," Viveca said sarcastically, trying to hold back tears of shame. "You're on a roll."

"What are your intentions toward Ray?"

"What?" Viveca asked, surprised by her mother's question.

"He came by to see me when I was in the hospital, just to make sure I was all right. After everything you put him through, the man is compassionate enough to still be your friend. Don't take advantage of that. He deserves better."

Viveca stared out her window. She was fuming.

"And what do I deserve?" she asked her mother quietly.

"Nothing until you can appreciate what you already have. I know you're going to find this hard to believe, but I'm really not trying to hurt you."

Viveca turned to her mother and said, "Too late."

"Well, maybe that's a good thing. Shows you have some feelings after all. I was beginning to wonder."

Viveca had heard enough. She threw the car in reverse and hit the gas pedal.

"Honey," began Joyce softly, "there's no gain in using people. I think you've seen that already. Material things don't add up to much when you're all alone."

"Thanks for the sage advice. I'll tuck those words of wisdom deep in my heart along with the other life lessons I learned from you and Daddy."

This time it was Joyce who spoke angrily. "Don't try to blame your father and me for your greed or your unhappiness, Viveca. We did the best we could with what we had. If we didn't do anything else we made sure you had everything you needed growing up. You may not have had all the pretty clothes and trinkets your friends had, but you had a roof over your head, decent clothes and food to eat."

"And very little else."

"I'm not going to apologize for your upbringing. Yes, there may have been some things your father and I could have done differently, but sooner or later, you're going to have to take responsibility for your own actions."

"That's exactly what I plan to do," Viveca said pulling into the driveway of the house. "And if my actions are a problem for you, then I guess that's going to be something you'll have to deal with."

After her mother had taken her medication and laid down to rest, Viveca sat at the kitchen table nursing a warm beer and hurt feelings. She was still very angry and hurt by her mother's accusations although none of what they'd argued about that afternoon was unfamiliar. However, this was the first time her mother had been so vocal. It was no secret that Joyce disapproved of her daughter's lifestyle, but she'd never said a great deal about it, only warned her to be careful of the choices she made.

Viveca needed to get out of the house for a while, clear her head. Calling on her mother's next door neighbor to keep an eye on Joyce for a few hours, Viveca got in her car and began to drive with no particular destination in mind.

After driving around the outer belt for nearly an hour she thought about calling Dr. Hammond and inviting him out for a drink but remembered that she'd left the piece of paper he'd written his numbers on at her mother's. She wasn't quite ready to go back there yet and she really didn't want to be alone, so she called Ray at work. He was getting ready to leave for the day and agreed to meet her at a café near his office.

Viveca sat at a small table near the café's front window as she waited for Ray to join her. As was typical for this time of year, it was barely six o'clock and it was already dark. This was another reason she hated the winters in Ohio. Nothing was green and there was very little sunshine. She needed the sun as much for its brilliant light as for its warmth. She'd go out of her mind if she had to spend an entire winter under the cloud cover that was typical for this region.

While she watched the general hustle and bustle of downtown workers leaving their jobs and going home for the evening, she found herself thinking about Claudia, more specifically, Claudia's relationship with Ray. Even though she never admitted it to him, she had always been jealous of the close bond he shared with Claudia.

During the time that they were together, Ray had tried unsuccessfully to bridge some form of friendship between Viveca and Claudia. But from their first meeting on, it was clear that the two women would never be friends. Viveca was resentful of how deep the bond ran between Ray and Claudia and she never let an opportunity go by without making him aware of how uncomfortable it made her feel. Along the same vein, Claudia had done very little to befriend her which always made Viveca feel as if she only wanted Ray for herself.

Now Viveca wondered if Ray and Claudia's relationship had grown beyond mere friendship. She had posed the question earlier to Ray but he had successfully skirted the issue. Sooner or later she would get an answer.

Viveca rested her chin in the palm of her hand and looked down into her cup of coffee. *Why should she care what was going on between Claudia Ryland and Ray?* She had pretty much blown any type of meaningful relationship between herself and Ray when she left him and married Clayton, but, she thought, it was the principle of the matter. Ray had been hers. Claudia wouldn't know what to do with a man like Ray if her life depended on it. A man like Ray would be wasted on Claudia, she thought cruelly.

"It's nice to see you smiling," Ray said as he sat down and joined Viveca.

Lifting her chin and looking up into Ray's handsome face, Viveca tucked away her previous thoughts.

"Well, I have a great deal to feel good about. Mom came home from the hospital today and seems to be doing quite well. On top of that, I'm sitting here with Mr. Fine himself. Life couldn't get much better than this."

Ray smiled and looked at the sadness in Viveca's eyes. "You always know the right thing to say. Now maybe I can return the favor."

Puzzled, Viveca asked Ray what he meant by that statement.

"You've clearly invited me here for a reason. When we spoke on the phone earlier I detected a slight edge in your voice. More to the point, you just mentioned that your mother came home from the hospital today and no matter how well she may be doing, you're not at home with her. That's a bit strange, don't you think? Care to fill in the some of missing details?"

Surprised that she was that transparent, Viveca turned up the charm a notch. She wasn't about to be read that easily and didn't need Ray trying to play therapist. She smiled sweetly and said, "You know how much I hate hospitals and being there every day was beginning to wear on me. Plus, I've been really worried about my mother. I know I should be home with her right now, but I just had to get out of the house for a little while. That's all. Mom isn't alone if that's what you were thinking. One of her neighbors is there with her. I'm glad that she's finally home and resting comfortably."

Ray gave his order to the waitress and returned his attention to Viveca. He wasn't a hundred percent sure that she was being completely honest about what was going on in her life, but he decided not to press the issue.

"How much longer are you planning to stay in town?"

Viveca shrugged her slim shoulders. If it wouldn't seem so heartless, she'd hire a private nurse to take care of her mother and leave the following day. But she felt the least she could do was to wait until she was sure that her mother would be all right on her own before she went back to California. "I'll probably be here for a few more weeks."

"And then what?"

"Then I'll pick up where I left off in California."

"Is that what you really want to do?"

"What's with all the strange questions today?"

"If you don't mind me being honest, I just get the feeling that you're not happy."

Viveca smiled. "On the contrary, I'm quite happy. I have everything I want and more. Life couldn't be better."

"What about things between you and your mother? Has there been some improvement over the years?"

Ray couldn't have asked that question at a more appropriate time. She wasn't about to let him know about the argument she had with her mother earlier that afternoon. She needed to answer the question carefully so that she would not arouse Ray's curiosity. "My mother and I are two entirely different people. I love her and she loves me. Sometimes we just don't like each other. With the two of us living so far apart we manage to maintain a civil relationship most of the time. It's when we're under the same roof for more than twenty-four hours that we tend to clash." Viveca hadn't intended to reveal so much, but Ray always seemed so understanding and caring that she almost got carried away and told him about the argument.

"Any clashing going on recently?"

Enough with the questions. She hadn't invited Ray out for a drink in order to spill her guts. She had just wanted some company, that's all.

"No. The only thing I've been able to focus on is helping my mother get better and she has had the same goal. So, with that out of the way, let's talk about something else."

"Like what?" Ray asked, checking his watch.

Viveca pretended that she hadn't seen him do that. "Let's talk about you."

"What would you like to know about me that you don't know already?"

Viveca laced her fingers together and placed them under her chin, leaning her elbows on the table. She carefully watched Ray's expression as she posed her question. "How are things between you and Claudia?"

Ray looked into Viveca's beautiful eyes and wondered if there was a scheme hidden behind them. This wasn't the first time she had asked about his relationship with Claudia and he was beginning to wonder why she was showing such interest.

"I believe we had this discussion before."

"Yes, and you avoided it then, too."

"I'm not trying to avoid anything. I'm just a little curious as to why you want to know about Claudia and me."

"Blame it on curiosity."

"Isn't that what killed the cat?"

"So I've been told. But if my memory serves me correctly, satisfaction bought it back."

Ray smiled. Viveca could be cunning. He remembered Claudia's warning to be careful around her. He wasn't sure why she was so curious but he wasn't going to give her ammunition if that was what she was looking for.

"Let's just say Claudia and I are still pals."

"Pals? That's cute." Viveca placed her hands on the table and leaned in close. "Is there room in your life for another pal?"

"That all depends."

"On?"

"What you really want from me."

"Your friendship, Ray. Is that asking too much?"

"No strings attached?"

"No strings attached," she said.

"I think I can live with that." Ray checked his watch again. "Viveca, I hate to leave you like this, but I have a meeting across town that I can't miss."

"That's okay. I've got to get home anyway."

Ray stood and placed some money on the table. "Are you going to be all right? It's really hard for me to read you anymore."

Viveca stood, pasted on a smile and turned for Ray to help her with her coat. "You don't need to read me, Ray, and you don't have to worry if I'm all right. Haven't you learned by now that I always land on my feet?"

Ray turned Viveca to face him and held her by the shoulders. "It's not a question of how you'll land, but where and what shape you'll be in when your feet touch the ground."

Impulsively, Viveca went into Ray's arms. She held on to him for only a moment and it wasn't the kind of embrace that lovers share, but one in which a soul reaches out for comfort.

Ray didn't pull away but embraced her because he knew that was what she really needed at that moment. Then she was gone.

Claudia waited patiently at the counter of the jewelry store while the clasp on her necklace was being repaired. While she waited, she looked at the tennis bracelets that were displayed in the case by the cash register and tried to calculate in her head whether she could afford the purchase or if she would have to be content window shopping.

After a little thought and a reality check she reasoned that even though they were all so pretty, they were also much too expensive.

Just another time when necessity beat out frivolity, she mused.

Passing the cuff links and men's rings she found herself in the front of the store by the bridal sets. If everything went as planned, she'd be wearing one of those sets within a year or so.

One of the salesmen noticed Claudia looking at the rings and asked her if she'd like to try on a set. He opened the case and picked out a set containing the largest and most magnificent diamond she had ever seen and slipped it on her finger.

It was a near-perfect fit. She held her finger up to see the light reflect off the dazzling stone. But it wasn't the brilliance of the stone that caught her attention.

In the lighted window of the café across the street she thought she caught a glimpse of someone familiar. Moving closer to the window, she realized that it was Ray - and Viveca.

The two of them stood face to face. Then they embraced. The whole scene looked very intimate and she was strangely disturbed by what she saw. A chill raced up her spine.

Claudia turned away from the window.

"If you don't like that particular solitaire, you can try on another one set," the salesman said when he noticed the expression on Claudia's face.

What were Ray and Viveca doing together? And why was he holding her?

"Miss?"

Claudia looked at the salesman as if he were speaking gibberish.

"Is everything all right?"

Claudia removed the ring from her finger and placed it on the counter. "Y-yes, everything is fine. Could you please tell the woman who's repairing my necklace that I'll be in tomorrow afternoon to pick it up?" She left the shop and stood outside looking across the street at the café. Ray was gone. And so was Viveca.

She stood there and wondered if the two of them had left together. *Was Ray getting involved with Viveca again?* she wondered. She was concerned, but this time it was more for herself than for Ray.

CHAPTER NINETEEN

As soon as Mark arrived back in town he called Claudia. He had been gone less than a week, but he had missed her. They had spoken on the phone a few times but he found that although he enjoyed their phone conversations, he really wanted to see her in person. He called to invite her to his house for Sunday dinner.

At first Claudia had declined. She knew she wouldn't be very good company and had planned on staying in bed all day. But it wasn't until after he promised to make chocolate cake with chocolate icing, which he'd learned was one of her favorite desserts, that she had accepted. She hoped that spending time with Mark would make her forget how she felt when she saw Ray and Viveca together.

Claudia hadn't spoken to Ray since she had seen him and Viveca together. When she called to cancel another Wednesday lunch date, he had been out of the office. She had left a message stating that she would have to sit in on a late morning conference call that was scheduled to last at least two hours and that she would catch up with him another time. She made a point to say that she didn't know when that other time would be.

The conference call had been just the excuse she needed to cancel lunch with Ray. Claudia was having a hard time dealing with her jealousy over what she thought was going on with him and Viveca. For all she knew it was nothing. But those two had a history. They shared intimacies that Claudia couldn't compete with. Ray had been in love with Viveca and had wanted to marry her. And at one time Viveca had a power over Ray that Claudia couldn't understand. Now Viveca was back in his life. In what capacity, Claudia didn't know and was a little afraid to find out.

Mark was an excellent cook and a gracious host. Claudia had arrived at his house promptly at six o'clock. She had brought a bottle of white wine to go with dinner, even though he told her the only thing he wanted her to bring was her appetite.

Mark lived in a part of the city that was undergoing a major facelift. Years before many of the homes and business in the area had been abandoned when the residents moved to the suburbs. It had been difficult trying to find buyers that were interested in the stately, old homes. Soon these abandoned houses became more attractive to gangs and drug dealers than to prospective buyers. The area quickly became crime-infested and rundown. Those who could afford to leave did. But some of the older residents and those with no other place to go had no choice but to stay in the dilapidated neighborhood and endure the onset of rapid decay.

When the few residents that still remained after everyone else had fled became fed up with what was going on right in their own backyards, they decided to take back their neighborhood. They had simply had enough of being afraid to leave their own homes.

Initially, it wasn't easy combating the unsavory element that had taken up residence in the neighborhood, but eventually they were able to get the mayor to pay attention to their plight. Soon after, positive changes began to occur. Law enforcement officers became more visible, making more arrests, and the residents set up a neighborhood watch program. Soon after, the city sold the abandoned homes, offering low interest loans as an incentive to potential homeowners if they made a commitment to stay in the neighborhood for at least five years. Partnering with several development firms to bring the houses up to code, at very little or no cost to the homeowners, many houses began to sell and the neighborhood once again became a desirable place to live and raise families. Ray's development firm had been instrumental in renovating the block of homes south of where Mark lived.

Mark lived in one of the homes that had undergone a complete renovation. He'd only been in the house for a little while but had added quite a few personal touches already.

The living room was warm and cozy with a huge fireplace, glistening hardwood floors, and vaulted ceilings. The furniture consisted of a leather sofa, loveseat and two matching recliners, all sitting on a colorful area rug that added a distinct splash of color to the room. Although very masculine the room was by no means overpowering.

Mark's kitchen was as spacious as the living room and just as cozy and inviting. At first glance Claudia noticed that he had more equipment in his kitchen than the housewares department of any major department store she'd ever been inside. For every task that needed to be performed, there was a tool for the job. Spotting an apple peeler mounted to the end of a counter, Claudia couldn't resist the urge to tease Mark about it.

Mark had completely modernized his kitchen. It was clearly evident by the appearance of the stainless steel appliances and especially by the large workspaces and spacious cabinets.

There was an island in the center of the kitchen on which Mark had placed a tray of fruit and cheese for Claudia to nibble on until dinner was ready. She had offered to help with the final preparations for dinner but he had refused. He simply wanted her to keep him company while he finished the meal, and it smelled wonderful.

Claudia obliged. She felt comfortable in Mark's kitchen and it reminded her of being a little girl and watching while her mother prepared Sunday dinner.

"You seem a little preoccupied this evening," Mark noted when he noticed the faraway look on Claudia's face.

"I have a lot on my mind."

"I'm a good listener. Care to talk about it?"

Claudia shrugged her shoulders. "Just some projects at work that I need to finish." She didn't like lying to Mark, but would he really want to hear what was on her mind?

"How are the preparations coming for the restaurant?" Claudia asked as she munched on a chunk of smoked cheddar cheese and attempted to change the subject.

"Very well, I'm pleased to announce. The contract on the building has been signed, sealed and delivered and we have already started interviewing for staff positions. I'm really pleased about our location and especially the building. Because it was previously a restaurant and the building is not very old, there are only a few renovations that need to be made to the inside. Of course my partner and I will be adding our own flavor to the décor."

"You two are moving rather quickly."

"I suppose. We're just really anxious to get things started and we're even a little ahead of schedule."

"Sounds like things are really happening for you."

"I think so. Even though I was a little hesitant at first, I knew moving here was a good idea. Things are finally starting to fall into place for me. A nice home, a new business venture and," he turned off the gas burner and joined Claudia, "a pretty lady to spend time with."

Claudia blushed.

"A toast," Mark said, pouring himself a glass of wine.

Claudia raised her glass. "Here's to good food, a thriving business and good friends."

After dinner, Mark and Claudia sat in the living room in front of the fireplace. Mark had added a few more pieces of wood to the fire and stoked it until it cast off enough light that they didn't need to turn on the room's lamps. Will Downing was singing softly in the background and the log on the fire crackled occasionally.

"That was an excellent meal," Claudia remarked. "Whoever thought chicken, pasta and vegetables could be so delicious. I usually find that vegetables are so boring and bland, but not the way you prepared them. I can't even remember the last time I enjoyed eating my veggies that much."

"I'm glad you liked the meal. That will be one of the dishes featured on our menu."

"I don't know if I can wait until the restaurant opens. You're going to spoil me preparing meals like that."

"Good. You deserve to be spoiled and I think I have all the qualifications to do just that." Mark moved closer to Claudia on the sofa. "You know," he began, "I still find something very puzzling."

"What's that?"

"How a big old country boy like me could be fortunate enough to have someone like you to spend time with."

"I consider myself to be the fortunate one," Claudia said, clearly flattered by Mark's compliment.

"Would it be too forward of me to ask you for a kiss?"

Claudia felt her heart beating rapidly. "No," she said softly.

Mark leaned forward and touched Claudia's lips with his own. Softly at first, he simply wanted to know the feeling of her lips against his, to taste a bit of her sweetness. Then, wanting to broaden the exploration and taste more of what she had to offer, Mark's tongue beckoned to enter. Claudia accepted the invitation and permitted the entry without hesitation.

Mark found Claudia's taste intoxicating as her tongue, warm and delicious, met his in a gesture that begged for more. Pulling her close to him, Mark could feel Claudia's hardened nipples against his chest. She felt good in his arms, just as he knew she would. But, he had to be sensible and stop before he got carried away.

"Mmm, that was nice," Mark said, as he ended the kiss. Claudia looked so beautiful in the soft light from the fire that he found himself thinking about things that he really shouldn't be thinking about, not this soon anyway.

Claudia's hair was pinned up in a mass of curls secured by a single gold barrette. The hairstyle was pretty but he liked it when she wore her hair down. Mark unclasped the barrette sending her hair tumbling to her shoulders. She looked so pretty with her hair framing her face that way, he thought.

"Was this what you had planned for dessert?" Claudia asked seductively.

Mark smiled. If only Claudia knew how much he really did want to have her for dessert. Exploring her sexy curves and touching her skin would definitely be a sweet treat.

Brushing a stray curl from her face, Mark pulled Claudia into an embrace and said, "Pretty lady, I'm sure what you have to offer would be much more delicious than anything I could ever come up with in my kitchen. But if we don't stop this right now, we'll be treading into some pretty dangerous waters and I don't think either of us is ready for that right now."

Claudia pulled away slightly and asked, "Do you see dangerous waters ahead?"

"I'm not quite sure," he replied and ran a finger along the side of her face. "All I can say right now is that when we get together the way I feel that we are intended to, I need for you to be one hundred percent sure that what I'm offering you're ready and able to accept. No doubts. No hesitation. No regrets."

Claudia searched Mark's face. *Did he sense something?* she

wondered. Could he possibly have known that while their lips touched passionately and his hands held her gently, thoughts of Ray never left her mind?

CHAPTER TWENTY

Ray dribbled the ball down the court, went for the lay up and missed. Frank got the rebound and scored without exerting too much effort.

"That's game," Frank announced. "I would say how much fun it was schooling you on the court today, but that would be bragging. And you know how modest I am."

Ray leaned over, resting his hands on his knees. He couldn't ever remember losing to Frank this badly.

"Let's hit the showers and you can buy me a congratulatory beer."

Ray nodded and headed toward the locker room.

Once Ray had showered and dressed, he waited at the front desk for Frank. Leafing through the recreation center's activity calendar, Ray wondered what was taking Frank so long to come out of the locker room.

"Finally," Ray said when he saw Frank meandering out of the locker room. "I thought I was going to have to send in a search party to look for you."

"You can't rush perfection," Frank said jokingly.

From the time they left the gym until they reached their favorite sports bar, Ray had barely said more than two words to Frank. The two men took a seat at the bar and ordered a pitcher of beer.

"If I keep beating you up on the basketball court, we're going to have to switch games. It's no fun playing one on none," Frank joked.

"Huh?"

"Man, what is wrong with you? First, I'm practically playing basketball all by myself, now it looks as if I'm going to have to keep up both ends of the conversation. You look like you've got the weight of the world on your shoulders."

More so my heart than shoulders, Ray thought. "Have you seen your sister lately?"

"Claudia? She was by our parents' house late Sunday evening, but other than that I haven't seen much of her lately. I heard Karen asking her about some guy she's dating, so I guess that's why she's not been around much. Why?"

Ray shrugged his shoulders and popped some pretzels in his mouth. "No special reason. I just haven't seen her much, that's all. She cancelled our lunch date again and I haven't spoken to her in a while. I left a couple of messages for her at work and home but she hasn't returned any of my calls. Probably pretty busy with work."

Frank and Ray watched a basketball game on the TV above the bar until a commercial came on.

"Have you met the guy?" Ray asked when Frank didn't offer any more information.

"What guy?"

Ray was doing his best to act nonchalant but Frank was making him work for information. "The one Claudia is seeing."

"Nope. You?"

Ray shook his head. He didn't want to bring up their brief meeting from before. "Do you know if it's someone named Mark?"

"Man, I don't know. Sometimes my sisters talk about so many different things at one time that I tend to tune them out. Honestly, I don't remember if they mentioned his name. If they did, I missed it. It's probably nobody that we know anyway." Frank ordered wings and asked Ray if he wanted some, too.

Ray shook his head.

After Frank finished his second glass of beer, he placed the glass on the coaster and turned in his seat to face Ray. "You're in love with her, aren't you?"

Ray looked at Frank and pretended to be absorbed in the game on television. "What are you talking about? In love with who?"

Shaking his head, Frank slapped Ray on the shoulder and laughed. "I knew it!" he exclaimed. "You're in love with my baby sister."

Ray was embarrassed that he could be read so easily and especially by Frank, who never really seemed to pay attention to much of anything except his job. "Am I that obvious?"

"Well, you weren't at first, but ever since Christmas you seem to be wearing that lost puppy dog look. And then tonight you seemed more interested in playing twenty questions than having a beer and watching the game. I thought maybe your behavior had something to do with your ex being back in town, but now I know differently."

Ray leaned his elbows on the bar and let out a long breath. "What am I going to do?" he asked.

"Tell Claudia how you feel about her. What's so hard about that?"

"If it were that simple then I would do that, but it isn't. Apparently you don't know about her plan."

"What plan?"

Ray explained to Frank Claudia's plan to be married or in a committed relationship by the following Christmas. He told him about the list she had prepared and her method for finding Mr. Right.

"And according to Claudia, you don't fit anywhere into this plan of hers?" Frank questioned, even though he already knew the answer. "That sounds like Claudia, all right."

"You know your sister about as well as I do, so you know what I'm up against."

"Well, you know I'm the last person on earth that is qualified to give advice to the lovelorn, but I do know my sister, and I know that you mean a great deal to her."

"You see," Ray began, "that's just it. I want to mean everything to Claudia. She already means everything to me."

"Then you're going to have to show her."

"How? And more importantly, how am I going to find out how she feels about me?"

"I think that's going to have to be up to you to figure out."

"And what if things don't work out? There's so much at risk here."

"What if they do work out? There's a lot to gain."

Ray nodded. "You're right. Man, I have been in love with your sister for a long time but I was afraid to do something about it. And then when she came up with this plan to get married, I got worried. What if she actually does find Mr. Right?"

"Then I suggest you get yourself in the running so the only Mr. Right she notices is you."

Frank was right and Ray knew it. He had to let Claudia know of his feelings for her. But before he did that, he had to know if Claudia loved him, too.

CHAPTER TWENTY-ONE

It was Jewel's birthday and her family had planned a special dinner in her honor. A big dinner surrounded by family and friends was how Jewel liked to celebrate and her children always complied with her wishes.

When Ray walked into the Ryland home, he found the house decorated with balloons, streamers and happy birthday signs that had obviously been made by the grandchildren. He knew Claudia and Karen would be in charge of the food and his mouth watered when the aromas wafting from the kitchen greeted him at the door.

Claudia's car was parked in the driveway but Ray didn't see her in the living room with the other guests. Before searching for her, he decided to present Jewel with her birthday gift. He had searched for more than a week to find her something really special and he hoped she liked the charm bracelet he'd had made for her.

Jewel hugged Ray and took the package from his hand. "Honey, you didn't have to buy me anything for my birthday. Just having you here is a treat in itself."

"There's no way in the world I would have walked in here tonight empty handed, Miss Jewel. And let me be the first to say that you don't look a day over twenty-nine."

Jewel swatted at Ray playfully and laughed. "And let me be the first to say that you lie like a rug."

Jewel removed the wrapping paper from the rectangular box and squealed with delight when she saw the charm bracelet nestled inside the velvet liner.

The gold bracelet contained charms made up of Jewel's favorite things with spaces to add more.

"Oh, Raymond, it's beautiful," she said, touching one of the ladybug charms.

Ray fastened the bracelet on Jewel's wrist and noticed with the pride of a five-year-old child giving his mother a bouquet of dandelions that she truly loved the gift.

After chitchatting with Jewel and several other guests, Ray eventually made his way toward the kitchen but was stopped before reaching his destination by Claudia's niece. Candace had been watching as her grandmother opened her gift from Ray and wanted to know if he had brought her a gift, too.

Ray knew better than to come around the children without having something special for them and slipped a piece of bubble gum into the child's hand and made her promise not to chew it until after she had eaten her dinner.

Delighted with her gift, Candace carefully placed the piece of gum in the pocket of her jumper. "Did you bring Aunt Claudia a present, too?" the child asked.

"No, honey, it's not her birthday," Ray reminded Candace.

"You can get presents even if it isn't your birthday. My daddy gives Mommy presents all the time and she really likes him. I bet Aunt Claudia would like you better if you got her presents."

"Do you think so?"

Candace nodded enthusiastically.

Ray knelt down so that he could speak to Candace face-to-face. "What kind of presents do you think your Aunt Claudia would like?"

Candace thought for a second and then answered, "Shiny stuff. Mommy likes it when she gets shiny stuff."

Ray nodded his understanding and tried to keep a serious

expression on his face, but he couldn't help but smile. He kissed Candace on the forehead and slipped another piece of bubble gum in her pocket. He watched her run off when she was called by her grandfather and thought about what she'd just said. Maybe he should get Claudia some shiny stuff.

When Ray finally reached the kitchen, he nearly collided with Karen who was rushing through the door with a plate filled with cheese and crackers in one hand and a bowl of fruit salad in another. She barely said hello to Ray as she hurried past him. After he let Karen pass, he stepped into the kitchen and stopped short when he saw Claudia leaning over the stove. But it wasn't the sight of Claudia that caught Ray's attention. It was the man standing beside her and the intimate way he looked at her when she spoke.

Sensing another presence in the room, the two of them turned around simultaneously. Claudia registered the strange expression on Ray's face and wondered what was wrong.

"Hey, there," she said. "Come in, roll up your sleeves and lend a hand. You remember Mark, don't you?"

Oh yes. He remembered Mark. Feeling as though he needed to make a stand, Ray walked over to Claudia and kissed her on the cheek, lingering a little longer than was necessary.

Mark wiped his hands on a towel and approached Ray with an outstretched hand, nodded his head slightly and said, "Good to see you again." He had noticed the length of the kiss.

It was pretty clear to Ray that Mark wasn't thrilled about seeing him again but he'd probably said what he said for Claudia's benefit. However, the feeling was mutual. Ray didn't like Mark being in the kitchen with Claudia. He didn't even like him being in the Rylands' house, which was like a second home to Ray. This was his territory and in his opinion Mark was trespassing.

Ray took Mark's hand in his own and matched his firm grip.

The two men stood toe to toe and for a few seconds, no words were spoken. The tension in the room nearly sent off an electric charge.

"Um, Mark was helping me put the finishing touches on dinner," Claudia remarked, feeling as if she had to explain what she and Mark were doing and not really knowing why.

"Well, she didn't leave much for me to do. She practically completed the entire meal all by herself." Mark looked at Claudia and smiled affectionately. "This woman is something else. Not only is she smart, talented and beautiful she can also burn in the kitchen."

Ray nodded. "Yes, I know that firsthand. Claudia has many talents, seen and unseen."

Claudia looked from Ray to Mark with a puzzled look on her face. *What were they up to?* she wondered.

"Mark, would you do me a favor?" she asked, turning toward the stove and feeling as if she needed to separate the two men.

"Anything, baby."

Baby? Ray didn't miss how easily the term of endearment rolled off Mark's tongue. Neither did Claudia.

"Would you take this platter into the dining room and start moving everyone toward the table? I'll bring out the rolls when they come out of the oven."

Mark winked at Claudia and said, "Consider it done."

Claudia watched Mark leave the room with a smile on her face. But as soon as he was gone, so was her smile. She whirled around to Ray who was casually leaning on the counter and looked at him with fire in her eyes.

"Are you out of your mind?"

"No."

"On drugs?"

Ray shook his head.

"Recently suffer a head injury?"

"No. Why do you ask?"

"Because you're acting like a complete idiot."

"And how am I doing that?

"For starters, what was that kiss all about? And the comment about my talents, seen and unseen?" Claudia rolled her eyes and snatched a dishcloth off the counter. She had to have something in her hands to keep from wringing Ray's neck.

"What? I can't kiss you on the cheek or give you a compliment? When did you become so sensitive? Afraid of what Marvin might think?"

"His name is Mark and you know it." Claudia was fuming. "I don't like this game, Ray, so stop it. The two of you were standing in here like two testosterone-crazed jocks. I was half expecting one of you to mark your territory. And to answer your question, no, I'm not afraid of anything except for what's gotten into you."

Ray walked over to the counter and stood beside Claudia as she placed hot rolls in a breadbasket. He was all up in her personal space and was close enough to smell her perfume and to see tiny beads of perspiration on her nose. That was a signal that she was really mad.

He reached out and wrapped a strand of Claudia's curly hair around his finger.

Even though she was angry with him, she didn't pull away.

"Nothing's gotten into me. Has something gotten into you?" Ray asked, his voice suddenly husky.

Karen was standing in the doorway of the kitchen and cleared her throat for a second time. Claudia and Ray turned toward the sound.

"You two are the only ones that are not seated at the table and everyone is waiting for you and the rolls. So, whatever is going on in here, put it on hold until after the party."

Karen's tone was sarcastic and Claudia wondered what all she'd seen or heard. Claudia grabbed the basket of bread and stormed past Karen.

Somehow Claudia was placed between Ray and Mark at the dinner table. She didn't know who was responsible for the seating but she would find out later and give them a piece of her mind. Throughout most of the meal, Mark kept his arm placed on the back of Claudia's chair.

Ray noticed and wondered what Mark was trying to prove.

Jewel had picked up on the tension between her daughter, Ray and Mark and tried to ease the mood a bit. "Mark, Claudia tells me that you're going to be opening a restaurant soon."

"Yes, my partner and I were able to find a prime location rather quickly and we've just about completed the renovations. We've even hired most of the staff."

Claudia's niece Candace had been staring at Mark ever since they'd sat down at the table. "Are you from another country?" she asked.

"No, Candace. What makes you think that?" Mark inquired.

"You talk funny," the inquisitive child answered honestly.

"It's called a southern drawl, Candy," Ray offered. "Women like that southern flavor in their men, don't they Claudia?"

Frank looked across the table at Ray, cleared his throat and tried to get his attention, but Ray ignored him. If Ray was attempting to win his sister's heart, he was failing miserably, Frank thought.

"Who's ready for dessert?" Karen asked after her brother nudged her when he saw the anger clouding Claudia's face.

Everyone went into the living room where the cake and ice cream would be served. Everyone, that is, except Ray.

He sat at the table with his head in his hands. He had acted like a fool and he felt like one. Claudia was angry with him and Mark probably thought he was crazy, even though at the moment he really didn't care what Mark thought.

Ray heard someone come into the room and looked up to see Jewel placing a plate containing cake and ice cream in front of him.

"You're not going to win her heart by being jealous," she said and took a seat beside him.

"You know, too?" he asked with a mixture of surprise and relief. "Did Frank say something to you?"

Jewel shook her head and looked at him knowingly. "Frank didn't have to say a word. I've known for a while now. It's quite evident in the way you look at her and by how jealous you are with Mark's being here."

"I'm sorry, Miss Jewel. I didn't mean to act up at your birthday party. It's just that when I saw Claudia and Mark together in the kitchen I immediately saw red."

"More like an explosion," Jewel remarked.

Ray smiled sheepishly. "Yes, I have to admit I am a little jealous."

"My daughter is very special to me, Ray, and so are you. Nothing would please me more than for the two of you to get together. But, on the other hand, I'd hate to have to track you down and skin you alive if you cause her any undue pain."

Ray held his hand up in protest. "I would never do anything to hurt her. I love Claudia and I want to spend the rest of my life showing her just that."

"Then I suggest you stop wasting time."

Ray looked over at Jewel, a little taken aback by her statement.

"You heard me," she said firmly. "Claudia has it in her head that the way to find the perfect man is by matching his characteristics with items on a check list. Good job, kind, compassionate, educated," she rattled off in a mocking tone. "Can you imagine such a thing?"

"No matter how impractical it sounds to us, it makes sense to Claudia. And to make matters worse, it seems as if Mark has what she's looking for."

"Maybe he does and maybe he doesn't. That's not really the issue. What matters right now is how Claudia feels about you."

"Let's see. Anger. Hatred. Disappointment."

"Raymond, we could go on and on with this all evening. Right now Claudia is probably a little upset with you, but that's only temporary. You need to look beyond tonight and really judge the competition. Just from my perspective, it appears as if Mark is quite taken with Claudia. You're going to have to deal with that without appearing to be mean-spirited or confrontational."

Ray nodded in agreement.

"If you want my advice," Jewel began, "don't just tell Claudia how you feel about her. Show her. Women like pretty words, but actions speak much louder and have a more profound affect. Now, come in the living room with everyone else and let's enjoy the rest of my party. It isn't everyday that I get to turn twenty-nine again."

Ray and Jewel walked into the living room arm in arm and he tried not to notice Mark and Claudia sitting together on the couch as Mark seemed to be hanging on to her every word. Someone had put on a CD and the kids were dancing in the middle of the living room floor, much to everyone's amusement. Pretty soon Jewel and her husband joined the children.

"Mark, can I steal Claudia away from you for a minute?"

Mark looked up at Ray and then back to Claudia to see if it was all right. She nodded her head.

Ray led Claudia by the arm into the kitchen. When they were alone she removed her arm from his grasp and folded her arms against her chest.

Ray walked over to the counter without saying a word. She was angry so he would have to choose his words carefully.

"What is it, Ray?" she asked irritably.

Turning to face Claudia, he began to apologize. "I was out of line earlier and I wanted to say that I'm sorry."

Claudia waited a moment before she walked over to Ray and sighed. As much as she wanted to, she couldn't be upset with him for long. Obviously something was bothering him and maybe he would feel better if he talked about it. She wondered if his behavior had something to do with Viveca.

"You have been acting so strangely lately. Is there something going on that you need to get off your chest?"

"Yes, and that's why I wanted to speak with you alone." Ray paused and took a deep breath before continuing. "I've been battling a bout of jealousy lately and I don't really know how to handle it."

Claudia looked confused. What could Ray possible be jealous about? Did he find out that Viveca was dating him and someone else at the same time? That would explain his strange behavior.

Ray continued with his explanation. "You're probably going to think this is strange, but when I walked in here earlier and saw you and Mark all hugged up over the stove, I was a little jealous."

Ray was jealous of Mark? Claudia was a little surprised but didn't let it show.

"Yes, I do find that to be strange. Seems rather odd to me that you have a problem with other men paying attention to me, but you can carry on with whomever you like."

"What are you talking about?"

"I knew you would pretend that you didn't know what I was talking about, so maybe I should break it down for you."

"I'm not pretending, Claudia. You're going to have to help me out here."

"Last week. You. Viveca. A quaint little café. A warm embrace.

167

Ring a bell?"

Understanding dawned. "You saw me with Viveca at the café?"

"Guess you didn't need too many clues after all," Claudia said sarcastically. "Yes. I saw the way the two of you were *hugged up* at the table," she said, throwing Ray's words back at him.

"Claudia, that was completely innocent. I don't know what you think you saw but nothing happened. She was feeling down and needed a friend to talk to."

"And you were the one friend that was conveniently available. It's funny how it always happens that way with you and Viveca. She calls, you come running. She gets in trouble, you bail her out. She sheds a tear, you wipe it away."

"Stop right there, Claudia. It's not like that between Viveca and me and you know it." Ray shook his head and put his hand up. "Wait, that's another conversation for another day. I didn't come in here to talk about Viveca. I came in here to talk about us."

"Us? There you go again with that us reference. What are you getting at?"

Things were getting out of hand. This was not how Ray wanted their conversation to go. Claudia was even more upset with him now than she had been before. And to top it all off, she had thrown Viveca into the mix.

Ray reached out to caress her cheek.

She pushed his hand away.

"I don't want to argue, Claudia."

"Why not? We're getting pretty good at it. It seems that's all we do lately, and I don't like it. I don't like how we can't have a simple conversation anymore. We don't spend time together the way we used to and when we are together, it all feels so different. I want my friend back, Ray. Am I asking for the impossible?"

Ray looked down into Claudia's pretty brown eyes and felt his heart constrict. She was angry, hurt and confused, and he was the cause of it. It all stemmed from one misunderstanding after another. They needed time alone to talk. But this wasn't the right time or place.

"We need to straighten some things out. There's something very important that I want to share with you but I'm really having a hard time putting it into words," Ray began.

"Just say it, Ray. After all this time there should be nothing that you can't say to me." Claudia sounded exasperated.

Ray took a deep breath and let it out slowly. This was it. He had to say what was in his heart, before it was too late. "Claudia, I-"

Claudia turned when she heard footsteps. It was Mark. She had almost forgotten that he was waiting for her in the living room.

"Am I interrupting something?" Mark asked as he looked at the strange expression on Ray's face.

Claudia turned to Ray and searched for a hint of the words that had been left unspoken, but she was puzzled by what she saw.

He couldn't do this now. He needed to have Claudia's undivided attention, with no interruptions. "No, you're not interrupting anything. Claudia and I were just discussing something about a mutual friend," Ray lied.

"Claudia, baby, it's getting late. Are you about ready to go?"

Ray's jaw tightened. If Mark called Claudia "baby" one more time he was liable to punch him.

She turned to Mark and noticed his questioning gaze. She tried to smile reassuringly to let him know that everything was all right. "Would you mind getting our coats from upstairs, Mark? I'll meet you in the living room in a few minutes and we can leave."

Mark nodded and left the room reluctantly. He didn't like what he saw. If he didn't know better he'd swear Ray was trying to make a play for Claudia. She had explained to him about her special friendship with Ray. She had also stressed then and on a few other occasions that they were simply close friends, and that there was nothing romantic about their relationship at all. But Mark had his doubts. Ray didn't like him and he knew it was because of Claudia.

If Claudia didn't see it, Mark sure did. Ray's feelings for her ran much deeper than mere friendship. Mark had to wonder just how deeply Claudia's feelings ran for Ray.

"Okay, Ray, what is it that you need to tell me? Make it quick because I can't keep Mark waiting."

Ray shook his head. "We're going to have to talk about this at another time. What I want to say to you won't be rushed. And it won't be said to you with your *man* waiting in the wings."

Claudia stood open-mouthed as Ray left the kitchen. Shortly after, she heard the front door close. She had never seen Ray act so strangely.

When Claudia joined Mark in the living room, he was thanking Jewel for inviting him to the party. Claudia kissed her mother on the cheek and took her coat from Mark.

On the ride home neither Mark nor Claudia said a word to each other. Both were deep in thought. When they reached her house Mark pulled in the driveway and turned off the engine.

"Would you like to come in for a few minutes?" she asked.

Mark shook his head. "No, but there is something I would like."

There was just enough light from the overhead streetlight for Claudia to see that his jaw was clenched.

"What?" she asked, already knowing the question before it was asked.

"I'd like an explanation," Mark said, turning to Claudia.

She knew it would be silly to try to pretend that she didn't know what he was talking about. The best thing to do would be to simply offer the most plausible explanation she could.

"Mark, I know you think there is something going on between Ray and me, but there isn't. I've explained this to you before. We are close friends. Ray is just going through some things right now and wanted to talk to me about them, that's all there is to it."

"What kind of things?"

Claudia shrugged her shoulders and shook her head. "To be really honest with you, I don't know. He said he wanted to talk to me about something tonight, but just when he was about to tell me he changed his mind."

Mark let out a deep breath.

Claudia turned in her seat. She couldn't quite make out his expression, but for some reason, she got the idea that he didn't believe her. "You think it's something more, don't you?"

"Yes, I do."

"Do you think I'm lying to you about my relationship with Ray?"

"No, but I think you're lying to yourself. Maybe you honestly don't see it, but there is more to your relationship with Ray than just being buddies. At least from Ray's point of view."

"I don't understand."

"Claudia, you mean more to Ray than you think. I can't believe you didn't notice the look on his face when he came into the kitchen tonight. He looked like a bull staring at a red cape."

"I think you've misunderstood Ray. The only thing I noticed was that he was acting like an idiot and I told him just that."

"Did you ever stop to question why he acted the way he did?"

"Because he's a man and men do crazy things sometimes?" she questioned with a smile.

Mark wanted to be serious, but he looked in Claudia's pretty face and all of his resolve melted away like sugar in water. He laughed softly and leaned over and placed a kiss on Claudia's lips. He didn't want to argue with her, and deep in his heart, he knew she was being honest with him. She really had no idea of Ray's feelings for her.

"Come on, honey. Your lips are cold and as much as I'd like to warm them up, I think it would be better if you just went inside."

Claudia unlocked her front door and she and Mark stood on her porch and he bid her good night.

"Are you sure you don't want to come in for a little while?"

Mark shook his head. There was something he wanted to say to Claudia and as good as she looked to him right then, he didn't trust himself to be behind a closed door with her. Instead he told her, "I know I've said this to you this before, but I think you're a very special lady. In the short time that we've known each other, I've become quite fond of you. It's strange but I find myself thinking about you at the oddest times. And I wonder if you're thinking about me, too, and secretly hoping that you are. When we're not together, I miss you and when we are together, I don't want to leave you."

Claudia shivered slightly as much from the low temperature as from Mark's words. The shiver didn't go unnoticed by Mark. She needed to be inside where it was warm. But there was one more thing he wanted to leave with her before he left for the night.

Mark knew Claudia was expecting a good night kiss and he delivered like FedEx, right on time. He reached out and pulled Claudia to him and kissed her long, slow and hard. He didn't want there to be one doubt in her mind how he felt about her and he used the kiss to relay that message.

When he broke the kiss, he opened the door for Claudia to go inside. Her breath came in short, clouded puffs of air that seemed to glow under the porch light. She had been expecting a good night kiss, but not quite like that.

"Tonight," he began in a voice that was low and sensual, "when climb into bed and lay your head on your pillow, I want you to know that there is someone who finds you incredibly sexy. From the crown of your head to the soles of your feet and along every generous curve in between, you have what it takes to bring a man to his knees." He paused before continuing and lifted Claudia's chin with his gloved hand and looked her straight in the eye. "The question is, which man will it be?"

CHAPTER TWENTY-TWO

It was Sunday morning and Claudia had decided to sleep in for a change. As she sat at her kitchen table holding on to a cup of coffee that had long grown cold, she recalled with mixed emotions the events of the previous night. It was obvious that Mark wanted to take things up a notch but she didn't know if she was ready for that just yet. According to her plan, she should be progressing to the next step. But her heart didn't agree. At the same time she felt as if things were changing between Ray and her and she didn't quite know how she felt about it. Mark had said to her the night before that Ray's feelings ran much deeper than she had imagined. *How did he know that?* she wondered.

The doorbell rang and interrupted her thoughts. Ginger sprang to her feet and began barking excitedly.

"Calm down, Ginger. It's probably no one to get excited about."

When Claudia opened the door, Ray stood on her front porch holding a small bakery box.

Ginger ran up to greet Ray and he gave her a doggie treat.

"At least Ginger still likes me," he said wearing a sheepish grin.

"She may be the only one."

Ray stood on the front porch as a gust of cold wind whipped around him. He was freezing and he knew Claudia had to be cold, too, standing in the doorway wearing her bathrobe. "Claudia, it's cold out here. May I please come in? I have a peace offering."

Claudia was cold, but she felt a need to hold on to her anger.

Ray patiently waited for permission to enter.

Claudia was unrelenting and without her saying it, Ray knew that she was still angry.

"Claudia, it's freezing. Please let me come in for a few minutes."

Feeling the icy wind whip around her bare legs she turned to walk back to the kitchen with Ray and Ginger following behind her.

"I suppose the hospitable thing to do would be to offer you a cup of coffee," Claudia said flatly, pulling the bottom of her robe over her cold legs.

Ray sat the bakery box on the table and went to the counter to pour his own coffee.

The two of them sat in silence and Ray sipped his coffee and Claudia pretended to read the newspaper. The only sound in the room came from the thumping of Ginger's tail against the hardwood floor and the ticking of the clock over the doorway.

As he sat across from Claudia, Ray noticed she was wearing the fluffy pink robe her sister had given her for her birthday last year. On anyone else, the robe would have looked frumpy, but on Claudia the color was a wonderful complement to her skin tone and seemed to wrap her in pink, fluffy softness.

Claudia was a natural beauty, Ray thought as he stole glances of her from across the table. She always had been and seemed to get more beautiful as time passed. But she never used her good looks to her advantage or seemed overly concerned about her appearance. Yes, she did care about how she looked, but it wasn't an obsession with her.

As a teenager Claudia had been uncomfortable with her ample breasts and full hips especially when the symbol of beauty at that time seemed to be life-sized Barbies. But as she matured so did her attitude about her body. Claudia learned to embrace her beautiful figure and celebrated it with a style and attitude that was truly complementary.

"You're staring."

"Am I?" Ray was lost in thought and was caught off guard.

Claudia's robe was open slightly and revealed just enough cleavage to send Ray's temperature up a few degrees. At that moment he wanted more than anything to reach out and wrap Claudia in his arms. Just to feel her warm skin against his would be intoxicating and he needed to know that she needed and wanted to be with him as much as he did her. Thoughts of lazy Sunday morning lovemaking came to mind.

He couldn't go on loving Claudia only in his dreams. It was killing him to know that he could say and do whatever he wanted with Claudia in his dreams, but in reality it was totally different. The words never came out right or the mood would be all wrong. He wanted to love her for real, to make her feel like a woman. His woman.

"Would you mind answering something for me?" Ray asked.

"That all depends on what you want to know." She didn't even bother to look up from the newspaper when answering.

"How serious are you about Mark?"

This time Claudia looked up with a frown on her face. *What was Ray getting at?* she wondered. "Why is that of any concern to you?"

"Could you please just answer the question?"

"It's too early to tell," she answered honestly. "We've gone out a few times and we talk on the phone a lot. I think with time things could get serious. Mark is a very nice man who knows how to treat a lady and I feel that I would be happy with him."

"Does he know about the plan?"

"No, but he does know that I'm looking for something a little more serious than a steady Saturday night date."

"Does he feel the same?"

"Yes, I believe he does." She didn't mention what Mark had said to her the previous night.

Ray nodded his head.

"All right, Ray, what's with all of the questions? Why are you so concerned about my relationship with Mark and why did you act like such an idiot last night at my parents'? And what is it that you've been trying to tell me but can never seem to get the words out?"

"What do you want me to answer first?"

Claudia pulled her robe together in the front, folded her arms and sat back in her chair. "Start wherever you like but make sure you cover it all."

"Okay, Claudia, I'll tell you why I'm concerned about your feelings for Mark and I'll explain why I acted the way I did last night." Ray took a deep breath. "First, I don't have anything against Mark. I think he's an okay brother, but I don't think he's right for you." Claudia started to protest, but Ray put his hand up to stop her. "Let me finish. Ever since the night of Lorna and Troy's wedding when you told me how you felt about being alone and wanting someone to love and wanting to be loved, I've been wanting to tell you just how I feel." Ray sighed and leaned back in his chair. He wanted to choose his words carefully and needed to cover everything he felt. He stood and walked over to the counter. Running his hand over the back of his hair, he continued. "Claudia, we have been friends since we were kids. There are times when I think you know me better than I know myself. But this is one time I wish you actually could read my thoughts or at the very least, know what is in my heart. You see, there is something that I've wanted to share with you for a while and just didn't know how to put what I felt into words. Or maybe I was afraid of telling you for fear that you wouldn't feel the same way."

"Ray, you know there is nothing that you can't tell me."

"Oh really? How would you feel if I told you that I loved you?"

Claudia looked at Ray with a wrinkled brow. "You've told me you loved me before. Am I supposed to all of a sudden think that's strange?"

Ray went to the table and turned Claudia in her chair to face him as he knelt in front of her. "Claudia, look at me. Look into my eyes. Have I ever told you that I think you're beautiful, inside and out? And that when I look into your pretty eyes, I want to just melt. Have I told you that no matter how many women I date, I find myself measuring them against you, and they always fall short? Have I told you that there are times when I want to take you in my arms and let you know that you don't have to search for someone to love because I'm right here and I want to give you all the love you need and deserve? I know I've told you that you're my best friend, but I want you to know that I want to also be your man."

Claudia looked at Ray. She couldn't believe what she was hearing. *He was kidding around, wasn't he?* She looked into his eyes as he requested and was surprised by what she saw. There was no doubt that he was very serious.

Claudia stood, shaking her head and walked over to the counter. "Ray, I-I don't know what to say. You're serious, aren't you?"

Ray followed her and stilled her hands from fidgeting with something on the counter. "Very," he answered.

"What do you want me to say?"

"You don't have to say anything right now. I just want you to think about what I've said. Claudia, I love you and I have for a very long time. I've been afraid to let you know what my feelings are because the one thing I didn't want to risk losing is our friendship."

"But, Ray, we've both seen what happens when friends decide to carry their relationship to the next step. It usually ends up being the final step. You mean too much to me to risk it all on a fling."

Ray reached out and lifted Claudia's chin, forcing her to look directly into his eyes. "I'm not looking for a fling and neither are you. What we've built over the years could be the foundation for something meaningful and fulfilling that I hope will last a lifetime."

Claudia backed away from Ray and tried to get a handle on what was going on. "Could be? We'd be risking a lot, Ray."

"But look at what could be gained."

"What about Mark?"

"What *about* Mark? Claudia, Mark could never love you the way I do. Listen," Ray began as he stood facing Claudia, "just think about what I said. All I'm asking is that you give us a chance."

"And how do I know that you want the same things that I do? With all of the different women you've dated over the past few years you have never mentioned getting married or having children. Those have been my goals, not yours."

"That's not true. I want those things, too. But I want them with you."

"This is happening so fast and I don't know how to handle it."

"There's nothing to handle. Just think about what I've said. That's all I ask."

"But you're asking a lot."

Claudia crossed the room needing to put some space between herself and Ray. "You know I've got to give Mark a chance, too. His feelings for me are sincere and I don't have a crystal ball that will predict which man is right for me. Part of me wants to build on what we've shared over the years but another part is afraid that if I do there won't be a happily-ever-after ending, and in the end I'll lose you and whatever chance there might be with Mark. I guess I'm really wondering if our friendship is strong enough to withstand a failed love affair." Claudia said sadly.

Logically, Ray knew what Claudia was saying made perfect sense, but in his heart he was sure that they were made to be together.

"Claudia, I can't promise you a fairytale life with a happy ending, but I do promise to be good to you and to love you with all my heart. I believe in us and I don't think we're going to fail at loving each other."

She still didn't look convinced and he didn't want to push her anymore.

"Okay, honey, I'm going to give you some time to think this over, but not forever. I've had this on my heart for a long time and now that it's out in the open I don't want to waste any more time. Three weeks."

"Three weeks?"

"Yes, that should be enough time for you to figure out what you want to do."

"You're asking me to decide if I'm willing to put our friendship on the line and you're giving me three weeks to make that decision?"

Ray approached Claudia and stood facing her. "Do you love me, Claudia?"

"Of course I do, Ray. You know that."

"But do you love me the way a woman loves a man, and more to the point, do you love me enough to take this chance?"

She didn't have to answer, for Ray saw the uncertainty in her eyes. He reached out and took Claudia in his arms. Regardless of what happened, he would always love her.

"I know you're unsure, and that's understandable. But I'm still going to hold you to the three weeks. And in that time, I want you to know that I'm going to do whatever it takes to win your heart."

CHAPTER TWENTY-THREE

"What was going on between Claudia, Mark and Ray last night?" Karen asked her brother as they sat in their parents' kitchen enjoying the lunch their mother had prepared.

"What do you mean?" Frank asked between bites of sandwich.

"Frank, I wish you'd pay more attention to the world around you. You can't tell me that you didn't pick up on the tension between Claudia and Ray. If I didn't know any better, I'd say Ray was a tad bit jealous."

Jewel came into the room just in time to hear the tail end of her daughter's comments. "I think you should stay out of your sister's business," she admonished Karen.

"Her business? An interesting choice of words. You know something, don't you, Mom?"

"I know what you know, Karen."

Okay, that door just closed, Karen thought. She looked at her brother as he pretended to read the newspaper. "What's going on, Frank?"

"Hmm?" Frank peered over the top of the paper.

"You heard me, I asked you what was going on between Claudia and Ray last night? I think you and Mom know something but you're not sharing it with me."

Frank folded the paper, looked at his sister and smiled. "Karen, I'd love to tell you what I know. But I really can't do that. If I clued you in on the Claudia-Ray situation you wouldn't keep it a secret. And we can't have that, can we?"

Karen wanted to wipe the smirk off Frank's face but then, understanding dawned. Frank had revealed more than he knew. "They're in love with each other, aren't they? I knew it! Candace said she saw Ray kissing Claudia but I didn't believe her. And Claudia has been acting like a confused teenager in love and Ray is the reason why. Last night when we were all waiting for them to come to the table, I walked in on an argument of some sort between them. You could have cut the tension in the room with a knife. If my instinct is correct, Ray wasn't too happy about Mark being here and Claudia was caught in the middle of a little love triangle."

Frank and Jewel exchanged glances. Karen was turning the whole thing into a soap opera. They had to nip this in the bud before she said something to Claudia or Ray, or both. And she had the tact of a drunken sailor.

"Karen, keep this information to yourself for Ray's sake as well as your sister's," Jewel advised. "If either of them want to discuss it with you, then fine. But in the meantime, let them work this out for themselves, without interference from you."

Mark called Claudia late Sunday afternoon to invite her to join him on a tour of his new restaurant. By the time he arrived at her house, she was more confused than ever about her feelings toward Ray. She still couldn't believe he'd had the gall to give her a time limit on making a decision about something that could change her life forever. But she knew that type of behavior was typical of Ray when he was determined about something.

On the way to the restaurant Claudia did her best to keep up her end of the conversation. Adding the appropriate responses and attempting to interject an opinion when one was needed was proving to be an effort. If she was going to be true to her word and give

Mark a chance as she'd told Ray, she would have to concentrate on only one man at a time.

"So, what do you think of The Gatehouse?"

"It's beautiful," Claudia remarked with sincerity. "I can't believe how quickly you were able to complete the renovations. And everything feels so warm and inviting. You and your partner have done an outstanding job. I am truly impressed." She was also surprised by the level of activity going on around them. Members of the wait staff were busily going over the menu and the wine list. Supplies were being delivered, and everywhere she looked someone was hard at work.

Mark beamed when he looked around the dining room. He'd spent a lot of time and energy creating something he hoped would please a lot of people, especially Claudia.

"Mr. Bishop, would you mind signing off on the wine delivery?" asked a pretty young woman whom Mark had previously introduced as Lynette, the restaurant's assistant manager.

"I have a surprise for you," Mark announced when he handed the paperwork back to Lynette.

Claudia braced herself. She wasn't sure if she could handle any more surprises today.

"Because we were able to complete the renovations earlier than expected and all of the staff has been hired and has nearly completed training, we're going to have the grand opening in three weeks. That is if winter ever decides to loosen its stronghold."

"Three weeks?" Claudia heard herself saying again.

Mark nodded and slipped an arm around Claudia's shoulder, leading her into the deserted kitchen. When he was sure they were alone, he lowered his voice and said, "More than anything, I'd like you to be here with me for the grand opening. I can't think of anyone I want to share this with more than you. Would you do me the honor?"

When Claudia looked at Mark, she didn't see a list of characteristics from a check list. She saw a man who obviously cared a great deal about her. She reached out and caressed his cheek, feeling a slight roughness against his strong jaw.

Mark lowered his head and kissed Claudia. Pulling her into an embrace, he deepened the kiss causing a definite reaction. As his tongue sought entry into Claudia's mouth she felt his hand leave her shoulders, traveling down her spine. Claudia could feel Mark's desire growing as their bodies meshed and the kiss ignited unexpected sparks.

Mark and Claudia suddenly broke the kiss when they heard something hit the floor. Turning toward the noise they saw Lynette picking up the clipboard she had dropped when she walked in on her boss and his lady friend. Lynette looked more embarrassed than they did.

"I am so sorry. I thought you'd left," she said apologetically. "I didn't mean to barge in. I'm really sorry."

"It's okay, Lynette, we are leaving."

Mark grabbed Claudia's hand and led her past Lynette, who was still blushing profusely.

When they were in the car, Mark turned on the ignition and moved in his seat to face Claudia. "You've come to mean a lot to me in the short time I've known you," he said. "I don't know when or if I've ever felt for anyone the way I feel for you. There's just something about you that feels so right. I just want you to know how much I enjoy having you in my life."

Mark didn't know it but he had just made things harder for her. Why did he have to be such a good catch?

As they drove away from the restaurant, Claudia couldn't help but think about the decision she would have to make. In three weeks, she would have to choose between Mark and Ray and no matter what her choice would be, someone would be hurt by her decision.

CHAPTER TWENTY-FOUR

Monday morning brought clouds, light snow showers and scattered thoughts. Claudia had had very little sleep the night before as she tossed and turned thinking about her situation. When she had first initiated her plan, she had no prospects and a string of bad dates. Now, she had two potential suitors. Most women can't find one good man and here she had two. From the outside looking in, this seemed like an ideal situation, but in reality, it was difficult.

Shortly after she arrived at work, Claudia received flowers from Mark with a card attached telling her how much he had enjoyed their evening the previous night. And, how much he was looking forward to their upcoming date on Wednesday. Later, Claudia received a telephone invitation to join her mother and sister for lunch to which she accepted.

For most of the morning Claudia sat at her desk deep in thought. What was she going to do? Ray was obviously very much in love with her and Mark, although not in love, was very taken with her and had made it quite clear the night before that she was someone he wanted in his life.

By the time she was ready to leave to meet Karen and her mother for lunch she was no closer to making a decision than she had been the day before. Perhaps a little motherly or sisterly advice would help put things into perspective, she thought with more hope than she felt.

Karen looked around the busy delicatessen for her sister but Jewel was the first to spot Claudia sitting at a booth near the back.

Karen and Jewel exchanged glances when they saw Claudia sitting with her head down, oblivious to the world around her.

"If I were a tall, dark, handsome man, you'd have missed out on a prime opportunity to make my acquaintance sitting there staring at that napkin," Karen said sarcastically as she nudged her sister to the other end of the seat.

Claudia looked up, surprised to see that her mother and sister had arrived.

"I don't need another man in my life right now, thank you very much."

Jewel noticed the frown lines creasing her daughter's forehead and gave Karen a look that meant "lighten up".

"Why aren't you working today?" Claudia asked Karen.

Karen flipped open her menu and replied, "I took the day off. Every once in a while I need a sanity day. Today was it."

After the waitress took their orders Karen began telling them how little Candace had decided that she wanted a baby sister and had asked her mother if she put an order in would the baby be here in time for next Christmas.

"Speaking of next Christmas, how's the man hunt going?"

Jewel threw Karen another sharp look.

Claudia ignored her sister's question and posed one of her own. "Mom, can I ask you a question?

"Of course you can. What would you like to know?"

"How did you know when you were in love and that the man you were marrying was the one you wanted to build a family with and be with for the rest of your life?"

Jewel looked at her daughters and smiled. "Well, honey, I'll be honest with you. I knew your father was the man I wanted to marry the first time I laid eyes on him. However, it took some influential wrangling on my part to convince him of that."

"What do you mean?" Karen asked.

"You two know that your father's mother, Grandma Ryland, and I attended the same church. Well, when your father came home from the army, his mother was bound and determined that he was going to make something of his life. She thought that with a good woman by his side, gently guiding and encouraging him, he could be quite successful at whatever he put his mind to. See, what she didn't know was that she didn't have to convince me of that. I could see your father's potential even if no one else could. Your father has always been smart, extremely determined and very likeable."

"When your grandmother first introduced me to him, I could tell he thought I was a little church mouse, and that was fine. There were plenty of girls trying to get your father's attention who were flashy and some who were prettier, but none of them saw in your father what I saw. All they were looking for was a good time. And he wasn't paying them any attention anyway." Jewel smiled at the memory. "You know, your father doesn't know that I know this, but the first time he took me out was because his mother had been urging him to all week. I think he only agreed to take me out just to get some peace at home."

"Why did you even bother?" Karen asked.

"It's like I said, I knew your father was special even if he didn't. On our first date your father had expressed a desire to become an attorney. He was fascinated by law and had taken a few legal courses when he was in the service. I told him that I thought he would be a wonderful attorney and could see him standing before the Supreme Court arguing an important case as everyone in the courtroom hung on to his every word."

"You buttered him up," Karen said, giggling.

"No," Jewel replied, wagging her finger, "I encouraged him. And it wasn't just a show, I was for real."

"So, when did you fall in love with Daddy?" Claudia asked.

Jewel leaned back in her seat and thought before she answered. "I fell in love with your father when I saw how hard he worked going to school while holding down a full-time job. And again when after his father died, he made sure his mother never needed or wanted for anything. And once again when he asked me to marry him and promised me that he would be by my side until the Good Lord called one of us home. And yet again when each of you were babies and I saw how lovingly and carefully he held you each night and rocked you and kissed your little lips and told you how special you were. And I continue to fall in love with your father whenever I look back on the wonderful life we've had, the beautiful children we've raised, and the trials and tribulations we've made it through. And even if it were to all end tomorrow, I feel truly blessed to have lived such an amazing life with an equally amazing man to share it with."

Karen and Claudia looked at their mother with a new-found respect, for they knew that through all of their parents' ups and downs, they were still very much in love.

While Karen and Jewel enjoyed their lunch, Claudia sat staring out the window.

"Honey, what's wrong?" Jewel asked her.

Claudia shrugged her shoulders. "I guess you could say I've gotten myself into a bit of a situation."

Karen was just about to bite her sandwich and stopped in midair. "Situation? This sounds serious." She was waiting for Claudia to open the door to the Ray and Mark dilemma.

Claudia rolled her eyes and turned to address her mother. "Do you remember what you told me when I told you about my plan to find a man?"

"Yes."

"Well, I was so busy trying to find the man of my dreams, that I was overlooking someone who was right under my nose."

"Ray?" Jewel asked, already knowing that she was correct.

Claudia nodded.

"Ray?" Karen asked sarcastically. "You're in love with Ray? I would have never guessed that in a million years."

Claudia continued to ignore her sister and went on, "And as fate would have it, Mark is in the mix, too."

"You have two men vying for your affection and you don't know what to do?"

Claudia nodded again. "Ray and I had a long talk the other night and he told me how he felt about me. Mom, how could I not have noticed that my best friend was falling in love with me?"

"We don't always see the obvious."

"No, we don't," Karen commented between bites of salad, as she attempted to interject her own level of wisdom into the conversation.

"I guess you've got some tough decisions to face," Jewel said.

"Yes, and I've been given three weeks to decide."

"Three weeks?" Jewel asked.

"Yes, Ray has given me three weeks to make a decision about our relationship. Also, the grand opening of Mark's restaurant is in three weeks and he wants me to be there to celebrate with him. I'm sensing that Mark is using the grand opening as a turning point in our relationship. I don't think he's going to propose or anything like that, but I do sense something. He said that he couldn't think of anyone else to share the evening with but me."

"Do you love Ray?" Jewel asked, pretty sure the answer was yes.

"Yes, I love Ray, but I'm not sure if what I feel for him is strong enough. To be honest, I don't know if what I feel for Ray is the kind of love you share with Daddy. You know the kind of love I'm talking about. The kind where you can't eat or sleep and that person is the only thing that's on your mind."

"Forget all that," Jewel scolded. "What you're talking about is infatuation, puppy love. That fades faster than good looks. What I have with your father is real and there is no mistaking that it's a lasting love."

"See, that's what I'm talking about, Mom. I don't know if I feel that for Ray."

Jewel asked, "What about Mark? How do you feel about him? It's obvious that he's quite taken with you."

"I really like him. He's sweet and kind and considerate. He sends me email letting me know that he's thinking about me, calls me just to say hello, and is always concerned about what I want or am interested in. And despite how silly my plan seems now, he is everything I thought I wanted."

"Thought?" Jewel questioned.

"Nothing is clear to me right now. I guess I just have to take my time and look at things logically. Hopefully, the answer will be right under my nose," Claudia said, smiling for the first time that day.

"Well, Claudia, whatever decision you make, I hope it's one you can live with. My only advice to you is to be careful. No matter what you decide, you can only give your heart to one man."

CHAPTER TWENTY-FIVE

Mark showed up at Claudia's house on time for their date. However, he was a bit too warmly dressed for a casual evening at home.

"Am I missing something?" Claudia asked, mildly amused. "I can turn up the heat if you like."

Mark had on snow boots, a heavy coat, a wool scarf, thick gloves and a knit hat.

"You're not missing anything but I do think you've forgotten something you promised me when we first met and I think it's time you delivered."

Claudia tried to think back to the dinner party at Kelly's but couldn't remember what it was that she had promised Mark.

Mark pulled back the living room curtain and said, "Look outside."

With Ginger at her heels, Claudia walked over to the window and did as Mark had asked. The moon was full and reflected off the new layer of snow that had fallen that afternoon. From what she could see, it was a typical winter evening. She turned back to Mark and shrugged her shoulders.

"The snow," Mark said excitedly. "You promised to show me how to enjoy the winter weather. So far the only enjoyment that I've gotten out of all of this snow is finding shelter from it."

She now remembered what she'd said. "You want to go sledding? Tonight?"

"Yes, and I've already called the park. Big Run, right? They have sledding tonight until ten o'clock. Apparently the area is lighted. Anyway, I've got a thermos of hot chocolate and I picked up two sleds this afternoon."

Claudia laughed. "I don't know if you're crazy or just spontaneous."

"I vote for spontaneous. But I am crazy about you," he said and winked.

"Okay, give me a few minutes to get dressed as warmly as you."

The sledding hill at Big Run Park was fairly busy for a weeknight, but Mark and Claudia managed to find an area that wasn't too crowded or too steep. Standing at the top of the hill they each tied a rope to their sled to give them some steering control on the way down the hill.

"What are the bales of hay for at the bottom of the hill?" Mark asked.

"They're what you smash into after you go careening down the hill," she answered, jokingly.

After Claudia gave Mark a few instructions and showed him how to push off, they went soaring down the hill. They both made it down at almost the same time and were laughing wildly as they fell off their sleds into the hay.

"Oh my goodness, that was fun!"

Claudia laughed at the boyish excitement in Mark's voice. "Go again?"

"Most definitely."

After a few more runs, Mark became rather confident in his sledding skills and decided he was ready for the bigger hill. He challenged Claudia to a race to the bottom.

She gladly accepted the challenge.

Mark started the race, "On your mark. Get set." But before he said go, he pushed off the hill before Claudia.

"Cheater!" she yelled and pushed off seconds after he did.

Soaring down the hill a few feet behind Mark, Claudia didn't catch him until they had reached the bottom.

He looked at her, laughing, as she picked up a handful of powdery snow and formed a snowball. Throwing it at Mark, she had almost perfect aim and hit him square in the chest.

"Oh, you want a snowball fight, huh?" he asked, moving out of the path of the other sledders and grabbing a handful of snow. His snowball missed Claudia by inches as she ran to find more packable snow.

Mark was on her heels and captured her just as she grabbed the tip of a tree branch that was covered with freshly fallen snow. The two of them lost their balance and fell into a snowdrift.

"Say uncle," Mark demanded playfully as he pinned Claudia beneath him.

"Never," Claudia said giggling. "I don't give in to cheater's demands. Besides, justice is about to be served."

Mark looked at Claudia questioningly, but before he had a chance to say anything, snow from the tree branch fell on top of his head.

Claudia laughed uncontrollably. Mark's massive frame had shielded her from being caught in the mini snow shower but he was covered from his head to his shoulders.

"I'm glad I can be a source of amusement for you," he said, still holding Claudia down with one hand while he brushed the snow off his shoulder with the other.

"See what happens when you sneak and do deceitful things?" Claudia asked, trying to hide her smile.

Mark smiled down at Claudia and was instantly struck by how beautiful she looked. Her eyes twinkled with amusement and her face practically shown in the soft moonlight.

Mark lowered his head for just a taste of her sweet lips. But just one taste was not enough. The passion that he had for Claudia surprised and excited him and burned more deeply than it ever had before. He wanted and needed more from her, possibly more than she was able to give.

"It would be so easy for me to love you," he said honestly, bearing a part of his soul that he'd never revealed to her before.

Claudia saw the passion and honesty in Mark's eyes. She searched for the right thing to say, but words escaped her.

Mark knew that she was struggling with her feelings for him, and he was afraid that if he pushed for more then he might push her away. That was something he wasn't prepared to risk.

"Let's get something warm to drink," he said, helping Claudia up.

As they sat in Mark's car drinking hot chocolate and munching on cookies, Claudia turned to him and said, "Despite what you might think, I really do care about you."

"I know," Mark replied. "But you're torn right now."

Claudia clearly understood Mark's comment. "You know, don't you?"

"That Ray loves you?" Mark nodded. "I've known it from the first time I met him. The way he looked at you and especially the way he looked at me."

"I thought he was friendly toward you the first time. How do you think he acted?"

"Like he wanted to rip my head off."

"I'm sorry about that. I never meant for any of this to turn into some type of love triangle. I'm just a bit confused right now. Will you bear with me while I try to sort all of this out?" she asked with such sincerity that Mark had no other choice but to say yes.

"The only thing I need from you is honesty," Mark said. "No matter what you decide, be honest with me. But more importantly, be honest with yourself. And know that I will not stop pursuing you, Claudia, until you tell me otherwise."

CHAPTER TWENTY-SIX

"Mr. Elliott, Mrs. Kidd is holding for you on line three."

Ray and Shawn had been going over plans for an upcoming project. When they heard who was holding they exchanged hopeful glances.

"Yes, Mrs. Kidd," Ray said smiling and nodding his head. "Of course. I think you'll be very happy with the development of the land. The EPA reports back up our findings just as I said they would."

Shawn could only hear Ray's part of the conversation, but from his expression, he knew the news would be good.

"That's good. I'll have my secretary keep an eye out for it."

Ray ended the call with the usual pleasantries and turned to face Shawn with an enormous grin on his face.

"Well, is the project a go or what?"

"It's a go," Ray announced excitedly. "They granted all of our exemptions and the board signed off on the paperwork last night. Mrs. Kidd said she sent everything out by courier this afternoon and it should be here before the close of the day today."

Shawn and Ray slapped high fives, clearly pleased with themselves.

"I'd say this calls for a celebration. Champagne and a big, juicy steak. How does that sound to you?"

"Sounds like the perfect end to a long work week," Ray said, still smiling.

"I've got a few things to wrap up and then I'll be ready to go."

Ray checked his watch. It was almost four-thirty. His secretary would be there at the office to sign for the package from Mrs. Kidd and he couldn't think of any reason to hang around the office any longer.

Ray and Shawn decided on a restaurant and Shawn went to his office to call his wife Leslie to invite her along. Ray called Claudia but was unable to reach her at work. He tried her cell phone and ended up leaving a voice mail message. He told her that he had some good news to share with her and left the name of the restaurant where they would be. He asked her to meet him there as soon as she could.

Ray, Shawn and his wife waited for Claudia to join them while they talked about finally being able to relax after waiting on pins and needles for the final word from Mrs. Kidd. But after forty-five minutes Ray suggested they go on with their celebration without her. He was about to call her once more but realized that in his haste he'd left his cell phone on his desk at work.

"Do you want to try to call her again?" Shawn asked, offering his cell phone.

Ray shrugged his shoulders nonchalantly. "No, it's all right. I left a message and hopefully she'll get it in time and join us."

He couldn't help wondering if Claudia was with Mark.

After a few glasses of champagne Ray and Shawn were in high spirits. Laughing and joking, it was easy to see that the party of three had a lot to celebrate.

"Did my invitation to the party get lost in the mail?"

Both Shawn and Ray looked up at the decidedly feminine voice and saw Viveca standing beside the table. Wearing a red knit dress with a dangerously low plunging neckline, she looked absolutely gorgeous.

"Viveca, what are you doing here?" Ray asked, surprised by

her presence and how beautiful she looked.

"I was supposed to be having dinner with a friend, but he was called away on an emergency."

After he made brief introductions, Ray noticed that Shawn hadn't taken his eyes off Viveca the entire time and after shaking her hand, stood to pull out a chair for her.

"Why don't you join us? There's no reason for your evening to be ruined just because of a badly timed emergency," Shawn said, wearing a lopsided smile.

Shawn's wife cleared her throat. She suddenly felt very frumpy next to Viveca who was dressed impeccably from head to toe and practically oozed sex appeal.

Shawn looked around the table. "I'm sure Ray won't mind."

Viveca smiled in Ray's direction and lowered her long lashes, giving her eyes a smoky, seductive look. "Do you mind if I crash the party, Ray?"

Ray shook his head.

"So, what are we celebrating?" Viveca asked, never taking her eyes off Ray.

"We just tied up all the lose ends on a huge project we've been working on for quite a while. The last few pieces fell into place this afternoon," Shawn answered.

"Well, congratulations." Viveca lifted the glass of champagne that Shawn had just poured for her and offered a toast. "To the brightest minds at Braxton-Smith, Ltd. Here's to many more successes."

Ray was beginning to feel the affects of the champagne and wisely suggested they order dinner.

While they waited for their meals to arrive, Viveca and Shawn chatted about a variety of subjects, much to his wife's chagrin. It was clear to see that Shawn was smitten. And Viveca played it to the hilt. She lavished him with compliments and practically ignored

Leslie the entire evening.

After they'd had dessert, Leslie complained of a headache and suggested to Shawn that it was time to go home. Disappointed, Shawn reluctantly agreed to leave but not before insisting that the two couples get together another time.

"Leslie's headache was rather sudden," Viveca observed once Shawn and Leslie left.

Ray folded his arms and shook his head.

"What?" Viveca asked innocently.

"How you can sit there and act totally innocent is beyond me."

Viveca removed an imaginary piece of lent from the table cloth and smiled. "I am innocent. I'm only guilty of crashing your party. Nothing more, nothing less."

"No, there is more. You flirted shamelessly with Shawn from the moment you arrived until Leslie whisked him out of here. The poor woman was practically reduced to a casual observer, thanks to you. She might as well have picked up her plate and moved to another table."

"That was the position she chose to take."

"Again, thanks to you."

"Oh, please. If she were secure in her relationship, my presence would have meant nothing to her and she wouldn't have cared one bit if he looked twice in my direction."

"Sweetheart, that dress is designed to evoke stares and grab attention. Looking twice or even three times in your direction is inevitable."

"Well, it's nice to know that I can still turn heads. Does my dress have the same affect on you?"

"Oh, I noticed how good you look in that dress."

Viveca leaned in and ran her tongue along her crimson colored lips. "Would you be interested to see how I look out of the dress?"

"Are you trying to seduce me, Viveca?"

"I just thought it would be a good idea to continue the celebration at your place. If my memory serves correctly, and I rarely forget anything, you were always a magnificent lover. I'd be willing to bet that you've perfected your skills over the years. Care to test my theory?"

Ray was beginning to sober up quickly. He took a sip of coffee. He needed to have a clear head when dealing with Viveca. She was a skilled seductress and by now a lesser man would have crumbled, but Ray knew that he needed to hold firm. Sleeping with Viveca would be disastrous and he had long ago stopped allowing his libido to dictate his actions.

"Viveca, if you had made this offer to me four years ago, even three years ago, there would have been no question as to whether or not I would have accepted. I was head-over-heels in love with you, even after you left, and I would probably have done almost anything for you."

"What's changed since then besides your feelings toward me? Wait. Before you answer that I feel that I need to make a point. Love is not an issue here. It's not what I'm looking for. I'm talking about a good time. Tonight. That's it. I can still turn you on, Ray, and as far as I know, you haven't taken a vow of celibacy. I still know what pleases you."

"No, I haven't taken a vow of celibacy but I am in love and I refuse to jeopardize my relationship for a fling."

Viveca laughed, almost cynically, and said, "Let me guess. The lucky lady is Claudia Ryland."

Ray nodded.

"Who says she has to know? We're both adults. What we do behind closed doors, stays behind closed doors. This is our business and no one else's."

"That's where you're wrong. I'll know. You see, Viveca, something pretty interesting has happened to me over the years. I've grown up. There are some things that are clear to me now that were unclear to me before. I realized a while ago that the kind of love I had for you wasn't the kind of love that could stand the test of time. The way I felt for you was one-sided and a bit selfish on my part. I expected way more from you than you were able to give, and that was wrong. If you hadn't left me when you did, we would probably have broken up soon anyway."

Viveca wasn't trying to hear a true confession and waved her hand in the air as if to dismiss what Ray had just said. She had something else on her mind and it had very little to do with deep emotional feelings.

Refusing to take no for an answer, Viveca continued to try and make her case. Turning up the charm a notch, she crossed her legs around to the side of her chair, giving Ray a full view of her shapely legs.

"Come on, Ray. Let me show you what you've missed over the past few years. I can reacquaint you with pleasures that you've probably forgotten, and show you new pleasures that you've never experienced before."

Ray moved uncomfortably in his seat. He couldn't let Viveca get to him and she wasn't, especially in the way she would have liked to. He just didn't like her coming on to him that way.

Viveca bit her lip and practically cooed, "I just want to feel you inside me, baby. That's not asking too much."

Ray sucked in his breath between clenched teeth. "No, Viveca, I can't," he said firmly.

"Can't or won't?"

"Both."

Ray called for the check and when it arrived, threw several

bills on the table.

"You might find this hard to believe, Viveca, but what I have, what I hope to have with Claudia means more to me than helping you fulfill your erotic fantasies."

Viveca watched Ray walk out of the restaurant seemingly unaffected by his rejection. But once he was out of sight, she leaned her elbows on the table and let her shoulders slump.

He must really love her, Viveca thought unhappily. But why did she care? Rejection was rejection no matter where it stemmed from.

Viveca finished her coffee and resigned herself to a lonely night at home with her mother. At least she had a chance to wear her new red dress. But as she was leaving the restaurant she nearly ran into Claudia.

"Hello," Viveca said sweetly.

"Hi," Claudia said curtly and tried to get past Viveca. "Could you excuse me please? I'm in a bit of a hurry."

Viveca moved aside to let Claudia pass and said over her shoulder, "Of course. I've got to get going myself. Ray and I just finished dinner and I'm supposed to be meeting him at his house for a night cap and you know how he hates to wait."

Claudia stopped and turned to face Viveca. "You had dinner with Ray? Here tonight?"

"Yes, we ran into each other by accident and he invited me to help celebrate the finalization of some big project at work. We had champagne and a scrumptious dinner, and now we're going to continue the celebration at his house. If you know what I mean," Viveca added with a wink.

Claudia looked shaken. Ray and Viveca? Every time she thought that chapter of his life had been closed, she realized just how wrong she was.

Viveca pretended to fumble around in her purse for her car keys. "Whew, found them. I think I had a little too much champagne. I probably should have taken Ray up on his offer to drive me to his house. But the way he was behaving, we may not have made it out of the parking lot. Well, gotta go. See you later, Claudia."

Claudia's mind was racing. Ray had invited Viveca to his house and she had made it quite evident that it was going to be for more than just a nightcap. Just earlier that week he had professed his love for her. It was clear to her now that those had just been empty words.

CHAPTER TWENTY-SEVEN

How dare Ray give her a time limit to make a decision about their relationship. Apparently, he still couldn't decide on his relationship with Viveca after all these years. And if he wasn't clear about Viveca after all this time, then he might never be.

Viveca. This woman was the proverbial bad penny. Absolutely nothing about her had changed over the years. Claudia couldn't help but notice the outfit she'd been wearing - tight, bright and designed to quicken the pulse of any male over the age of twelve.

Had Viveca caught Ray's attention with the form-fitting dress she was wearing? Despite everything she'd put him through, did Viveca still have some secret power over Ray that Claudia would never be able to understand or that he would never be able to break free from?

This was a terrible beginning to the weekend. Ray had left a message for her to meet him at the restaurant for a celebration. But she'd been in a meeting that ran much later than she had anticipated. By the time she had received the message it was late. She raced across town to get to the restaurant and hoped that Ray was still there.

Of all the restaurants in Columbus, Viveca happened to run into Ray at that particular one, or so she said. Claudia had wanted to wipe the smug look off her face when she talked about helping Ray celebrate.

Well, she hoped Ray enjoyed spending time with Viveca. As far as she was concerned those two could spend the rest of their lives unhappily ever after.

Ray hung up the phone. He had tried several times to reach Claudia but to no avail. It was almost eleven o'clock on a Friday night. Surely she had to be home by now.

He wondered if she'd ever made it to the restaurant. Celebrating his success with Claudia was something he'd been looking forward to since receiving the good news. In fact, she was the first person he wanted to tell besides Shawn. Ray knew she would have been proud of him and that meant a lot.

If all went well they would be celebrating other successes. Fifteen days. That's when he'd have an answer from Claudia. He hoped with everything he held sacred that she would choose to make the commitment to taking their relationship to new heights. Ray needed and wanted her in his life. She already held a special place as a friend, but he also wanted her as a lover, wife and companion. Having her only in his dreams was torment. Having her in real life would be paradise.

Ray had never had with Viveca or any other woman what he had with Claudia. His relationship with Viveca had been based on give and take. He gave, and she took until he had nothing left to give. Financially and emotionally spent, he'd been left wary of ever finding someone to love and someone to love him. But without his realizing it at first, Claudia had been that someone. It had taken him a long time to recognize that his feelings for her was something that went far deeper than mere friendship. Initially, he'd tried to deny those feelings. But once he stopped running away from the inevitable, he had to face what he already knew subconsciously. No matter how many women he dated, trying to dispel the notion that it was Claudia who had his heart wrapped up tight, it always came down to a comparison of those women against her. And it was

Claudia who always came out on top.

Their relationship would work and it would grow. He knew deep down in his heart that it would. The compassion and love they'd shared over the years had laid the foundation for which they would build a lifetime of happiness.

Two more weeks. Fifteen days to be exact and she could kiss this town good-bye. Viveca longed to be back on her own turf and away from the tension that had built up over the last several weeks between herself and her mother.

They would never be close, she'd decided. They were just too different. Joyce didn't approve of her daughter's choices and never missed an opportunity to say so. And Viveca had long ago adopted the live-and-let-live attitude that had served her well over the years. But there was one thing she was having a difficult time dealing with-Ray and Claudia's relationship.

It wasn't so much that she was bothered by the knowledge that Ray was in love with Claudia. She had expected that to eventually happen, it was the fact that she had counted on Ray being there for her during her visit. Yes, he had been there for her emotionally but she'd wanted more.

Viveca poured a drink and thought about her evening with Ray and his friend. Shawn had practically drooled over her and she was sure if his wife hadn't been present, he would have been easy prey. She smiled imagining the wild time they could have shared. She would certainly have given his little wife something to be jealous about.

But what Viveca had really wanted was Ray. She wasn't sure if his rejection of her had fueled her desire for him or if she just needed to be wanted.

Her evening had started out on a good note and held promise. Dr. Hammond had finally called to invite her to dinner. And with his invitation Viveca had decided she would provide dessert. Through their conversations over the phone, she'd learned that the good doctor was in his early forties, had been divorced for two years and had no children. He had just built a house in a section of town where Viveca knew that only those who had money, influence and power resided.

Long hours at work inhibited the doctor's social life. He admitted to Viveca that he had dated very little since his divorce and as a result, he was lonely.

Viveca was more than willing to spend her remaining days in the capital city keeping Dr. Hammond company. And experience told her that their relationship would be mutually beneficial.

But the evening took a downturn when a page from the hospital summoned the doctor to emergency surgery. After answering the page he had apologized profusely for having to leave and promised to make it up to her another time. Before he left he had even instructed the waiter to give Viveca whatever she wanted.

But she hadn't wanted to spend the evening alone or at home. On her way out she had spotted Ray and his friends. The champagne was flowing and they were laughing and having a good time. This scene was certainly more of an attractive alternative than what she had been faced with only moments earlier. And she'd had a good time. That is until she attempted to extend the celebration.

Viveca sat back in her chair and took a swallow of her drink. Ray didn't want to play. It wasn't as if she'd asked for his hand in marriage. She simply wanted to have a little fun. But closer to the truth was that she wanted to be close to someone who she knew cared about her. It had been a long time since that had happened. One night stands and sugar daddies were generally the norm for her.

That was usually how she liked to roll, until tonight. And maybe just for tonight.

Viveca's life was empty and she knew it. That's why she tried to fill it with as many material possessions as possible. But something her mother had said over and over again, echoed in her mind. Mere possessions could never be an equal substitute for love.

CHAPTER TWENTY-EIGHT

Claudia had successfully avoided seeing or talking to Ray for most of the week, but the one thing she couldn't avoid doing was thinking about him.

After what seemed like a long, exhausting day, Claudia had decided to call it quits around six o'clock. She made a mental note to call Mark at the restaurant later that night. He had called earlier to let her know that he was thinking about her and that once things settled down after the grand opening of the restaurant they would be able to spend more time together.

She hadn't seen Mark in several days and was secretly glad that he was too busy to spend time with her. She wouldn't have been good company anyway. Since her run-in with Viveca she'd been trying to put her relationships with Mark and Ray into perspective, again. This seemed to be a recurring mission.

She had been hurt by Viveca's announcement that she was going to spend the evening with Ray. *What could Viveca offer him?* she wondered over and over again. It certainly couldn't be anything substantial. Ray couldn't be so callous as to think a romp in the hay was just innocent fun.

And then there was Mark. There was no question that she was fond of him. Who wouldn't be? Mark was the ideal man and, given time, she was sure that they could have something special together. At least that's what she had been trying to convince herself to believe.

When Claudia left work she could think of nothing other than going home and relaxing. Something along the lines of a bubble bath, a large pepperoni pizza with mushrooms and a good movie seemed to be in order. But when she reached the parking lot she was surprised to see Ray casually leaning against her car.

Claudia walked slowly to her car and kept her gaze straight ahead as she forced her mind to think of anything other than how rapidly her heart was beating.

She looked tired, Ray thought. He had concluded that Claudia was attempting to avoid him and he was determined to find out why.

When she finally reached the car Claudia knew she couldn't pretend that Ray wasn't standing less than five feet away from her so she just decided to face the situation head on. She would say what she had to say and go home.

"Would you mind explaining to me why you haven't returned any of my phone calls?" Ray asked, thinking how much he'd missed seeing and talking to Claudia. She looked tired, he thought again, and sad. It hurt to know that somehow he knew he was the cause. He wanted to reach out and hold her and show her how much he loved her, but instinct told him to hold back.

"I suppose I could pretend that I don't know what you're talking about, but why should I? Let's just say that I choose not to be a second string player in your game."

"You're going to have to explain that one to me because I don't have a clue as to what you are talking about."

Claudia lifted her chin and said, "I showed up at the restaurant last Friday after I received your message, which wasn't until later that evening because I was tied up in a meeting."

"Why didn't you just come by the house or at the very least, call me? I had some good news that I wanted to share with you."

"I didn't want to be a third wheel."

Ray saw what he thought was a flash of pain in Claudia's eyes and he was more confused than ever.

"Let me fill in the missing gaps for you, Ray. When I arrived at the restaurant, I ran into Viveca. She was kind enough to let me know that I had just missed you.

Viveca. He should have known. *What had she done now?*

"Seems like the two of you shared a nice intimate dinner together. She also made it clear that she was on her way to your house to continue the celebration that was started earlier in the evening."

Ray let out a long breath. "And you believed her? Honey, she was lying."

Not completely convinced, she said, "Oh, really?"

"Yes, Claudia, *really*." Ray was becoming angry. "When I told you I loved you, those weren't empty words. When I told you I was over Viveca, that was also the truth. Why do you have such a hard time believing either of those things? And why after all these years and everything we've been through with each other, why is it that you do not seem to be able to trust me all of a sudden?"

"Because you've asked me to put my heart on the line. Where everything else is concerned, Ray, I can trust you. But when Viveca is involved, things get a little shaky."

"And why is that?"

"Maybe you should ask yourself that question. Maybe you should ask why Viveca goes out of her way to make it clear to me that she is still a very important part of your life."

Ray threw his hands up in despair. "I don't know why Viveca does the things she does. It's probably just some crazy mind game she likes to play because she knows she can get under your skin. Maybe you should ask yourself why you continue to allow Viveca to come between us."

"She has always been an issue in one way or another. There is nothing new about this. I think there's some unresolved business between you two and until it gets cleared up, my vision about the two of us will remain cloudy."

Claudia had said all she needed to say and got in her car and drove away.

Ray didn't stop her but watched as the taillights from her car grew smaller and smaller as the distance between the two of them seemed to widen. He sat behind the wheel of his car and slammed his fist against the dashboard. Then something caught his eye. Claudia's Valentine's gift. The rectangular velvet box that he'd placed there earlier served as another reminder as to how far apart the two of them seemed to be growing. Did she even know or care that it was almost Valentine's Day? And would she accept the diamond tennis bracelet that he'd brought for her? She had been so hurt and angry.

Claudia had never reacted this fiercely to anything Viveca had said or done in the past. And Viveca had never been this conniving. Or had she? Either way, he needed to set things right. And his first step would be to talk Viveca.

CHAPTER TWENTY-NINE

Whoever was ringing the doorbell was going a little overboard. Viveca hurried to the front door to see who was being so persistent. Seeing Ray standing on the front porch she smiled and quickly opened the door.

"We've got to talk."

Viveca's smile faded when Ray blew into the room like a raging storm. The look on his face let her know immediately that this was not a social call. He looked tired, angry and hurt. Sure that she was responsible in part, she immediately put up her defenses.

"Good evening to you, too, Ray. I was just on my way out to the club. Care to be my escort for the evening?"

Ray had been pacing and went over to the door and nearly slammed it shut. He grabbed Viveca's arm, leading her to the nearby couch. "Sit down and listen. We are going to get some things straight and we are going to do it right now." Not wanting Viveca's mother to hear him Ray kept his voice as controlled as he could and his tone low, but deep down inside he was seething.

This wasn't the first time that Viveca had ever seen Ray angry but this time she knew that she had pushed too far.

"What are you talking about, Ray?" Her best defense was to feign innocence, she thought.

"You know damn well what I'm talking about. You ran into Claudia the other night at the restaurant. From what I can tell, she believes that something is going on between us. Now, where do you suppose she got that idea?"

"I'm not responsible for the way Claudia interpreted our conversation nor am I concerned about her insecurities."

"No, but you are responsible for what you say and how you say it. Don't play games with me, Viveca."

"I don't play games, Ray."

Ray laughed bitterly. "You've perfected the art of game playing and I want it stopped. You are hell-bent on making everyone around you miserable and I refuse to be sucked into your plan. What Claudia and I have, what I hope to have with her, is something you will never understand. To be honest, I don't care if you understand it or not, just don't get in the way. You've hurt Claudia once, but you won't do it again."

Viveca didn't know what to say. Ray had never spoken to her like this before.

"I have done everything I can to be a good friend to you and you've done nothing but throw it all back in my face. No more, Viveca. If you want to be miserable your whole life, then go right ahead. I won't let you pull me down with you. Continue to live in that empty, pathetic existence that you've created for yourself, if you can call that living."

"The next time you need a friend," Ray said on his way out the door, "remember, I no longer fit into that category."

The phone call Viveca received that morning was as unexpected as it was unwanted. After nearly a year and a half her ex-husband, Clayton, decided to resurface. This was the last thing she needed after her blow up with Ray the previous evening.

Clayton called just to say hello, he'd said. Supposedly he was passing through Columbus on his way to Pittsburgh.

What did he really want? Viveca wanted to know. Perhaps his latest meal ticket had wised up and sent him packing. Well, she wasn't about to be the shoulder he undoubtedly was looking for to cry on, or worse, the gravy train he was looking to climb aboard.

Viveca met Clayton at the K and S lounge shortly before ten P.M. He had called several times asking to see her and finally she had agreed to meet him. Maybe after he saw her he would leave her alone once and for all.

Viveca pulled into the parking lot of the K and S and cringed. The bar and grill that had once been a hot spot had become so run down that now it was little more than a hole in the wall.

Oh well, she thought, it was a fitting location for her meeting with Clayton.

The inside of the bar was as dark and dreary as the outside. It smelled of stale beer, cheap perfume and cigarette smoke. Viveca looked around the dimly lit bar for Clayton and saw him waving from atop his barstool.

He looked exactly the same, maybe even a little better, Viveca thought as she strolled casually across the room. Wearing an off-white sweater that she knew was cashmere and chocolate colored wool pants, to the casual observer Clayton looked handsome and debonair. But a snake was a snake no matter how well it was dressed.

"Have mercy," he said grinning. "Girl, I swear you look good."

Viveca ignored Clayton and leaned against the bar. "What do you want, Clayton?" She tried to keep her voice curt and her attitude crisp. Just seeing her ex-husband again brought about a plethora of emotions and none of them did she care to experience at the moment.

"Sit down and take a load off those pretty feet," he said gesturing to the empty stool beside him. "Order yourself a drink. On me."

The bartender had been at the other end of the bar cleaning glasses and seemed to magically appear when he heard the word order.

"I'll have a cup of coffee. Black." Viveca sat down on the edge of the stool, not wanting to get too comfortable.

Clayton raised his eyebrows. "Just coffee? Are you trying your hand at being a good girl or are you on the wagon?"

"No, I'm just particular who I drink with."

"Damn, Viveca, you act like I'm some kind of low-life criminal."

"You said it, not me."

"Look, baby, I just wanted to see you that's all. I'm not here to run a game on you or anything like that."

Viveca checked her watch. She didn't have anything to do or any place to go, she just wanted to let Clayton know he was wasting her time. "What is it that you want, Clayton? I know you and sentimentality is not one of your traits. So spit it out so I can get out of this place before the police raid it."

Clayton shook his head slowly and smiled. He could be quite charming when he put his mind to it, or if there was something he wanted.

Viveca was used to his charming ways and remained unaffected. As far as she was concerned, he didn't have any tricks that she hadn't seen before.

"Okay, I get it," he said. "You hate my guts and I can't really say that I blame you. I admit, I did you wrong. But you can't hold that against me forever."

"Why not? Because you don't deserve it? Because you treated me like a queen the whole time we were together? Or maybe, it's because you've never shown me anything but respect and have always treated me like a lady? Oh, I know. It's because you're looking for another benefactor and you think I'm foolish enough to be it."

Clayton smiled again, showing capped white teeth that she was sure had been financed by one of his ex's. He had a beautiful smile that cleverly hid the coldness in his heart. "Do you feel better now that you've gotten that off your chest?"

"Actually, I'll feel better when I know that you're out of my life. For good. And I never, ever have to see or hear from you again."

Clayton reached out to touch Viveca's arm and she pulled away.

"Did I make you hate me that much? We used to have some good times together. Doesn't that add up to anything?"

"Yes, and unfortunately the interest on those credit cards is still accumulating." Viveca thought she saw a flash of shame in Clayton's eyes, but then thought better of it. He wasn't capable of such feelings, she thought sarcastically.

"Baby, I wish you could put all of that behind you. I have."

"I can just imagine how you've struggled to do that. Suffered through a lot of sleepless nights I'm sure."

"I know you won't believe me when I say this, but I have struggled with everything I put you through."

Viveca rolled her eyes in response.

"I realized something tonight, Viveca, when I saw you walk in that door. I realized how much I've missed you."

Dumbfounded, Viveca turned in her seat and looked at Clayton to see if he was serious.

"How much you've missed me? You mean how much you missed my money. How long has it been since your wife threw you out, Clay? Couldn't find anyone to keep you in the lifestyle that you've become accustomed to?"

"No, baby, it isn't anything like that. I've really missed you.

Things between Denise and me didn't work out. I was a fool to ever think that she could be half the woman you are. These last few years I've been miserable without you. I've come here tonight to ask you to forgive me. But what I really want to know is if you will give us another chance."

Viveca took a sip of coffee. This was too much. Clayton thought he could play her for a fool. Boy, was he wrong. It took every ounce of reserve she had to keep from tossing hot coffee in his lying face. She took a moment and paused before speaking, as she wanted what she had to say to be clear and to the point, with no room for misinterpretation.

"You know what, I think I will have something a little stronger than this coffee." Turing to the bartender, she ordered a glass of red wine.

"So, what do you say? Do you want to give us another chance?"

Viveca took a sip of wine and ran her tongue along her bottom lip. Crossing her legs, she made a point to show just enough thigh to remind Clayton how sexy her legs were.

"You know, Clay, I have to say you're the same man that I fell in love with years ago."

Clayton smiled. *She was remembering the good times,* he thought. Things were looking better than they had when she first arrived.

"You still know all the right things to say and are just as charming as always. When we first got together, I was so naive and you seemed to have it all together. You taught me things that I never knew existed, but along the way, I began to see things from a different perspective. My own. I've changed, Clayton. I'm not the same woman I used to be. Now, I can see through you like glass. And what I see is something I don't ever want to be a part of again."

Clayton's smile faded.

"I knew you were up to something the moment I heard your voice over the phone. So, I made a few calls myself."

Squirming in his seat, Clayton bit his lower lip and crossed his hands in front of himself on the bar.

"Seems as if you've racked up quite a bit of debt playing the horses and your luck wasn't very good, which doesn't surprise me. Denise refused to pay for your fun? I guess she finally saw you for what you really are. Word around town is that you have to come up with a large sum of money soon or else there are some people who aren't going to be very happy with you."

"Naw, baby, it's not quite like that. I don't know who you've been talking to, but they need to get their facts straight. I admit that I've run up a little debt but that's not the reason I'm here."

"That's precisely the reason you're here. I guess you think I'm the same fool that I was when you first met me. Think again. I'm a force to be reckoned with, Clayton, and I refuse to be used by anyone, especially by the likes of you. I make the rules and I pull the strings now. No one tells me what to do or when to do it. You got that? Now, if you'll excuse me, I must be going."

Clayton was desperate. He couldn't let Viveca go. She was right. He needed money and he needed it fast. He knew she always kept a stash for hard times and these were indeed hard times.

"Wait, baby." He stood and put his hand on Viveca's arm to stop her. "Everything I told you was the truth. I do miss you and more than anything I want us to give our relationship another try."

"And?"

"And I am also in a bit of a financial jam," he admitted, shame-faced. "I need help, Viveca, and I don't know where else to turn."

"Clayton, I have always been there to get you out of jams. But not this time. I can't help you."

"Can't or won't?"

"A little of both."

Anger flashed in Clayton's eyes. "After everything I've done for you I can't believe you're turning your back on me now. I made you what you are today. If it weren't for me, you'd still be nickel and diming old men for money to pay your light bill."

That was a low blow and Viveca had to hold back to keep from slapping the smirk off Clayton's face. "So, what you're saying is that I owe you?"

"Damn right!"

Viveca's expression softened.

His words had hit home, he thought. She was remembering what they'd been through and how he had been there for her more times than she could count, Clay thought smugly.

"You're right. You did make me the woman I am today and I owe you for that. Almost everything I learned came from you. You may not know it, but you were a very good teacher and I was an equally attentive student. How to lie, cheat and use people to get what I want were skills that I perfected thanks to you. "

Viveca loosened her arm from Clayton's grasp and picked up her glass of wine, flinging it into his face and watching as it dripped onto his sweater. "My debt to you," she said before leaving the bar, "is now paid in full."

CHAPTER THIRTY

This year's health fair at Mt. Pisgah A.M.E. Church was by far the most successful one they'd had in years, due in part to partnering with several local hospitals, grocery stores and the community blood bank. The opening of the health fair featured a heart healthy breakfast, which included cooking demonstrations, presentations by nutritionists and a special nutritional segment for children.

When the blood drive had first begun that morning, Karen and Claudia were busy handing out cups of juice, cookies and fruit. But now there was a bit of a lull.

Karen took the opportunity to look over and make sure her children were behaving. Candace and Eric were engrossed in a puppet show and sat spellbound as the puppets entertained the children while instructing them on what to do when approached by a stranger, what to do if offered drugs and how to find help if they were lost.

"So, little sister, how's your little love triangle going?" Karen asked, munching on a cookie.

Claudia refused to be Karen's source of entertainment for the day and instead asked, "Why are you eating the snacks? Those are for the blood donors and that doesn't include you."

Karen sucked air through her teeth and leaned back in her chair. "They won't miss this little package of cookies. Besides, I have to keep my strength up, too."

"For what? All we're doing is handing out snacks."

"I'm trying to work up my nerve to give blood today. I saw you

221

do it and I know Frank is also coming down later today to donate. I don't want to be the only member of this family who hasn't done my part."

"I don't think anyone will think badly of you if you don't give blood, Karen. A lot of people are afraid of needles and simply can't work up the courage to donate."

"Okay, enough talk about blood. Now, answer my question."

Claudia rolled her eyes and sighed. "I was hoping you'd forgotten about that."

"Please, you've known me for how many years? This is prime drama. I'm not about to forget about it."

"Karen, I really don't want to talk about what you like to refer to as my love triangle. This all may seem entertaining to you but it's serious business with me."

"Has something happened? Come to think of it, I haven't seen or heard from Ray in a while. What's up with that?"

"I really don't want to talk about Ray."

Karen leaned in a little and said in a whisper, "Well, I don't think you're going to have much choice. Here comes Mr. Elliott right now."

Claudia turned around right as Ray walked up to their table. He said hello to Karen but never took his eyes off Claudia.

He looked tired, Claudia thought. Good, maybe he was thinking about everything she had told him when they were last together. Or maybe he was worn out from spending time with Viveca.

Ray had gone over to fill out the paperwork to donate blood. Claudia busied herself straightening up the tray of snacks while she tried to pretend that he wasn't in the room.

"Claudia!"

Claudia looked over at her sister and wondered why she was shouting.

"Maybe you should have your hearing tested today. I've said your name three times and you act as if you can't hear."

"Did you ever think I might be ignoring you?"

Karen ignored Claudia's question and continued. "What's wrong with Ray? He looks as if he's lost his best friend. Did he?"

"I already told you, Karen, I don't want to talk about this right now," she said and left to go into the kitchen.

Jewel and the other members of the kitchen committee had just finished cleaning up after the breakfast. Claudia found her mother drying silverware and asked if she needed help.

"No, but Mrs. Lawless is in the supply room and she could probably use a hand."

Claudia had to pass the blood donation station in order to get to the supply room. She walked past Ray who was lying on a cot while a bandage was being applied to his arm. She tried not to look at him but felt his eyes on her as she quickly walked by.

"Mrs. Lawless, Mom said you might need some help."

Fran Lawless placed a box of napkins in the supply cabinet and locked it. "I just finished, Claudia. But thanks for the offer."

She turned to leave but Claudia stayed behind. If she timed it just right she could hang around in the supply room until Ray left. She knew he would want to talk to her but there wouldn't be anything new to say. If so, he would have said it by now.

"You're hiding from me."

Claudia didn't have to turn around to know who'd just made that statement. She knew it was Ray. She had felt his presence even before he had made himself known.

"No, I was helping Mrs. Lawless," she said looking around the tiny room for something else to do.

Ray knew she was lying but decided not to press the issue.

"Are we going to talk?" he asked.

"Do you have anything new to tell me?" she asked.

"Claudia, nothing has changed. The way I feel about you and everything I've told you are the same. I love you. I don't know what more I can do to prove that to you so that you will believe me."

"Well, actions speak louder than words and lately your actions have said something contrary to what you want me to believe."

"That's not true. You're punishing me for something someone else has done. You're not being fair and you know it."

Claudia thought about what Ray had just said. Was she punishing him unjustly or was he simply buying time thinking that she would cool off after a while? "You know what, Ray? I need some time to think things over and I think you do, too. Maybe some time away from each other would do us some good."

Ray had been standing in the doorway partially to prevent Claudia from escaping, but also to keep anyone else from coming into the room. He reached over and closed the door and walked toward Claudia. "Are those words from your heart or your head?"

Ray's cologne filled the tiny room with a heady scent that went straight to Claudia's head. If she could manage to focus on the spot on the wall behind Ray, she would be all right. But if she looked into his eyes the tough exterior that she was working to maintain would crumble like a saltine cracker.

"I'm listening to my heart and my head," she said unconvincingly.

"I don't think so. I think your heart is telling you one thing and your head is telling you something else. Listen to your heart, Claudia."

Ray stopped within inches of Claudia and could see that her breathing had quickened. Her chest rose and fell quickly as she tried to show ambivalence.

"And your body," he said in a voice that was a little above a whisper. Ray leaned in and his lips found hers, ready and wanting to return the unspoken passion that hung between them. He pulled Claudia into his arms and felt her body respond to him exactly as he knew it would.

Claudia welcomed the kiss but at the same time battled conflicting emotions. It felt like heaven being in Ray's arms. She wanted nothing else to matter when they were together like this. He made her feel safe and secure and loved. But she needed to be sure that what he was offering her was for her alone, not just hers only when Viveca wasn't around.

"No, Ray," she said, pulling away. "I won't do this. I have to be sure about us and right now, I'm not." She pushed past Ray and walked quickly out of the room, never once looking back.

After Claudia left, Ray stayed behind and thought about what had just happened. Claudia was his but she didn't know it yet. Her body and heart told him one thing, but what he needed to hear from her lips, to know, still only existed in his dreams.

CHAPTER THIRTY-ONE

If Claudia didn't already feel confused and conflicted, falling into Ray's arms and kissing him as if she were starved for love, pushed her to that point. What was wrong with her? She couldn't go on like this. She missed Ray. But not Ray her buddy, Ray who made her body yearn for his touch and sent her emotions into a tailspin. Claudia was tired. Weary, even. She wanted to climb into bed and pull the covers over her head and stay there until everything was crystal clear to her. Unfortunately she didn't have that luxury.

Claudia sat curled up in her living room on her sofa and thought about what she was going to do. Her mother had told her to make a decision that she could live with. But how could she determine if the choices she made were the right ones? She couldn't even control herself when she was around Ray.

As she pondered this question over and over again, she heard Ginger whine softly. Someone had pulled into her driveway and now Ginger was barking loudly.

Claudia pulled herself off of the sofa and went to the door when she heard the doorbell ring. She hoped it wasn't Ray. Then again, she hoped it was.

When Claudia opened the door, it wasn't Ray who stood on the other side. It was Mark.

"Hi. Is everything all right? I wasn't expecting to see you this evening."

Without responding, Mark stepped inside and pulled Claudia into an embrace. She felt like heaven in his arms. He had needed to see her, touch her and to feel reassured by her presence.

Pulling away, he said, "Don't be upset with me for dropping by like this. I've just missed you so much and had to see you."

Claudia led Mark into the living room and they sat together on the sofa.

"How's everything going?" she asked, still a bit puzzled by Mark's behavior.

"With the restaurant, fine. With me, not so good."

Concerned, Claudia asked, "Why? Is something wrong?"

"Just this," Mark said and leaned over and gave Claudia a fiery kiss. "Baby, I've missed kissing those sweet lips of yours and holding you in my arms. You don't know how good you feel to me right now. With all the craziness that's surrounding the opening of the restaurant, you are the one thing that keeps me sane."

Claudia didn't know what to say. She had missed Mark, too, but unfortunately there was so much drama going on in her life right now that she'd unintentionally placed Mark in the back of her mind.

"Is something the matter?" he asked when Claudia didn't respond.

She felt like dirt for not giving Mark the time and attention he deserved. She was going to have to make it up to him, but not tonight. "I'm just tired, that's all. Remember, I told you about the health fair at my church?" *Convenient excuse.*

"Oh, that's right. I'd forgotten that was today. I wanted to stop by but I was so busy."

"I know," was all that she could think of to say.

"Claudia, is something else wrong?"

That was a loaded question if ever there was one. Good thing he couldn't read her mind but apparently he could read what was on her face. Could Mark see that she was a bundle of emotions? Did she know that she was having a hell of a time trying to straighten out the mess she'd created with the men in her life?

Time to be honest. "Mark, I'm going away for a few days. I need to get my head and my heart together and I need to be away from here to do it."

Mark hadn't been expecting that. "Baby, what's bothering you? Is it something I've done or that I can help you through?" he asked, clearly concerned.

"No, Mark, this is something I have to work through on my own."

"Does this have something to do with us?" he asked hoping that he wasn't losing Claudia.

"In a sense, yes."

Mark wanted to find out more but he knew that when the time was right, Claudia would confide in him. "What about the grand opening? I really want you to be there with me, by my side."

"I know and I won't disappoint you. I'll be there. I promise."

"Are you going to tell me where you're going? How will I be able to get in touch with you?"

Claudia looked into Mark's eyes and pleaded for understanding. "To be honest with you, I'm not really sure where I'm going. But I'll call you when I get back."

When Mark left that evening, Claudia went to her room and made a few phone calls. When she got off the phone she packed her bag and got ready for bed. She had a long drive ahead of her the next day and needed a good night's sleep.

CHAPTER THIRTY-TWO

Rolanda lived in a high rise luxury apartment that boasted vaulted ceilings, spacious rooms, easy access to downtown shopping and restaurants, and a spectacular view of Lake Michigan. Claudia was impressed with how tastefully decorated Rolanda's apartment was, but more so with how welcome her friend made her feel.

Claudia had arrived in Chicago around eight that evening. She had stopped only once in a small town in Indiana for something to eat and to buy gas. Overall the ride had felt good and hadn't been too tiring, even though she'd gotten very little sleep the night before. She found that the more distance she put between herself and home, the better she felt, and she was looking forward to spending time with her friend.

Before she had left town, Claudia had taken Ginger over to her parents' and explained to them that she would be going away for a few days for some rest and relaxation. Claudia left a number where she could be reached and had asked her mother not to tell anyone where she was, especially Ray.

Jewel had agreed but she'd also warned Claudia that she could not run away from her problems, and sooner or later, she would have to deal with the inevitable, whatever that may be.

Claudia and Rolanda had been talking for the better part of the evening about the different things that were going on in their lives, but Claudia didn't mention anything about Ray or Mark.

"So, what would you like to do tomorrow?" Rolanda asked.

She had cleared her work schedule and taken the week off in order to spend time with Claudia.

"The first thing I want to do is to sleep for as long as my body will allow. No alarms, no real need to get up, just sleep."

"And after that?"

"Oh, I don't know. Having a little food would be nice. Then, maybe go shopping or see a movie."

"I'll tell you what. You get a good night's sleep. I'll come up with something to do tomorrow that will knock your socks off."

Claudia yawned. She was more tired than she'd realized. "Sounds like a plan."

Rolanda showed Claudia to the guestroom and gave her a set of towels and an extra blanket.

After Claudia had taken her shower, Rolanda stopped in to say good night. "Get some rest, Claudia. You look tired and I don't think it's from the drive."

"You're right, Ro. But I don't feel like talking about it tonight."

"Tomorrow or whenever you're ready is fine with me."

Claudia turned off the lamp by the side of the bed and snuggled under the warmth and security of the covers. She had done the right thing, she reassured herself. Getting away for a few days was what she needed to do in order to get her head straight. Everything was going to work out. It had to.

It wasn't long before she drifted off into a deep, peaceful sleep.

Claudia was gone. Ray had tried to reach her at home, at work and at her parents'. He figured she had turned off her cell phone since he'd been unable to reach her that way. At least her voice mail message from work had indicated that she would be out for the week. Now all he had to do was to find out where she was.

When Ray went by one evening to talk to Jewel to find out what was going on with Claudia, he was greeted by Ginger at the front door. He was too tired to beat around the bush and had asked Jewel straight out where Claudia had gone and if she had heard from her.

Jewel told Ray that she couldn't tell him where Claudia was but that she was somewhere safe and would be back at the end of the week.

Ray was hurting. There had never been a time when he and Claudia couldn't work through their problems. And now, the one time when it mattered most, they couldn't be further apart.

Hot water streamed down Claudia's body and warmed and refreshed her skin. All of the day's tension seemed to melt away as the water trailed over her shoulders, breasts, stomach and down the length of her legs.

It was hot and steamy in the shower, just the way she liked it.

Claudia heard a knock on the bathroom door and then the sound of the door opening. A rush of cool air invaded the room and caused goose bumps to rise on her arms.

"May I join you?"

"I'd be disappointed if you didn't," she said, forgiving the intrusion.

Claudia moved the shower curtain aside to allow entry into her warm space.

"You're cold," he said, tracing a line of goose bumps down the length of her arm and back up again. "Let me warm you."

Claudia's skin tingled from his touch as he followed a trail of water from her neck, to her shoulders and down to her breasts.

He leaned her against the wall of the shower and placed his lips where his fingers had previously explored. He found a nipple with his lips and suckled until it was a hardened nub.

As he took each nipple in turn and drew circles around it with is tongue, occasionally clamping his lips around the brown bud, he heard Claudia moan softly. Without looking, he knew that she was resting her head against the wall of the shower and her lips were slightly parted. He needed to kiss those lips. He needed to taste her and to feel her lips against his, with her tongue exploring the depths of his mouth.

The steamy water continued to flow, as did her juices. With one hand he followed the contour of her hips, around her thighs, and over the beautiful mound of black curls that was the passageway that led to exquisite delights. His explorations did not take him to depths unknown but to a place that was more familiar to him than home and more wonderful than paradise.

His fingers continued their exploration and he was delighted by the warmth and wetness he found there. Again, she moaned and the sweet sound fueled his need for her. He could no longer distinguish between the rushing waters from the shower and the spring that flowed from the depths of her desire.

When he found the spot that he knew would unleash unbridled ecstasy, he worked it and worked it until the sweet sensation forming in the base of her stomach overtook her entire body and permeated through her soul.

He knew how to please her and she, him, and neither was left disappointed.

Now, it was his turn. She covered his mouth with her own and kissed him longingly, for she could never get enough of his taste, his touches or his expressions of love.

While she kissed him, she placed her hands on his shoulders and turned him so that this time it was his back that was against the wall of the shower. One hand stroked his face, then his chin, neck and chest. She broke the kiss and began placing playful bites on his neck, then his chest. The hair on his chest tickled her lips and she smiled. Lowering her head she flicked her tongue over each nipple, causing them to grow rigid.

Then she continued her exploration of his magnificent body, seeking the one part of him that she knew would most welcome her touch. When she found what she sought, there was no doubt that he was ready to make love to her, but there were different pleasures that she wanted to bring to him. She found that the temperature and force of the water were no match for the heat and hardness that signaled an impending release.

He was weak with desire and that was exactly where she wanted him to be. She wanted him to want her and she delighted in pleasing him.

Her very touch caused his knees to grow weak and his body to react with familiarity and need. Her fingers magically stroked him and he wanted to tell her how good she made him feel and how much he loved her, but the words caught in his throat as his last coherent thought before being overtaken by desire was how much he loved his woman.

CHAPTER THIRTY-THREE

For most of the week Claudia and Rolanda spent a lot of time shopping on Michigan Avenue, going out to eat and sightseeing. Rolanda was an excellent host and tour guide. She took Claudia everywhere. They ate and shopped at Navy Pier, traveled up and down the Magnificent Mile, and even went to a Bull's game. Rolanda's company had provided them with tickets for floor seats, much to Claudia's delight.

The morning before she was to return home, Claudia awoke to the aroma of coffee, bacon and something that smelled like cinnamon. Looking at the clock on the nightstand she was dismayed to find that it was barely eight o'clock in the morning. All week long she had managed to sleep in at least until ten, but not this morning. She needed to get up. Something sweet and flavorful was calling her name.

Whatever Rolanda was baking smelled absolutely heavenly, Claudia thought as she pulled herself out of bed and slipped on her robe.

"Good morning, sleeping beauty," Rolanda said over the top of her newspaper. "I was wondering when you'd finally roll out of bed."

"Who can sleep when there's bacon sizzling, coffee brewing and something baking. What is that?"

"Coffee cake."

"You've got to be kidding," Claudia remarked. "I can't believe you got up this morning and baked coffee cake."

"Correction, I'm heating up coffee cake."

Claudia sat down and poured herself a cup of coffee. She felt underdressed compared to Rolanda who was wearing tan knit pants and a black sweater.

"I thought you'd be sleeping in, too. Why are you dressed already?" Claudia asked, munching on a piece of bacon.

"I know you haven't seen much evidence of it this week, but over the years I've developed into quite a morning person. I get up early, exercise, read the paper, have breakfast, meditate, and take care of whatever needs to be taken care of before I go to work. That way, when I get home I can relax and unwind."

"You do all that before you go to work? I'm sure there's a good reason to why you'd put yourself through that," Claudia said yawning.

"I manage to get a lot accomplished. You should try it sometime."

"No thanks."

"Did you sleep well last night?" Rolanda asked, ignoring her friend's sarcastic tone.

Had she slept well? Claudia placed her coffee cup on its saucer. Good question. She had been tired and had no trouble falling asleep but she had had an odd dream. She wanted to tell Rolanda about it, but wasn't sure if she should. She might be giving away more about herself than she was willing to right now.

"Yes, you could say that I slept well," she answered, deciding not to mention the dream.

"I was wondering. I heard you moan once or twice during the night."

"You heard me?" Claudia asked, trying to hide her embarrassment.

"Yes, I had gotten up to get a drink of water and at first I thought I heard you talking, but when I stood outside your door, I heard you moan."

Claudia put her head in her hands. Now she was really embarrassed.

"Claudia, when you called me last week to see if you could crash here for a few days, I said yes without a moment's hesitation. I knew something was going on that you needed to get away from or maybe it was just that you needed a change of scenery. Whatever was going on I was hoping you would share it with me and maybe we could work through it together but you haven't mentioned anything yet and quite frankly, I'm a little worried about you."

Claudia sighed. "Ro, I have gotten myself into such a mess and I don't know how I'm going to get out of it."

"What kind of mess? Is it money? You know I can help you out if that's what you need."

"Thanks for the offer but it's not money."

"Is it your job?"

Claudia shook her head and sighed.

"Man trouble?"

Claudia laughed cynically and nodded. Man trouble. That's exactly what she had.

"Okay, let's hear it. Take your time and start at the beginning."

Claudia filled Rolanda in on everything that had happened from the kiss she shared with Ray on Christmas Eve to his declaration of love and up to when she confronted Ray about Viveca.

"Sounds to me like you've got a very important decision to make."

Claudia frowned. "Thanks for clearing that up for me, Ro."

"Look, Claudia, I don't know what you expected to gain by running away from your problems. You know I love you like a sister, and I have enjoyed this week probably more than you, but I'm sure when you get back home very little will have changed."

"I wasn't trying to run away from anything. Or maybe subconsciously I was. But the bottom line is, I'm confused, probably more now than when I left."

"Okay, before we look at the big picture, let's look at both men."

"First, there's Mark. The brother is fine, talented, kind and all the rest."

"You sound like you're reading from a check list."

"Actually, Mark does fit all of the criteria on my list."

"What list?"

She knew Rolanda was going to give her a hard time about her plan, but if she was going to be up front with her she had to tell her everything. Claudia bit the bullet and explained the plan and the list to Rolanda.

"Claudia, I can't really get with that plan of yours. It sounds like your head was in the right place but your heart was nowhere in the mix. That may be part of the problem. But, go ahead. Finish telling me about Mark."

"That was pretty much it."

"Does he love you?"

"No, but I don't think he's too far from it."

"Do you love him?"

"Given time, I probably could."

"Okay, that doesn't sound too promising. You make falling in love with Mark sound like saving for retirement. You're heart's not in it, love. Now let's talk about Ray. You already know he loves you. How do you feel about him?"

"I don't know."

"What do you mean, you don't know? According to you, you've been friends since before you could spell the word and you know everything there is to know about the man."

"Apparently, not everything. I don't know what this fascination is that he has with his ex."

"Did you ever think you might be overreacting to that? This girl sounds like she's just out to make trouble and you're giving her the green light to do just that."

Sounding a little more defensive than she intended to, Claudia said, "No, Ray continuously allows her to re-enter his life at her whim. She snaps her fingers, he comes running. I don't want to play second string to her."

"Then don't. Take a stand. If Ray is who you want, then don't let anything or anyone stand in your way."

"That's just it, Rolanda, I don't know if it is Ray that I want."

"I think your heart knows but your head is afraid to follow. You seem to have a big problem getting those two together."

"I'm glad it's that clear to you," Claudia said half-smiling and wondering why Rolanda was sounding like Ray.

"It'll be clear to you, too. Just give it a little more time, and throw away that damned list. By the way, what were you dreaming about last night that had you moaning like a deacon at revival?"

Claudia flushed remembering the erotic shower dream. "Let's just say, if I make you privy to that information, I'll have to kill you."

CHAPTER THIRTY-FOUR

The grand opening of The Gatehouse was a tremendous success. From the moment the doors opened until the last patrons left the restaurant, the place was jumping with excitement.

Mark and his partner Cornell were pleased with their apparent success. Throughout the course of the evening there had been a few minor glitches, but nothing that wasn't handled quickly and efficiently by the well-trained staff.

Once the last three patrons left the restaurant it was time for the staff and owners to celebrate on their own. Mark called all of the staff into the dining area and opened a bottle of champagne.

Claudia stood off to the back and watched the pride and excitement on everyone's face. From the waiters and waitresses to the busboys to the chef, it was clear to see that everyone was pleased and excited with the new venture.

Cornell raised his glass. "Before I make a toast I just want to say a few things first. I know it was hectic tonight but Mark and I want you all to know that you did an outstanding job. Mark, if I wasn't sure before, now I'm positive. I think we've assembled a pretty good group of folks here."

Mark nodded his agreement and everyone applauded.

Mark continued, "From the moment the doors opened today, until the last few people trickled out of here, each and every one of you showed a tremendous amount of professionalism, efficiency and fortitude, especially when we found out a food critic from the *Dispatch* picked tonight of all nights to patronize our establishment."

"With all that said, here's to a packed house every night." Everyone joined Cornell in the toast.

After some lighthearted teasing from the wait staff about the potential to make some substantial tips and joking from the busboys, everyone went about cleaning and preparing the restaurant for the next day. Mark took the opportunity to grab a private moment with Claudia.

"I haven't had a chance to say much to you tonight, but I wanted to say congratulations," Claudia said. She was holding something in her hand and handed it to Mark. "This is for you. I think you're going to be very successful with The Gatehouse and I was glad to share this occasion with you. And judging by the few comments I managed to overhear, you'll be having many repeat patrons."

Mark took the package from Claudia and began to remove the wrapping. "I certainly hope we have crowds every night like we did tonight. I especially hope to see the pretty lady sitting at the corner table who looked absolutely scrumptious in the little black dress."

Mark winked.

Claudia blushed.

"A dollar? In a frame?" Mark looked puzzled when he removed the final wrapping from the package.

"That's the first dollar The Gatehouse made tonight."

"When did you have time to do this?"

"Well, I don't want to reveal all of my secrets, but Lynette gave me a hand."

Mark was touched. He'd been so busy running around trying to keep everything flowing smoothly that he hadn't been aware of anything else.

"Thank you," he said, taking Claudia in his arms and planting a kiss on her lips. "Sharing this evening with you meant a lot. It may not have seemed as if I noticed you throughout the evening, but I did. I just want you to know that."

"It was my pleasure being here and I think I had as much fun as you getting caught up in all the excitement."

Mark was pleased. He had been worried that she had felt neglected during the evening, but now he knew that she was enjoying the success of the restaurant as much as he was.

Now, the time was right, Mark thought. He turned Claudia around so that her back was to him and he asked her to close her eyes.

"Have I mentioned how sexy you look in that black dress?"

Claudia giggled and said, "Only three or four times. But you can say it as much as you like."

Claudia felt Mark's fingers brush her as he placed something around her neck.

"Open your eyes," he instructed softly.

Claudia opened her eyes and looked down.

"I wanted to give this to you on Valentine's Day but you were gone."

Around her neck Mark had placed a delicate gold chain with a diamond heart pendant.

She turned to face Mark and said, "It's beautiful, but I can't-"

Mark shook his head and took her by the shoulders, "Don't say you can't accept it, Claudia. The gift is my way of letting you know how much I appreciate and care for you. Tonight was very special for me and it meant more having you to share it with."

Claudia was touched and it showed in her eyes.

"What do I need to do to have you here every night? In fact, what will it take to have you in my life on a full-time basis?" Mark looked into Claudia's eyes, searching for the answer that he wanted to hear. "It's no secret that you've come to mean a lot to me. I'm still not sure about your feelings toward me and even now I can see that you're wrestling with those feelings."

Mark sighed and let Claudia rest her head against his chest. "I'm a patient man, baby, but when it comes to having you in my life completely, I don't know how much more patient or unselfish I can be. I'm willing to give you some time to make up your mind because when you come to me, I don't want there to be any doubt about your decision."

Claudia didn't know how to respond. She knew Mark was looking for something more than "let's take things one day at a time", but in her heart of hearts she had to be honest with herself and Mark.

They were interrupted when Mark's desk phone buzzed. Reluctantly, he let Claudia go in order to answer it.

"Go ahead, Lynette, and put it through," he said. "Yes, Karen, she's right here."

Puzzled, Claudia took the receiver from. "Hey, Karen. What's going on?"

Mark nodded. He was concerned. Why was Claudia's sister calling her here?

"What?"

"Oh, no!"

"When?"

"I'll be right there."

Mark saw the stricken look on Claudia's face and heard the terror in her voice. "Honey, what's wrong?"

Claudia looked from side to side, trying to remember where she'd left her purse and her coat. Tears were streaming down her face as she began to sob. Mark grabbed her by the shoulders and turned her to face him. "Claudia, what's wrong?" The terror in her eyes frightened him.

"M-my keys. Where did I put my purse?" she asked in a shaky voice that was barely above a whisper. "I-I need my keys. I need to get to the hospital."

"What's happened?"

"It's Ray," she said. "He's been in an accident."

CHAPTER THIRTY-FIVE

Mark drove as quickly as he could through the wet streets. The snowfall from earlier that week had started to melt during the day but was quickly re-freezing as temperatures began to drop, making the streets wet and slick in some spots.

Mark held Claudia's hand as he steered with his other. She sat motionless and stared straight ahead, not really looking at anything in particular. Even in the darkness Mark knew she was quietly crying, and praying.

The brightly-lit emergency room entrance was in stark contrast to the dark street they had just turned down to get to the hospital.

"I'll park and meet you inside."

Mark had barely gotten the last word out before Claudia leapt from the car. Once inside she searched for the front desk attendant.

"Claudia."

Claudia turned and saw Karen and her parents approaching.

"They're prepping Ray for surgery," Lawrence said gently. The pain stricken look on his daughter's face nearly broke his heart.

Mark had joined them but Claudia barely noticed.

"Can I see him?" she asked her father, almost pleading.

"No, baby girl, not until the doctor says so."

"Is he going to be all right?" Claudia asked, searching for something that would let her know that things weren't as serious as they seemed.

Jewel and her husband exchanged glances but neither of them answered. Jewel took Claudia's arm and led her to the waiting area.

"It was a pretty bad accident, Claudia, and it doesn't look good right now. The doctor said Ray lost a lot of blood."

A small sob escaped from Claudia's lips and Mark, feeling more helpless than he'd ever felt in his life, reached out and took her in his arms. The only thing he could do was to hold her as she cried.

After what seemed like an eternity, a nurse came out and gave them a progress report. It was just as Jewel had said earlier. Things did not look good for Ray. His right leg was broken. He had three cracked ribs, multiple contusions on his face and untold internal injuries.

When Mark went to get everyone coffee, Claudia turned to Karen and asked if she knew what had happened.

Karen bit her lip and looked at her mother.

"What?" Claudia asked. "What happened, Karen? Is there something you're not telling me?"

"It was my fault."

Claudia turned toward the small voice behind her and there stood Viveca looking battered and bruised and very frightened.

"What are you doing here?" Claudia asked angrily.

Viveca's lip trembled when she saw the hatred in Claudia's eyes.

"Claudia, I'm so sorry. It's my fault that Ray is lying in that operating room right now."

Hot tears streamed down Claudia's face as she asked, "What did you do, Viveca? What did you do to Ray?"

Viveca tried to compose herself as she tried to explain what had happened earlier that evening. "I was upset about something that happened earlier and I went out drinking. I only meant to have a few drinks to calm my nerves, but before I knew it, I'd had more to drink than I realized and was in no shape to drive. I called Ray, more for company than a ride home."

Viveca sat down across from Claudia and her family and continued. "When Ray arrived to take me home, I asked him if we could just drive around for a bit. I needed someone to talk to and I didn't feel like going back to my mother's house yet. We drove around for a little while and eventually ended up outside the city. We were driving down a back road that had started to ice over and before I knew it Ray had lost control of the car." Fresh tears flowed as Viveca relived the accident. "We were spinning around and it was so hard to see. But then, out of nowhere, there was a tree. I screamed when I saw it and I knew there was no avoiding it. It was dark and the road was so icy. Ray tried but he couldn't get control of the car. He tried," she repeated.

"Ray is lying in there right now fighting for his life because you were feeling sorry for yourself and had gotten too drunk to drive yourself home?"

The anger in Claudia's voice surprised everyone, including Mark who had returned with the coffee.

Viveca was ashamed and embarrassed. She didn't know what to say because Claudia was right. Just then the nurse came out to give another progress report. Ray was out of surgery. She advised that the doctor would be out soon to answer any specific questions they might have.

"When can we see him?" Claudia asked what everyone else had been thinking.

"He's in recovery right now. It might be a while."

They waited on pins and needles for the doctor to emerge.

"Mom, Dad, I just got the message about Ray." Everyone turned when they heard Frank's voice. "How is he?"

"He just came out of surgery and he's in recovery. We're waiting for the doctor to give us an update on his condition," Karen said.

Viveca stood away from the group, wanting more than anything for Ray to be okay. She would never forgive herself if…

The doctor walked somberly through the double swinging doors looking tired and worried. He wanted to be able to give everyone good news, but he had to be truthful.

"We found the source of the hemorrhaging and managed to stop it."

"Does that mean he's going to be all right?" Claudia asked, hopeful. When he didn't answer right away she sensed that he was holding something back. She didn't know if she could bear to hear it, but she had to know. "There's something you're not telling us, isn't there?"

The doctor nodded his head and exhaled. "Ray is in a coma."

CHAPTER THIRTY-SIX

Jewel begged Claudia to go home and get some rest, but she refused. The nurse and doctor had both explained that no one would be allowed to see Ray until sometime in the morning, but she wouldn't leave. She needed to be there, just in case.

It was by far the longest night of Claudia's life. Whenever she drifted off to sleep, images of Ray trapped in the twisted metal of his wrecked car haunted her.

Around six the next morning Jewel arrived at the hospital with a change of clothes for Claudia and some breakfast. One of the nurses showed Claudia an area reserved for patients' families where she could shower and change clothes. She was still wearing the black dress that she'd worn the night before at the grand opening of Mark's restaurant.

As Claudia stood in the narrow shower stall she let the hot water wash over her tired body. She repeated the same prayer that she'd prayed over and over throughout the night, for Ray to make it through this horrible nightmare.

Claudia emerged from the shower and went through the mechanics of getting dressed and combing her hair. She folded her dress and placed it in a bag for her mother to take home.

"Honey, you need to go home and get some sleep."

Claudia looked at her mother with a pleading look in her eyes. Surely her mother had to understand how she felt. "I can't, Mom. I need to be here for Ray. If the situation were reversed, I know he would do the same."

Jewel nodded her understanding.

A nurse knocked lightly on the door of the family lounge. "Miss Ryland, you can see Mr. Elliott now, but only for a few minutes."

Claudia hugged her mother and followed the nurse down the hall to the intensive care unit. They passed the nurses station where several nurses sat around a desk talking about everyday goings on. It seemed odd to Claudia that they were able to go on about their business when the tragic event of Ray's accident had brought her life to a screeching halt.

The nurse took Claudia to room three twenty-six. Ray's room.

When she walked into the room and saw Ray for the first time, Claudia heard her breath catch. The room was filled with every kind of medical machine imaginable. Monitors of every type spit out paper readings. Tubes and wires wound in all different directions carrying vital fluids. But in the midst of it all lay Ray's battered and bruised body. To say that his appearance shocked Claudia was an understatement. She hardly recognized him. His bandaged face was discolored, swollen and cut.

"I know it's a little overwhelming at first, but all of this equipment is important to monitoring the patient's progress and let's us know if he's in distress. If everything goes well, many of his bandages will be removed in a few days."

Claudia nodded and fought unsuccessfully to hold back tears.

"He isn't in pain is he?" Claudia asked trying to sound strong.

"No, he's on some pretty strong pain killers."

"Can he hear me?"

The nurse placed a reassuring hand on Claudia's shoulder. "Some people say yes, and some say no. I believe that although some coma patients don't respond right away, they can and do hear conversations directed toward them and are aware of what goes on around them."

The nurse pulled up a chair for Claudia and placed it at Ray's bedside. After she checked the readout from a monitor and scribbled something down on the chart, she left Claudia alone with Ray.

The rhythmic sound from the oxygen machine seemed unusually loud, as did the heart monitor and blood pressure machine. Claudia watched Ray as he lay so still in the narrow bed. Almost afraid to touch him, she reached between the guardrail and gingerly placed her hand on his arm.

"Ray, it's me. I'm not sure if you can hear me but if you can I want you to know that everyone is praying for you, especially me. I know you've been through a lot but right now you're going to have to fight, Ray. You're going to have to fight to pull through this. I wish I could help you do it, but I don't know what to do."

Tears flowed from Claudia's eyes as Ray remained unresponsive. She bit her bottom lip to keep him from hearing her cry. She felt as if she needed to talk, to get him to know that she was there and that he was going to be okay. "Mom, Dad, Karen and Frank were all here last night to make sure you made it through surgery, and Mom came back this morning."

Still nothing.

Claudia turned when she heard a sound. The nurse walked over to Claudia and placed a hand on her shoulder.

"It's time," she said.

Claudia nodded. "When will I be able to see him again?"

"If you'll be in the family lounge, I'll have someone come and get you in about an hour."

Claudia walked down the hall to the lounge with a heavy heart feeling completely powerless.

Jewel saw the look on her daughter's face and reached out to her. Claudia collapsed in her arms and wept silently.

"Baby, he'll make it through this. You've got to believe that. Ray is strong and healthy and he's got a lot of living left to do. Right now you're going to have to be strong, too."

Sniffing, Claudia took the tissue her mother held out and looked at her with bloodshot eyes. "I hope you're right, Mom. I can't lose him. I just can't."

CHAPTER THIRTY-SEVEN

Claudia sat with Ray for most of the evening. The shock she'd felt earlier that morning at seeing him so badly injured was beginning to wear off. Even though he really didn't look like himself, he was still Ray.

When it was time for the nurses to change shifts she had to step out of the room. To kill time until she could go back to be with Ray, Claudia sat in the family lounge and stared blankly at the news on TV. A bank had been robbed that day. A group of school children had raised money for cancer research. There was fighting in Afghanistan. Consumers were being advised of a recall on canned chili. Again it seemed strange to her that the rest of the world went on as normal when her whole world had been turned upside down.

All afternoon and most of the evening she had sat with Ray, praying for a sign that he was going to be all right. But there was nothing. Undaunted and afraid to give up hope, she continued to pray.

"Would you like some company?"

Startled, Claudia looked up to see Mark. She had been so deep in thought that she didn't hear him enter the lounge.

"I didn't mean to startle you," he said apologetically. "You were so still that for a moment I thought you were asleep." He noticed that she was no longer wearing the necklace he'd given her.

Claudia rolled her neck, trying to relieve some of the tension. "Just have a lot on my mind, that's all."

Before Mark took off his coat, he handed Claudia a white carryout container and a can of juice. "You look like you could use some food and something to drink other than coffee."

Claudia opened the lid to the container. There was chicken, rice, and broccoli. The aroma that wafted from the food was comforting and offered a welcome reprieve from the gallons of coffee and cold sandwiches she'd been consuming.

"Mario made that especially for you."

Claudia ate a bite of chicken and rice and was surprised at how good it tasted and at how hungry she was. "Please tell Mario that I said thanks, and that the food is as delicious as usual."

While Claudia ate Mark stepped behind her and began to massage her shoulders. She was more tense than he had imagined and he knew without asking that she wasn't getting much sleep.

"Mmm, that feels nice."

"How is Ray doing?"

"About the same. He had a fever last night but it was gone by this morning."

"Has he been responsive at all?"

Claudia shook her head and put her fork down. "No, but the doctor said he could come out of this today, tomorrow or…" Her voice trailed off as she remembered the doctor's exact words. *Ray might not come out of the coma at all.*

Mark sat down beside Claudia and took her hand in his.

"If I were in Ray's position right now it would be a tremendous comfort to me to know that someone that loved me as deeply as you was by my side. Honey, it's going to take a combination of love, strength and prayers to bring Ray through this."

Claudia searched Mark's face for a sign of understanding and what she saw touched her heart.

"Mark, I'm-"

He placed a finger on her lips to silence the words that he

already knew in his heart. "It's all right. I've known for a while that you were in love with Ray, even when you didn't want to admit it to yourself. If there was ever a doubt that you loved him, there isn't now. I know that was what you were going to tell me last night. I'd be lying if I said that I wasn't disappointed with the way things turned out between us, but from the beginning I should have recognized the special bond you and Ray shared."

Claudia felt a small sense of relief. Mark understood. She hoped that she hadn't hurt him. "Would it be asking too much for us to remain friends?"

Mark smiled and kissed the back of Claudia's hand. "It would be my pleasure, pretty lady."

Frank arrived at the hospital shortly after six the next morning and ordered Claudia to go home and get some sleep. After much protest and under the threat of being thrown over her brother's shoulder and carried out of the hospital, they decided upon a compromise. Instead of going home, she agreed to lie down on a cot in one of the private areas in the family lounge.

Claudia walked from Ray's room with her head down, shoulders slumped and fatigue blanketing her body like a heavy quilt. She was tired and it was beginning to affect her in more ways than one. It was hard watching Ray lie helpless and not be able to do anything about it. More than anything she needed to keep up hope. Not only for Ray's sake, but hers as well.

"Claudia."

Claudia had been so deep in thought that she hadn't seen anyone approach her. She lifted her tired eyes as Viveca stood before her looking very small and tired.

"What are you doing here?" Claudia seethed.

The usually poised Viveca struggled to find something to say. She'd been watching and waiting for a chance to visit Ray alone, but Claudia rarely left his side. Her chance finally came when she saw Claudia leaving Ray's room. At first she was going to slip quietly by her and not say a word, but it seemed as if Claudia were carrying the weight of the world on her shoulders and Viveca knew that she was to blame.

"I-I was…"

"You have no business being here."

"That's not true, Claudia, and you know it. Despite what you and everyone else may think, I do care about Ray. He's probably the only person I do care about and it's killing me to know why he is lying in that hospital bed clinging to life. It's all because of something that should never have happened."

"I find it hard to believe that you care about anything or anyone. If you did then you'd have called a cab to take you home from the bar that night. You'd have thought about how icy the roads get at night. And, maybe, just maybe for once in your selfish, scheming, lonely, pathetic life you'd have thought beyond the wonderful world of Viveca Roberts and realized that the world does not exist to serve you."

Viveca stood before Claudia with tears streaming down her face. She didn't have a rebuttal because Claudia was right. She had been selfish when she called Ray. If she had taken a cab home from the bar that night, Ray wouldn't be fighting for his life right now.

Viveca's meeting a few weeks ago with her ex-husband had had more of an affect on her than she knew at the time. Seeing Clayton again had opened up old wounds and had been a bitter reminder that she had no one in her life that really cared about her, except Ray. The night of the accident she was feeling sorry for herself and tried to drown her sorrows with a bottle of cognac. When that didn't work she decided to call Ray. He was probably still upset with her but she hoped he would at least talk to her. Being with him would make her feel better, she thought. It always did.

When she called him he had been asleep and sounded tired. She apologized for waking him but told him that they needed to talk.

Viveca could tell that Ray didn't want to talk to her. Any other time that she'd called he was more than willing to come to her rescue, but this time was different. She had crossed an invisible line with the stunt she'd pulled at the restaurant and she knew it. Ray clearly didn't want to have anything to do with her and that hurt more than she could have imagined. After practically begging to see him so that they could "clear the air", Ray finally agreed to meet her.

Over the phone Ray could tell Viveca had been drinking, but he didn't realize until he arrived at the bar that she was in a worse state than he had originally thought. She was drunk and depressed and all he wanted to do was take her to her mother's so that she could sleep it off, but she begged him to drive around for a while so that they could talk. She needed to be around someone who loved her despite all of her faults, she'd said.

Several times Ray had suggested a good night's sleep and a strong hangover remedy, but again, all she wanted to do was talk. So he drove and let her talk.

Viveca talked about her failed marriage, the relationship she had with her mother and the empty life she had in California. She was supposed to be leaving on a late flight the following evening but she admitted that she had nothing to go back to in California except a lonely house and no real friends.

But what had surprised Ray the most then and Claudia now, was Viveca's next confession. She was jealous of Claudia and had been for a long time. She had even apologized to Ray for trying to sabotage his relationship with Claudia and admitted that everything he'd said about her being miserable and wanting everyone else to be miserable was the truth.

"Viveca, I'm too tired for this," Claudia said as all the fight went out of her. She wasn't Ray and didn't have to listen to Viveca's confessions.

"Claudia, what I've been trying to say is that Ray is and has been the only good thing in my life for a long time. I have been jealous of his relationship with you probably just as long. It's not because I want Ray for myself. I guess it's just because I'm miserable and I couldn't stand to see someone else happy, especially when at one time that happiness had been offered to me and I threw it back in Ray's face. I can't hate you for accepting something that I didn't want. Ray loves you dearly, Claudia."

Viveca sighed and looked just as tired as Claudia. "You were right when you said that my selfishness led to Ray lying in that bed. If I could change things, I would. But I can't change the past."

"Are you trying to ask me for forgiveness to ease your conscience?"

"No, I realize that would be asking a lot, maybe too much. All I'm asking is that we not fight. Ray needs you right now and I need to make sure that he pulls through. I couldn't live with myself otherwise."

Claudia wondered if Viveca was being sincere. There was a part of her that knew how conniving and manipulative she could be. Yet now, Viveca stood before her and asked for a truce. Could she trust that there were no ulterior motives?

"When this is all over and I'm sure Ray is okay, I'll be gone. You won't ever have to worry about me trying to interfere in your relationship again. In the meantime, Claudia, I'm going to do everything I can to make sure Ray is all right and I promise to stay out of your way if you will promise me something."

Here it comes, Claudia thought wearily. She knew the old Viveca would surface sooner or later. What could she possibly want from her?

"Promise that you will love Ray and treat him like the jewel that he is."

Claudia stood before Viveca at a loss for words. When she realized that Viveca was serious and awaited her reply, Claudia simply nodded and the two women went their separate ways.

It had only been a week since the accident but it seemed like an eternity. Claudia continued to keep a vigil at Ray's beside. The minutes ticked by like hours as he remained in the coma and Claudia struggled to remain hopeful.

As she watched his still body she remembered what the nurse had said about Ray possibly being able to hear her when she spoke. Willing to try to get a response from him, she reached out and took his hand.

"Ray, I hope you can hear me. I hope that you know I'm right here beside you and I'll stay right here as long as you need me. So many people are praying for you right now." Ray remained unresponsive but Claudia continued undaunted. "This is a lot different from the time you had your tonsils out. At least now I don't have to hide to be with you."

"I wish you would wake up, Ray. There are so many things that I need to say to you and I don't even know if you can hear me. If you could just open your eyes or squeeze my hand. Something. Anything to let me know that you're in there and fighting to come back to me."

"We have so much to look forward to together. And I do mean together. I love you and I've fought against those feelings for a while now. Some people live out their entire lives without ever experiencing a friendship like ours. And others never know what it's like to be loved unconditionally. I've been blessed to experience both with the same person. And what do I do? Try to hide from my feelings. Crazy, I know. But isn't that one of the reasons you love me?" Claudia smiled and felt a warm tear trickle down her face.

"Do you want to know what I've been thinking these past few days? I've thought about all of the good times we've had over the years. And the bad times. I was thinking back to when I was away at college and it was my first birthday away from home. You drove over three hours in that car your roommate called the sloppy jalopy just so you could surprise me for my birthday. I had been so homesick and I had a major case of the blues and was feeling sorry for myself big time. Then, out of the blue, here you show up at my door with balloons, cupcakes and a large pizza with extra cheese. You thought I was being so sappy when I cried, but I was touched. That was one of the best birthdays I've ever had."

"Ray, you've proven over and over to me just how much I mean to you. I want the chance to show you just how much you mean to me."

"Please, please come back to me so I can spend the rest of my life showing you just how much."

CHAPTER THIRTY-EIGHT

The church was filled to capacity. Those who had arrived late would have to view the service on closed circuit television in the overflow room.

Claudia had arrived at the church before anyone else. She needed the extra time to get herself together and to pray. There had been a lot of that going on over the past few months and since she had done more than her share of crying she had promised herself that on this day, there would be no tears. But from the moment she walked into the church she had been overwhelmed with emotion.

Now, as she stepped from the vestibule into the sanctuary, she felt everyone's eyes upon her. Again, she promised herself that she wouldn't cry. Ray wouldn't want her to.

The music from the organ was mere background noise to Claudia as she clung to her father's arm for support. She could see her mother sitting in the front of the church and although she couldn't really see her eyes, Claudia knew that she was probably crying, too.

"You're going to be all right, baby girl," he said reassuringly with a smile.

Slowly Claudia walked forward. Her knees shook and her feet felt unsteady, but she heard her father's words repeated over and over again in her head. In her heart, she knew everything was going to be all right.

When they reached the end of the aisle, Claudia felt her father squeeze her hand as they stopped next to Ray. The music grew silent and the minister began to speak.

"We are gathered here this day in the presence of God and man to join this man and this woman together in holy matrimony."

Ray leaned heavily on his crutches as he stood next to the woman he was going to marry and spend the rest of his life with. He looked at Claudia with all the love, respect and passion that had blossomed over the years. He loved this woman with every part of his being and couldn't imagine anyone that was more perfect for him.

When he turned to face Claudia to recite the words he'd written for his wedding vows he intended to tell her just that.

"Today," he began, "I want to say thank you to my best friend. Thank you for loving me all these years and realizing that the love we've shared has grown into something so deep and wonderful that I can't find the words to fully express it. You've been there for me through the good times and the bad and that is one of the many reasons I love you. There were times that for whatever reason I was sad, but you were there and you smiled and brought joy to my life. Once when I was brokenhearted, you let me know that your love was unconditional and readily available. And when I lay bruised and battered and fighting for my life, you prayed for God to see me through and you never left my side."

"Claudia, I didn't know it was possible to love anyone the way that I love you or to be loved so completely by you. This is how I want to spend the rest of my life. Today, I promise to continuously strive to be the kind of man that you can proudly call your husband and more importantly, your friend. I will love you and stick by you and treat each day we have together as a precious gift. Claudia, I won't make empty promises to you that I don't intend to keep, but at this place in time, before our family and friends, I want you to know that I promise to love you for the rest of our lives."

Through her tears Claudia looked at the man whom she loved deeply as his words brought joy to her heart. Throughout the terrible ordeal of the past few months there was never a time that she didn't want to keep up hope that this day would come.

According to Ray's doctors, his recovery from the injuries sustained in his accident was accredited to luck. Claudia knew that it wasn't luck that brought Ray back to her. It had been the love, prayers and support of the many people whose lives he had touched.

Following the accident she had spent a great deal of time by Ray's bedside talking to him and hoping that soon he would answer her back or show that he knew she was there. Then when her prayers were answered, the long road to recovery began. Through another surgery followed by months of physical therapy, Claudia was more determined than ever to help Ray make a complete recovery.

When Ray was released from the hospital after his second surgery he and Claudia sat together that evening and had a heart-to-heart talk.

"Sooner or later I'm going to have to admit that I almost made a huge mistake," she'd said.

"I wasn't worried. I knew you would come around." Ray tried to make light of what they'd almost lost, but he was elated that Claudia had finally listened to her heart and realized that his love for her was just for her. She was all the woman he ever needed and he was going to do everything within his power to make sure that he was all the man that she would ever need.

"You say that with such confidence but you really didn't have any way of knowing how things would turn out."

"That's not entirely true. The night we kissed under the mistletoe, I felt something from you that surprised me and I think you felt it, too. Our feelings for each other had changed before that night but neither of us wanted to acknowledge it. Let's face it. We were meant to be together. I think I was the first one to recognize those feelings and accept them even though I didn't know what to do about it, and to further complicate things, you were hesitant."

Claudia had remembered vividly how she'd felt. Her hesitation stemmed from the fact that there had been so much uncertainty and mistrust on her part. Throughout it all Ray had been patient and understanding and his love for her never wavered.

"I never told you this before, but there would be times that I would have dreams about us that seemed so real that when I woke up and realized that what I had just dreamt wasn't real, the sense of loss was almost too much to handle. Claudia, everything felt so right with us that all I could do was hope that you realized it, too, and wanted everything wonderful that we could have together."

She told Ray about the dream she'd had when she was staying at Rolanda's. They had laughed about it and wondered if it had just been some cosmic coincidence or proved that they really were meant to be together.

"Ray, it took some time, but I did realize what we could have together. I had to figure things out on my own even though I was getting a lot of advice from everyone from Pastor Gray to my friend Rolanda. It seemed like everywhere I turned, someone was giving me advice. But it was my mother who gave me a piece of advice a while ago that I should have taken sooner rather than later. She told me that what I was looking for might be right under my nose. I know you think that it took almost losing you for me to realize my love for you, but I had realized it before then."

"The night of your accident and the grand opening of The Gatehouse, I was ready to give you an answer. First, I needed to let Mark know what was going on in my heart. But before I had a chance to tell him, Karen called with the news of your accident. From that day forward there was never a question of what was important to me. Nearly losing you did bring us closer together but, I was already headed in that direction."

It was now Claudia's turn and she began to recite her vows, "This day is a dream come true. For a long time, Ray, I've loved you as my best friend even though I didn't fully understand the depth or expanse of what I felt. You were patient and willing to give me time and space to see just how wonderful you really are." She smiled and continued, "We've weathered many storms together and laughed, cried, and stayed beside each other through them all. Those were the times that cemented our relationship and made it strong. And I know it took some serious strength for you to have to deal with me during many of those times."

Ray smiled.

"Right now," Claudia continued, "as you stand before me I can't help but offer a prayer of thanks. I almost lost you, in more ways than one. But my prayers were answered and you made it back to me. Your friendship is more than a precious gift to me, Ray, so much more. Whenever I needed someone to talk to, you were there. If I was sad, you gave me a reason to smile. If I needed to feel safe, you protected me. And when I was lonely and asked for someone to love, God sent you."

Following the reception the bride and groom left the banquet hall and made their way to the waiting limousine as well-wishers shouted their congratulations. The bright autumn sun reflected off of Claudia's diamond tennis bracelet as the couple waved from the open window. The festive spirit brought about by a new season, coupled with that of the wedding, filled the air with gaiety, love and romance. And all of that was felt by Claudia and Ray.

EXCERPT FROM FUTURE TITLE: HART & SOUL, BY ANGIE DANIELS

She glanced at him again and desire continued to course through her veins in hot spurts of awareness. She felt herself being pulled in by his charm as she went all soft and warm inside. David still elicited feelings she had long forgotten. Her cheeks burned with the humiliation of their last encounter.

Another wave of longing coursed through her. For almost a heartbeat a part of her wanted him to take her in his arms and tell her everything was going to be all right. The other part of her knew better. There was no way she was going to fall into that trap. She had seen too many others that had fallen victim to him and she refused to be the next. The smartest thing to do was to put some distance between them so she could regain her senses.

"I need to get back inside," she finally said. In an effort to try and keep her mind on track she rose. As she turned away David reached out and gently touched her hand.

Hearing the underlying tone in her voice he knew there was something else on her mind she had yet to reveal, but now was not the time to inquire further. Instead he asked, "Why the rush?"

"Because I have a job to do," she murmured. His touch was making it almost impossible to get her body back under control.

Releasing her arm, he chuckled knowingly. "I see you're still running away from uncomfortable situations."

"I am not," Calaine defended.

"You are too," he retorted. "I can see that delicious pulse throbbing in your throat. I still make you nervous."

The expression on his face told her he was thinking about the last time she had run away. With that very incident in mind her heart felt like she had just ran a marathon, making it impossible to retort this time.

"If you're not afraid then prove it and have lunch with me."

Her chin lifted aggressively. "I don't have to prove myself to you." How could she have only seconds ago thought she felt attracted to him? David hadn't changed a bit. He still had that same wolfish gleam in his eye. He was trying to use her weakest moment as an opportunity to get close to her. Then he smiled that wonderful heart-melting smile she remembered and had to look away to keep from returning it.

She propped her fists on her shapely hips unaware the gesture had drawn attention to the fullness of her breasts. "I'll see you inside." With that she turned on her heels and departed.

2003 Publication Schedule

January	Twist of Fate	Ebony Butterfly II
	Beverly Clark	Delilah Dawson
	1-58571-084-9	1-58571-086-5
February	Fragment in the Sand	Fate
	Annetta P. Lee	Pamela Leigh Starr
	1-58571-097-0	1-58571-115-2
March	One Day At A Time	Unbreak my Heart
	Bella McFarland	Dar Tomlinson
	1-58571-099-7	1-58571-101-2
April	At Last	Brown Sugar Diaries
		& Other Sexy Tales
	Lisa G. Riley	Delores Bundy &
		Cole Riley
	1-58571-093-8	1-58571-091-1
May	Three Wishes	Acquisitions
	Seressia Glass	Kimberley White
	1-58571-092-X	1-58571-095-4
June	When Dreams A Float	Revelations
	Dorothy Elizabeth Love	Cheris F. Hodges
	1-58571-104-7	1-58571-085-7
July	The Color of Trouble	Someone To Love
	Dyanne Davis	Alicia Wiggins
	1-58571-096-2	1-58571-098-9
August	Object Of His Desire	Hart & Soul
	A. C. Arthur	Angie Daniels
	1-58571-094-6	1-58571-087-3
September	Erotic Anthology	A Lark on the Wing
	Assorted	Phyliss Hamilton
	1-58571-113-6	1-58571-105-5

October	Angel's Paradise	I'll be your Shelter
	Janice Angelique	Giselle Carmichael
	1-58571-107-1	1-58571-108-X
November	A Dangerous Obsession	Just An Affair
	J.M. Jeffries	Eugenia O'Neal
	1-58571-109-8	1-58571-111-X
December	Shades of Brown	By Design
	Denise Becker	Barbara Keaton
	1-58571-110-1	1-58571-088-1

Other Genesis Press, Inc. Titles

A Dangerous Deception	J.M. Jeffries	$8.95
A Dangerous Love	J.M. Jeffries	$8.95
After the Vows	Leslie Esdaile	$10.95
(Summer Anthology)	T.T. Henderson	
	Jacqueline Thomas	
Again My Love	Kayla Perrin	$10.95
Against the Wind	Gwynne Forster	$8.95
A Lighter Shade of Brown	Vicki Andrews	$8.95
All I Ask	Barbara Keaton	$8.95
A Love to Cherish	Beverly Clark	$8.95
Ambrosia	T.T. Henderson	$8.95
And Then Came You	Dorothy Elizabeth Love	$8.95
A Risk of Rain	Dar Tomlinson	$8.95
Best of Friends	Natalie Dunbar	$8.95
Bound by Love	Beverly Clark	$8.95
Breeze	Robin Hampton Allen	$10.95
Cajun Heat	Charlene Berry	$8.95
Careless Whispers	Rochelle Alers	$8.95
Caught in a Trap	Andre Michelle	$8.95
Chances	Pamela Leigh Starr	$8.95
Dark Embrace	Crystal Wilson Harris	$8.95
Dark Storm Rising	Chinelu Moore	$10.95
Designer Passion	Dar Tomlinson	$8.95
Eve's Prescription	Edwina Martin Arnold	$8.95
Everlastin' Love	Gay G. Gunn	$8.95
Fate	Pamela Leigh Starr	$8.95
Forbidden Quest	Dar Tomlinson	$10.95
From the Ashes	Kathleen Suzanne	$8.95
	Jeanne Sumerix	
Gentle Yearning	Rochelle Alers	$10.95

Glory of Love	Sinclair LeBeau	$10.95
Heartbeat	Stephanie Bedwell-Grime	$8.95
Illusions	Pamela Leigh Starr	$8.95
Indiscretions	Donna Hill	$8.95
Interlude	Donna Hill	$8.95
Intimate Intentions	Angie Daniels	$8.95
Kiss or Keep	Debra Phillips	$8.95
Love Always	Mildred E. Riley	$10.95
Love Unveiled	Gloria Greene	$10.95
Love's Deception	Charlene Berry	$10.95
Mae's Promise	Melody Walcott	$8.95
Meant to Be	Jeanne Sumerix	$8.95
Midnight Clear	Leslie Esdaile	$10.95
(Anthology)	Gwynne Forster	
	Carmen Green	
	Monica Jackson	
Midnight Magic	Gwynne Forster	$8.95
Midnight Peril	Vicki Andrews	$10.95
My Buffalo Soldier	Barbara B. K. Reeves	$8.95
Naked Soul	Gwynne Forster	$8.95
No Regrets	Mildred E. Riley	$8.95
Nowhere to Run	Gay G. Gunn	$10.95
Passion	T.T. Henderson	$10.95
Past Promises	Jahmel West	$8.95
Path of Fire	T.T. Henderson	$8.95
Picture Perfect	Reon Carter	$8.95
Pride & Joi	Gay G. Gunn	$8.95
Quiet Storm	Donna Hill	$8.95
Reckless Surrender	Rochelle Alers	$8.95
Rendezvous with Fate	Jeanne Sumerix	$8.95
Rivers of the Soul	Leslie Esdaile	$8.95

Rooms of the Heart	Donna Hill	$8.95
Shades of Desire	Monica White	$8.95
Sin	Crystal Rhodes	$8.95
So Amazing	Sinclair LeBeau	$8.95
Somebody's Someone	Sinclair LeBeau	$8.95
Soul to Soul	Donna Hill	$8.95
Still Waters Run Deep	Leslie Esdaile	$8.95
Subtle Secrets	Wanda Y. Thomas	$8.95
Sweet Tomorrows	Kimberly White	$8.95
The Price of Love	Sinclair LeBeau	$8.95
The Reluctant Captive	Joyce Jackson	$8.95
The Missing Link	Charlyne Dickerson	$8.95
Tomorrow's Promise	Leslie Esdaile	$8.95
Truly Inseperable	Wanda Y. Thomas	$8.95
Unconditional Love	Alicia Wiggins	$8.95
Whispers in the Night	Dorothy Elizabeth Love	$8.95
Whispers in the Sand	LaFlorya Gauthier	$10.95
Yesterday is Gone	Beverly Clark	$8.95
Yesterday's Dreams, Tomorrow's Promises	Reon Laudat	$8.95
Your Precious Love	Sinclair LeBeau	$8.95

Alicia Wiggins read her first romance novel when she was in the seventh grade and has remained an avid romance reader ever since. As a writer, she draws on her professional background in computer science to create characters who are strong, independent, and successful, yet who are also vulnerable, believable, and most importantly, true  romantics. She lives in Columbus, Ohio with her three children. Read more about Alicia at www.Aliciawiggins.com.

ORDER FORM

Mail to: Genesis Press, Inc.
315 3rd Avenue North
Columbus, MS 39701

Name _____

Address _____

City/State _____ Zip _____

Telephone _____

Ship to (if different from above)

Name _____

Address _____

City/State _____ Zip _____

Telephone _____

Qty.	Author	Title	Price	Total

Use this order
form, or call
1-888-INDIGO-1

Total for books _____

Shipping and handling:
    $5 first two books, $1 each
    additional book

Total S & H _____

Total amount enclosed _____

Mississippi residents add 7% sales tax